STRANGE JOURNEY BACK

STRANGE JOURNEY BACK

Paul McCusker

TYNDALE
Tyndale House Publishers, Inc.
Carol Stream, Illinois

ISBN-10: 1-58997-325-9
ISBN-13: 978-1-58997-325-1

A Focus on the Family book published by
Tyndale House Publishers, Carol Stream, Illinois 60188

TYNDALE is a registered trademark of Tyndale House Publishers, Inc. Tyndale's quill
logo is a trademark of Tyndale House Publishers, Inc.

All Scripture quotations, unless otherwise indicated, are taken from the *Holy Bible, New
International Version*®. NIV®. Copyright © 1973, 1978, 1984 by International Bible
Society. Used by permission of Zondervan Publishing House. All rights reserved.

The books in this collection were originally published as:
Strange Journey Back, copyright 1992 by Focus on the Family
High Flyer With a Flat Tire, copyright 1992 by Focus on the Family
The Secret Cave of Robinwood, copyright 1992 by Focus on the Family
Behind the Locked Door, copyright 1993 by Focus on the Family

A note to readers: The Adventures in Odyssey novels take place in a time period prior to
the beginning of the audio or video series. That is why some of the characters from those
audio and video episodes don't appear in these stories—they don't exist yet.

Editor: Liz Duckworth
Cover design: Greg Sills
Cover photo: Gary Locke
Cover copy: Larrilee Frazier

Library of Congress Cataloging-in-Publication Data
McCusker, Paul, 1958-
    Strange journey back : four original stories of fun, intrigue, and friendship / Paul
McCusker.
        p. cm. — (Adventures in Odyssey flashbacks ; 1)
    Summary: Presents an anthology of four books from the Adventures in Odyssey series,
which introduce Mark Prescott, Patti Eldridge, and the Imagination Station.
    ISBN-10 1-58997-325-9
    ISBN-13 978-1-58997-325-1
    [1. Conduct of life—Fiction. 2. Time travel—Fiction. 3. Friendship—Fiction.] I. Title.
    PZ7.M47841635Str 2006
    [Fic]—dc22
                                                                2005025566

Printed in the United States of America
1 2 3 4 5 6 7 8 9 /10 09 08 07 06

To Nancy L. Freed.
It is an honor to be your son.

To Chuck Bolte,
For more reasons than words permit.

To Bob Adams,
Who shaped my understanding of friendship.

To Phil Lollar,
Friend and fellow adventurer.

Contents

Strange
Journey
Back

Chapter One

MARK PRESCOTT WALKED DOWN the sidewalk with grim determination. In his hand, he clutched an envelope. In his heart, he carried a single desire: More than anything else, he wanted things to be the way they used to be.

He wanted things to be the way they were earlier in the spring before his dad left them; before Mark and his mom moved from his neighborhood and friends in Washington, D.C.; before they came to this little town called Odyssey; before . . . before, well, before everything went wrong.

No matter what Mark was doing or thinking about, that one desire stayed with him—to change things back.

He didn't have time for the hot June day or the gentle breeze that whispered the first secrets of summer. He was on a mission. He had written a letter to his father, and he had to get it mailed.

Mark walked quickly, glancing from one side to the other. The tarred street to his left looked like a steaming black river. To his right, the last Victorian house slipped away like the last car on a long train. Odyssey Elementary School slid into view. It would be Mark's school in the fall, if he were still living in Odyssey, if he couldn't make things the way they used to be.

He was looking ahead when his attention was suddenly

drawn to the playground. Two kids were wrestling on the grass. Next to them, a couple of bikes lay like crippled horses that had fallen to the ground.

"Ouch," cried one of the wrestlers.

"Cut it out," hollered the second kid.

The one with sandy hair, dirty jeans, and T-shirt sat triumphantly on the chest of the darker-haired one.

"Say you're sorry," the victor kept shouting.

"Ow! Get off!" the dark-haired kid whined.

Mark felt sorry for the kid on the bottom. He knew what it was like to be bullied. One time Cliff Atkinson sat on Mark's chest at recess and tried to take his lunch money. Just as Mark was about to give in, Lee Brooks grabbed Cliff and pulled him off so Mark could defend himself. Lee did crazy things like that. From then on, Lee had become his best friend.

Remembering how Lee had rescued him, Mark started across the field toward the fighters. Maybe he could help. Maybe he would make a new friend like Lee Brooks. His pace quickened to a run as he shoved the letter into his back pocket.

"Say you're sorry," the sandy-haired kid shouted again.

"Let me go!" the darker-haired kid on the bottom cried.

Mark locked his arms around the one on top and pulled hard.

"Hey, stop it!" the kid cried out with surprise.

The one on the bottom jumped up like a freed animal. His dark hair was matted to his sweaty forehead; his face was dirty and streaked with tears. A drop of blood bubbled out of his nose. He was taller than any of them.

"Hah," the boy shouted, as if he had gotten free without any help. "You're in big trouble. I'm going to get you for this!"

The boy pulled his bike upright, climbed on it, and pedaled off without even saying thanks to Mark.

The sandy-haired kid broke loose from Mark's grip and turned on him. Bright blue eyes shone with fury, and the face contorted into an expression that could have withered houseplants.

Mark gave a startled gasping sound and exclaimed, "You're a girl!"

Chapter Two

THE GIRL THREW A PUNCH at Mark. As her hand flew past his face, he stepped backward, tripped, and fell. Catlike, she pounced onto his chest and pinned his arms to the ground.

"Do you know what you did?" she screamed. "I waited the whole school year to get Joe! He picked on me. Called me bad names. And just when I—" She let out an angry huffing sound, swallowed, and then asked in a hoarse growl, "Do you know what you did?"

Mark considered wrestling his way out from under her. He knew he could, but he didn't. Instead, he said calmly, "Get off my chest."

"You ruined it! You ruined everything! Joe Devlin's been needing a good pounding all year."

"I'm sorry," Mark said. "I didn't know."

"You're sorry!" she shouted.

"Yeah," Mark answered quietly.

She looked puzzled. "You're sorry?"

"Yeah."

She blinked a couple of times. Her weight on Mark's chest lessened as she climbed off.

"Oh," she said and sat on the grass next to him. She looked confused.

Mark propped himself up on his elbows and took a deep breath.

"Well . . ." the girl fumbled, "you should be sorry."

Mark got up and pulled the letter out of his pocket. It was wrinkled and sweaty. *It doesn't look too bad*, he thought.

He turned back to the girl. "I have to leave," he said and started to walk across the field toward the post office.

By the time Mark reached the sidewalk, she was at his side walking her bike.

"I don't know you," she announced. "You're new in Odyssey, right?"

"Yeah." Mark picked up his pace.

"You live in old lady Schaeffer's house, right?"

Mark nodded. *Old lady*, Mark mused. *Is that what they called her?*

"Old lady" Schaeffer was Mark's grandmother, his mom's mom. The house had been his grandmother's until she died a couple of years ago and left everything in a will to Mark's mom. He hadn't known his grandmother very well, only through the usual Christmas and birthday cards.

"You're there with your mom, right?"

Mark wished this girl would leave him alone. She asked too many questions. Sooner or later, she would ask about his father.

"Look," Mark said, suddenly stopping. "I said I was sorry for ruining your fight. But I have to go. Nice to meet you." He took longer strides, hoping she wouldn't follow anymore.

The bike rattled behind him. *Maybe she'll climb on it and ride away*, he thought.

But she was at his side again. "Are you going to Whit's End? Looks like you're headed that way. I'm going to Whit's End, too."

"I'm going to the post office. I don't know what a Whit's End is."

"You don't know about Whit's End? Guess you've been hiding somewhere since you moved here."

"We've been busy. We had to unpack lots of boxes," Mark said defensively.

"Oh. Well, Whit's End is the best place to go in all of Odyssey! It's kind of an ice cream shop, but it's also got a bunch of inventions and displays and . . ." she paused. "You'll just have to see it. I'll take you after we go to the post office."

After we go to the post office? Mark didn't like the sound of it. His mission didn't include a strange girl.

"But I . . ." he stopped. He could be rude and tell her to get lost, but his mom had taught him better. "Okay," he finally said.

The rest of the walk to downtown Odyssey took only five minutes. It could have been five hours. Except to tell her his name when she asked, Mark never got a word in because the girl didn't stop talking.

She told him that her name was Patti Eldridge, and then she went on to say, "I like to do a lot of things boys usually like, but the kids make fun of me because I'm a girl. And Whit's End is owned by a man named John Avery Whittaker who used to be a teacher, but he quit because he likes to invent things for kids."

Her sentences never ended; they just kept going with the word "and." Eventually, Mark did what he always did with people who talked a lot. He stopped listening and let his mind drift to other places.

He was in his bedroom again. Not the bedroom at his grandmother's house but *his* bedroom, the real one in Washington, D.C. He was buttoning his shirt, rushing to get ready for school. He was feeling nervous.

In another part of the house, he heard the voices of his mom and dad. Another fight. They seemed to be having more and more of them. Mark suspected they had tried to hide their fights from him, but they couldn't. He heard them in the morning and sometimes late at night. And even when they weren't fighting, he suffered through the silences at mealtimes. He knew what the late hours his dad kept at the office really meant.

He fumbled with the buttons on his shirt and listened to the voices. His name was mentioned. He froze. As the questions sneaked into his mind, he felt like a fist was punching his stomach. They weren't questions like he had on tests. They were more like feelings with question marks at the end of them: Why did his parents have to fight so much? Why did they say his name?

Maybe he was doing something to make them fight. Maybe it was because he had woken up late for school again. Maybe he had left his shoes in the middle of the living room floor again. Maybe . . . maybe . . . it was his fault. Maybe that's why they didn't fight around him, so he wouldn't hear their list of terrible things he had done to make them fight.

The voices reached a peak and stopped. It was as if a bell had rung, sending the fighters to their corners after another round.

Mark heard a soft shuffle of feet coming up the stairs, down the hall, then stopping at his bedroom door. Mark's dad opened the door and surveyed the room with that familiar frown.

"You're not ready yet," he said. "You want to be late for school again?"

"No, sir," Mark whispered.

"And look at this room. How many times do I have to tell you to clean it?" He shook his head. "Hurry up. Your mother has breakfast waiting for you downstairs."

Mark's father turned and walked away. Shortly afterward, his parents' bedroom door slammed.

In the kitchen his mom didn't say anything. Her eyes were red and wet as she served Mark his breakfast. At one point, she kissed him on the forehead while he ate. She had never done that before. He usually got a kiss on the way out the door. It scared him, and he didn't want to eat anymore.

Finally he put on his coat, grabbed his books, and braced himself for the cold morning air. His mom opened the door, leaned down, and kissed him again. One of her tears smeared his cheek. And the tear was warm.

Mark stepped out into a nippy February day, thrusting his hands into his coat pockets. He heard the laughter and chatter of the other kids waiting at the end of the block for the school bus. He wondered if they had mornings like he did. Did their parents have fights before breakfast?

He walked down the front porch steps and glanced back to see his mother close the door. His eyes drifted up to his parents' bedroom window. The curtain moved slightly. For a brief moment, Mark thought he saw his father looking down at him.

Later that afternoon when he came running in after school, Mark's mom asked him to sit down and listen carefully. With a quavering voice, she explained that his dad had left them. She gave some excuses about why he had. She said he was overworked, they had some problems, and he was confused about things.

But Mark knew the truth. His dad had left because of him. He had left because Mark had woken up late again, his room wasn't clean, and his dad couldn't take it anymore. It was Mark's fault.

"There's the post office," Patti said, bringing Mark back to the present.

Mark rushed into the small brick building, waited in line, then handed over his letter when it was his turn.

The woman behind the counter smiled wearily and handed it back. "It's too crumpled," she said. "Put it in another envelope, honey. You don't want it to get lost, do you?"

He shook his head and stepped away from the counter. He had to get the letter to his dad soon.

Outside the post office Mark said to Patti, "I have to go home right away."

"But we were going to Whit's End."

He started to protest, but she grabbed his sleeve and tugged him along. "It's right over there," Patti pointed, "across from McAlister Park. Come on."

He didn't want to be rude; he figured he could escape soon enough. Patti identified the various buildings for Mark as they walked through the park. She showed him the gym, the basketball courts, and sports facilities, but he didn't care. Then a different sort of building came into view. It was a large house sitting off by itself, as if it didn't belong.

As he got closer, Mark noticed that the house looked more like a collection of odd-shaped boxes with small, medium, and large squares and a rectangular section with windows. It also had a jutting tower and roofs that angled every which way, as if the creator couldn't make up his mind which way to build them.

"That's Whit's End," Patti said.

For a moment Mark was drawn to the strange-looking place. But his mission came to mind again. He didn't want to go to an ice cream shop. He wanted to go back home. He wanted to get a new envelope and mail the letter to his dad. He wanted to get away from Patti Eldridge, who kept talking even when he stopped listening. Mark was about to tell Patti he had to leave when—BOOM!

Chapter
Three

THE EXPLOSION SHOOK THE PARK, sending echoes through the trees and scattering the birds like a shotgun blast.

"Come on!" Patti said, running toward Whit's End.

By the time they reached the front of the house, a group of kids and a few adults were filing out in orderly fashion. Mark was surprised by the lack of panic. No one was running or screaming. He didn't see any signs of damage. Small clouds of smoke drifted from the basement window.

What a strange place, Mark thought.

"Let's try to get in," Patti said, as they reached the front door. "I want to see what happened."

That was as far as they got.

A man stood in the doorway with a fire extinguisher in his hand. White foam dribbled from the nozzle. "Nothing to worry about," the man announced. "Everything's under control."

His voice was low and fuzzy, and his face was lifted into a large smile. His friendly eyes were bright and clear beneath white, bushy eyebrows. The eyebrows matched his mustache and hair, which were thick and untamed.

A fire engine siren screamed in the distance, growing louder as it approached Whit's End from Main Street.

"Completely unnecessary," the man said quietly. Glancing at Mark, he winked.

"What happened, Mr. Whittaker?" Patti asked.

Mr. Whittaker. So this is the one Patti kept talking about. Mark studied the man more seriously.

"A fractured filament," Mr. Whittaker answered. He put down the extinguisher and moved toward the firemen who were jumping off the parked fire engine. Their red helmets and yellow coats looked bright against the green of the park. Whit waved them back. "False alarm, boys. A lot of smoke, that's all."

As the fire chief approached Whit, he ordered the others to go in and check the building.

"The third time in two weeks, Whit," the chief said with a hint of disapproval.

"There's no danger," Whit replied.

"Uh-huh, and what was it *this* time?" the fire chief asked.

Whit hesitated, his cheeks turning red. "The Imagination Station."

"Huh?"

"A time machine, sort of," Whit offered reluctantly.

A time machine! Mark thought. *Can people really travel through time?*

The fire chief shook his head. "Whit, you're a wacko."

Mark heard affection in the man's voice.

Patti leaned toward Mark. "This happens all the time," she whispered. "Whit's always inventing stuff like that."

"Do . . . do the inventions work?" Mark asked.

"Of course!" Patti exclaimed proudly.

Then Mark heard a breathless puffing and a high-pitched voice muttering behind them.

"Uh-oh, here comes Emma Douglas," Patti said with a snicker.

Emma Douglas went straight to Whit. "Mr. Whittaker, please!" she said in a voice full of shaky nerves. "I . . . I told you when I took this job that I'm . . . I'm not very good with . . . with this." She gestured toward Whit's End. A strand of her silver hair came loose from the knot at the back of her head.

Whit smiled, his upper lip disappearing beneath his mustache. Mark thought the smile was reassuring.

"I'm sorry, Emma," Whit said. "I must have made a mistake in my figuring."

Her small hands twisted her apron, as if she were strangling it. "I know you're sorry, Mr. Whittaker, but I . . . I don't think I can stand it anymore. All the tinkering you do, the strange inventions, kids everywhere, loud noises." Emma Douglas caught her breath. "It's too much for me."

Whit pleaded with her. "Emma, give it a little more time."

"I quit, Mr. Whittaker. This minute. This very second. I quit." Emma Douglas turned and went back through the door into Whit's End. The knot of hair at the back of her head bobbed up and down like the tail of a rabbit.

Whit shoved his hands deep into the pockets of his work overalls. "Another one," he said. "That's the third worker I've lost in less than a month."

"No surprise," the fire chief chuckled as he walked away, calling orders to the other firemen to return to the station.

Patti tugged at Whit's sleeve. "Hey, Mr. Whittaker, you have to meet Mark."

Whit turned, giving his full attention to the two of them.

Patti went on, "He's old lady Shaef—" she caught herself and started again, "He's Mrs. Shaeffer's grandson. He lives in her house."

"Ah," Whit said. He reached out, took Mark's hand, and shook it vigorously. "I knew your grandmother well. A wonderful woman. Are you Julie's son?"

Mark nodded, suddenly shy.

Whit nodded too. "Of course. Your grandmother talked a lot about your family. There were pictures of you in her living room. I remember now."

Mark relaxed. There was something comforting about Whit's knowing who Mark was. He imagined Whit in his grand-mother's living room, maybe drinking tea, looking at the family photos and talking about them like old friends would.

"You're better-looking in person." Whit grinned. "Don't you think so, Patti?" he asked with a nudge.

Patti blushed. "I don't know. I never saw the pictures."

Mark's mind went back to the Imagination Station. He had a lot of questions he was bursting to ask. He had to say something, anything.

"It's very nice to meet you, Mark," Whit said with sincerity. "You should come on into the shop and have a look around. Meanwhile, I need to figure out how I'm going to replace Emma Douglas. Poor woman." He started to walk away from them.

"Mr. Whittaker," Mark blurted suddenly.

Whit stopped and looked back.

Mark didn't know how he was going to say what he wanted to say, but he didn't want to lose the chance to get closer to the Imagi-nation Station. "If you need help, I . . . maybe I could help you."

Whit cocked an eyebrow.

Mark continued, "Maybe until you find someone else, I could be an errand boy or something. You don't even have to pay me."

Whit rubbed his chin thoughtfully. "Hmm, an errand boy."

Mark wanted to say something else, something to convince him, but he couldn't think of anything. His stomach tightened with anticipation.

"Not a bad idea, as a temporary measure."

"It's a great idea," Patti said.

"Come on inside, Mark." Whit motioned to him. "I'll call your parents. If it's okay with them, it's okay with me. I could use the help, and I'll even pay you for it."

Mark's heart raced as they stepped into Whit's End to make the phone call.

Chapter
Four

WHILE WHIT TALKED WITH MARK'S MOM on the phone, Patti offered to show Mark around the shop. He wanted to tour the place, but more than anything he wanted to see the Imagination Station. He had it all worked out in his mind. If the Imagination Station could really do what they said it could, then Mark might be able to go back in time and change what had happened with his dad. He could make things like they were before his dad left them.

Mark's excitement surged like a current of electricity. He had to find that machine. As Patti guided him through the soda shop, he looked anxiously for something that might resemble an Imagination Station. He noted the snow-white refrigerators and shining silver dispensers. Was the time machine white? Or silver?

Next they went into a room with shelves filled with books. "This is the library," Patti explained.

Mark nodded, imagining that one of the bookcases slid away to reveal a secret room. If one did, Patti didn't give him the chance to see it.

Then she led him into a large auditorium containing a stage for theatrical performances. Looking at Whit's End from the outside, Mark wouldn't have guessed the building was so big.

Upstairs, Patti showed him the county's largest train set. At least that's what the sign beside it declared. The train layout featured scale replicas of classic engines chugging around lifelike hills, valleys, and miniature villages.

Kids and adults were everywhere. No one seemed to be concerned about the earlier explosion. Everyone was involved in one game or another. Mark had to admit that Whit's End really was unlike anything he had ever seen before.

They had finished the tour, but Mark hadn't seen anything that looked like an Imagination Station. Patti took him back to the kitchen, where Whit was still talking to Mark's mom on the phone. It was an endless conversation about his grandmother. Finally Whit asked if it was all right for Mark to be his errand boy. The tension was growing in his stomach again.

Whit finally smiled at Mark and gave him the okay sign.

Mark's mind spun with plans. Now that he was an official employee, he hoped Whit would hurry up and show him the Imagination Station.

Whit hung up the phone and slipped behind the ice cream counter to serve some newly arrived customers. As he dished out scoops of ice cream, he said, "For now, I'll need you to run some errands for me. I'll show you how to take care of things around the shop later. I don't think it'll be too hard for you."

What about the Imagination Station? Mark wanted to ask. *Where is it? When can I use it? Put the ice cream away and show me how to go back in time!*

Whit glanced at Mark. For a moment he was afraid Whit had read his mind.

"I know what you can do," Whit said. "You can run out to Tom Riley's place and pick up a box for me."

"A box?" Mark asked.

"Not a big one," Whit assured him, lowering his voice to a near-whisper. "It's top secret, though. It's a very important part that I need to get the Imagination Station working again. It broke in the explosion."

"Can I go?" Patti asked.

Mark darted a disapproving look in her direction. He wanted to explain to her that this wasn't a job for a girl. Top secret stuff was for guys. He was just about to say so, but Whit spoke first.

"Good idea, Patti," Whit said. "You can show Mark how to get to Tom's house."

Patti straightened up proudly. "I know a shortcut."

"I figured you would. You'll make a good team." Whit dropped a scoop of vanilla ice cream into a cone and handed it over the counter to a customer.

Patti tugged at Mark's sleeve. "Let's go."

Mark looked to Mr. Whittaker for any final instructions. Whit smiled at him and nodded. "Tell Tom I sent you. He'll know what to do."

Mark followed Patti outside, but he didn't like having to depend on her. *She's nice enough*, he thought, *but she still talks too much.*

"I know a shortcut," she said in the same proud voice she used back at the shop.

"I know, I know," Mark said. He didn't care how they got there. He just wanted to get the missing piece to the Imagination Station.

Patti began to talk again, but Mark's mind wandered off into another daydream. He replayed every detail in his mind of the day his father left, and it gave him new resolve to change things back.

"Hey! Look over there," Patti said.

Mark looked around, surprised to find that he had followed Patti into a clearing. She was pointing to a small grove of trees. Beyond them, Mark saw a large white house and behind it, a barn.

"Are you hungry?" Patti asked.

Mark was, but he shook his head no. "We have to get to Mr. Riley's, Patti."

"I'm hungry," Patti said firmly.

"Okay, okay. You're hungry, but we didn't bring any food."

Patti grinned knowingly. "We didn't need to bring any food. See those trees over there? They have the best apples in the whole county. Come on!"

Before Mark could say anything, Patti dashed off toward the trees. Mark grumbled to himself but ran after her. She was already climbing one of the trees by the time he caught up with her.

"Go on, Mark. Get an apple out of that other tree." Mark hesitated.

"What are you, a chicken? Get yourself an apple! You know you want one."

Mark reached for a lower branch, but a question nagged him. Will the owner mind? He shrugged it off. He didn't want Patti to think he was a coward, so he climbed up into the tree.

Patti was back on the ground by the time he found an apple that looked good enough to eat. She called to him, waving her apple proudly. "I found a big one! Hurry up," she said. "You don't want to get caught."

"Caught?" Mark asked, as he snapped off the apple he wanted.

"By the owner," Patti replied. "He's kind of, well, crazy. He gets real mad when kids climb his trees."

"What!" Mark nearly fell out of the tree as he started scrambling down the trunk.

Then he heard a screen door slam.

Mark peeked through the leaves. An old man was working his way down the front porch steps, yelling, "Aha! Caught you!"

Mark looked at the ground and considered his chances of getting down before the old man reached the tree. Then he saw the long barrel of a shotgun.

Patti shrieked, screaming at Mark, "Hurry!"

She stepped back, stumbled, and then took off running. Mark reached the lowest branch and swung his legs down to jump. It was as far as he got. He was helplessly hanging on the branch when the old man rounded the tree.

"I've warned you kids!" he shouted, aiming the shotgun at Mark's rear end.

Mark closed his eyes, his heart pounding wild rhythms in his chest.

"Don't," he squeaked.

Just then, the old man pulled the trigger.

Chapter
Five

MARK LISTENED FOR THE TELLTALE ROAR and tensed, fearing the sting of shotgun pellets. Instead he heard a gentle spraying sound, as warm water soaked through his clothes. He opened his eyes and looked down at the wet seat of his pants.

"I got you fair and square!" Tom Riley shouted, laughing as he pulled the trigger on his water-squirting shotgun.

Then he turned and called, "You can come out from behind that tree, Patti Eldridge. I got your friend!"

Patti stumbled out of her hiding place doubled over with laughter.

Mark dropped from the tree and landed with a squish. He brushed at the water on the back of his pants while Patti continued laughing helplessly. Tom did, too.

Everyone in this town is crazy, Mark thought.

"It's a game," Patti finally said. "If Mr. Riley finds anyone climbing his apple tree, he gives them a shot from his water gun."

"Thanks for telling me." Mark frowned, tugging at his soaked pants.

Tom put out his hand for Mark to shake. "We haven't been properly introduced. I'm Tom Riley."

"I'm Mark. Mark Prescott." As they shook hands, Mark felt the calluses on Mr. Riley's palm.

"Mark is living in Mrs. Schaeffer's house," Patti explained. "She was his grandma."

"I see," Tom said and hitched his thumbs into his overalls. "Your grandma was a good woman. Now tell me what you're doing out here besides picking my apples and getting a shower."

"Mr. Whittaker sent us," Patti blurted out.

"He sent me," Mark amended. "I'm his new employee."

"Oh," Tom said, "then you must be here for the part to the Imagination Station."

"Yeah, both of us!" Patti added.

"Then you'd better come with me."

They walked to the house while Tom explained how he helped Whit with some of the inventions and kept the extra parts on his workroom bench. Mark imagined the two men working under a dim light as they discussed and created and invented all sorts of magical things. The thought held wonder for Mark, and he looked at Tom Riley with different eyes.

The summer heat hadn't pierced the walls of the Riley home. It was cool down in the basement, back where the workroom was located. The workbench had a large assortment of tools and gadgets. Some of them Mark recognized, others he didn't.

Tom glanced around with confusion.

"The part for the Imagination Station," Mark reminded him.

"That's right," Tom chuckled, patting Mark on the shoulder. Then he reached to an upper shelf and brought down a mysterious object wrapped in white cloth. "This is what you came for," he said, carefully setting the component on the bench.

Mark stepped closer as Tom pulled the cloth aside. The thing looked like a black grapefruit with all sorts of transistors and computer parts attached to it. Tom gently placed it in a box and cushioned it with rags.

"What does it do?" Patti asked.

Tom stuffed more rags into the box. "It's a power unit. It's one of four in the Imagination Station. Together they make it work. Whit said one blew out when he tried it this morning."

"It must be pretty wonderful to make such a big noise," Patti said.

"Mostly noise and smoke," Tom replied. "We built it so it wouldn't blow up if anything went wrong. That's one reason it's so heavy."

"Still scary," Patti said quietly.

Tom nodded. "I reckon it is, if you don't know what to expect."

As if struck by a new thought, Tom reached up and grabbed another gadget from the shelf. "Oh, tell Whit I finished the alarm. He knows how to hook it up."

Mark looked closely at this new piece. It resembled a clock.

"Next time the Imagination Station has a mind to blow up, this alarm will warn Whit before it happens." Tom patted the alarm proudly. "It even has a test button," he added, pushing a small red circle on the top. The alarm started to tick.

Mark took a step back.

Tom continued, "You push this button, and in thirty seconds the alarm will go off. That gives you time to prepare for it. It's a little loud."

They watched intently for the remaining fifteen seconds or so. Even though they knew the time was up, the bell blasted so loudly it startled them all when it finally went off.

"Wow!" Mark exclaimed.

Tom laughed, "If that doesn't warn Whit something's wrong, nothing will." Tom put a lid on the box and handed it to Mark. "Be careful, son. I only have a couple more of these left."

"I'll be very careful," Mark promised.

Tom led the way back upstairs for homemade lemonade. Afterward, he walked them toward the woods, chatting cheerfully about Whit and Odyssey and expressing his hope that they would come to visit again sometime. Patti said they would. As they said good-bye, Tom gave Mark an apple, which he put inside the box.

Mark remembered his promise to be careful and clutched the box so tightly his arms began to ache. He could have asked Patti to carry it a while, but he was too proud.

Once again they took Patti's shortcut through the woods. This time Patti asked Mark questions about himself. It was awkward at first. He didn't like to talk about himself, but she persisted. Finally he told her why they had to move to Odyssey, being careful not to mention that all the trouble was his fault. He didn't tell her his plans for the Imagination Station, either.

"That's sad," Patti said about Mark's parents. He thought she meant it.

"I wrote my dad a letter," he added brightly.

"Is that the one we took to the post office?" Patti asked.

Mark nodded and said, "I asked him to come visit for the Fourth of July."

Mark felt funny telling her. He hadn't told anyone—not even his mom—what was in the letter.

Patti's face lit up. "Do you think he will?"

"Yeah! He said on the phone if I ever wanted anything to write and ask, so I did. It's a long weekend. He has to come."

"How long before he answers it?" Patti asked.

"He'll probably call when . . ." Mark stopped, suddenly remembering. The letter was still stuffed in his back pocket. With all the excitement over the Imagination Station, he had forgotten all about it. His heart sank.

Patti searched Mark's face. "What's wrong?"

"I was going to mail the letter today." Mark's voice was low again.

How could he have been so forgetful? He had a mission.

He quickened his step. He had to get the box to Mr. Whittaker, find a clean envelope, and mail the letter. They came out of the woods on Glossman Street, the road leading to the center of town. They had followed it only a short way when they heard the rattle of bikes behind them. By the time they turned to see who it was, they were surrounded.

Mark groaned quietly.

Joe Devlin and five of his friends climbed off their bikes. "Hello, Patti." Joe smiled viciously. "Guess it's time to finish the fight we had this morning."

Chapter
Six

"I'M NOT AFRAID OF YOU, JOE," Patti said with a sneer. "I beat you this morning; I can beat you again."

"Quiet, Patti," Mark whispered.

"You sneaked up on me this morning, that's all," Joe said, angrily. "Let's see how you do in a fair fight."

"My dad said boys shouldn't hit girls," Mark offered feebly.

"My dad says the same thing," Joe mocked, "but Patti isn't a girl. Are you, Patti? You dress like a boy, and you act like a boy. I guess you think you can fight like a boy, too, huh?" Joe stepped closer, and so did his gang.

"You want to fight? Then let's fight," Patti challenged, positioning herself for the attack. "And Mark won't rescue you this time, either!"

"He won't have to rescue me. He'll have to rescue you like boyfriends are supposed to." Joe laughed. His friends joined in, taunting and cackling.

"He's not my boyfriend," Patti countered with a blush.

Joe and his boys laughed louder. "Patti's got a boyfriend. Patti's got a boyfriend," they chanted.

"You guys are idiots!" Patti shouted. "Come on, Joe, you think you're so tough. I'll show you how tough you are!" Her face turned red.

She thinks she's going to fight them all! Mark thought.

Joe crouched slightly, as if he were going to jump at Patti.

Mark tensed and did the only thing he could think to do. "Wait!" he yelled.

All eyes turned to Mark.

"We can't get in a fight. We might break what's in this box," Mark announced.

"What do I care what's in your box?" Joe snorted.

"It's not my box," Mark explained. "It's Mr. Whittaker's box. And there's no telling what might happen if it gets broken."

Joe squinted, looking at the box. "That's Mr. Whittaker's? My dad says he's a crazy old man."

A wave of laughter went through the gang.

"Maybe he is," Mark said. "That's why we have to get this box back to him."

Joe shrugged it off. "Mr. Whittaker can't do anything to us," he countered. "Come on, Patti, your boyfriend's stalling."

Patti looked at Mark with a puzzled expression on her face.

"You remember the explosion at Whit's End earlier?" Mark asked.

Joe eyed Mark suspiciously. "Yeah? What about it?"

"I heard it blew up the whole bottom floor!" said one of Joe's gang.

Mark attempted a scowl. "Yeah, well, what's in this box caused it. It could happen again if I want. You guys should get out of here before you get hurt. I'm through messing around with you small-town bullies."

"Yeah, sure," Joe said in disbelief. "Nobody's going to get hurt."

"Okay, you asked for it," Mark said and put down the box. "I'll show you!"

Maybe it was curiosity or maybe it was fear, but everyone stood still and watched carefully. Mark took the lid off the box like a magician who was about to pull a rabbit out of a hat. Everyone stepped back.

"I'm telling you, you better get far away from here. You don't know me. I might be crazier than Mr. Whittaker," Mark warned.

Joe and his gang exchanged uneasy looks.

"What are you doing?" Patti asked, moving closer to Mark.

"Quiet," Mark whispered. Then he said aloud, "You guys have thirty seconds to get away."

Patti glanced at the box and realized what he was up to. Her eyes smiled at him.

Suddenly she shouted, "No! Don't do it!"

Mark punched the red test button on the top of Tom Riley's alarm. It ticked loudly.

Patti bolted away. "I'm getting out of here."

"See you guys later," Mark said, running a short distance away.

Joe's gang looked at the box, and then Joe, and then back at the box. They got tangled up with their bikes as they dragged them off to a safe distance.

Not Joe—he leaned forward to get a better glimpse of the contents.

Mark yelled, "Twenty seconds!"

Startled, Joe jumped and backed up a little.

"Joe," one of his friends called out, "get away from there."

Joe's confidence decreased with each tick.

"Fifteen seconds!" Mark shouted.

Joe moved toward his bike one slow step at a time, never taking his eyes off the box.

His entire gang screamed, "Run!" "Come on, Joe." "Get out of there!"

"Ten seconds!" Mark and Patti called together.

"Nine," Mark continued.

Joe grabbed his bike.

"Eight!"

Joe stumbled as his bike slipped from his hands. He got up and moved quickly away from the box.

"Seven!"

The gang moved farther away, tripping over one another as they did.

"Six!"

Joe's walk turned to a jog.

"Five!"

"Hit the dirt!" Patti screamed.

"Four!"

Several of the boys crouched near the ground.

"Three!"

Joe started to run.

"Two!"

Joe fell to the ground with the rest of his gang.

"One!"

They all watched expectantly.

Nothing happened.

Patti looked at Mark with concern.

Mark shrugged. "The timing must be off."

Joe and his gang growled and slowly stood. Joe started to issue a new threat.

But the alarm went off with such a shrill blast that Joe and his company dropped to the ground again.

"Into the woods!" Mark exclaimed, rushing for the box. Without breaking his stride, Mark grabbed the box and took off running.

Joe shouted, his anger growing with each word, "We've been conned! Get 'em!"

Patti ran through the woods. Mark was close behind, struggling not to drop the box. His heart pounded furiously. He dodged piles of leaves and broken branches. The shouts and curses of Joe and his friends followed them.

"This way," Patti gasped, moving off the path into a deeper part of the woods.

She ducked behind a tree and gestured for Mark to do the same. He tripped, knocking them both into a cushion of leaves. They lay still and struggled to quiet their hard breathing. The alarm had stopped. Mark heard thumping sounds of running feet. Threats and curses were swallowed by labored panting as Joe's gang ran down the path, passed by, and then faded away.

Mark relaxed and sighed with relief.

Patti began to laugh softly. "I've never seen them so scared," she said between giggles.

Mark smiled.

"Great idea about the box," she said, laughing harder. "I wish I'd thought of that."

"You were too busy trying to get yourself killed," Mark stated with a hint of sarcasm.

He closed his eyes, enjoying the soft bed of leaves. For the moment he was so tired that he didn't care about the letter to his father or the Imagination Station or any of the problems that weighed on his mind. He smiled, feeling relieved they had escaped.

"Oh!" Patti's startled gasp jolted him back to reality.

Then she shouted, "Watch out!"

A group of strangely dressed boys stood over Mark, their spears and arrows pointing directly at his chest.

Chapter
Seven

HAVE WE GONE BACK IN TIME? Mark wondered. His captors were carrying homemade shields, spears, and bows and arrows. They also had on vests that made them look like they had stepped out of an old Bible movie. *But are these characters real?* he wondered.

Patti quickly ended the notion. "I know who you are," she said. "I recognize you behind that disguise, George Baldwin. You, too, Billy MacPherson."

"We do not know these strange names," one of them said.

Another one stepped forward. "I am Jonathan. Are you Amalekites or are you with the forces of King Saul?"

"Quit playing around. You know who I am, Pete." Patti's tone was mocking. She started to get up, but the spears and arrows persuaded her otherwise.

"Cut it out!" she said.

"Well?" the one called Jonathan asked more forcefully.

Mark thought back to the Old Testament stories, remembering how David was best friends with Jonathan, son of Saul. But Saul, king of Israel, had chased the boy David. King Saul was jealous because God had chosen David to be the next king. Saul had also fought the Amalekites, the enemies of Israel.

Mark decided to play along with this Jonathan's game. "We are not Amalekites. And we are not servants of the king," Mark said, trying to sound official, "except as loyal subjects."

"Oh, brother." Patti rolled her eyes in disbelief.

"Why are you in our woods?" Jonathan asked. "We are true Israelites and do not look kindly to foreigners in our lands."

"We're trying to get this box back to Mr. Whittaker. But Joe and his gang tried to stop us." Then Patti said with anger, "Get those sticks out of my face!"

Jonathan gestured for them both to rise. "Come with us," he said.

Mark obeyed, clutching the box tightly. He considered trying the alarm clock trick again but decided that this gang wouldn't fall for it.

"Where are we going?" Patti asked.

"You'll see," Jonathan answered.

As they walked through the woods, Mark hoped Patti knew where they were because he was lost. He also hoped this band of "Israelites" wouldn't hurt them, but he couldn't be sure.

Suddenly Jonathan signaled for them to stop. "Blindfolds," he said.

"Oh, no you don't," Patti said, stepping away from them. A couple of Israelites grabbed her.

"Hey, let go!" she yelled, straining against them.

"You won't get hurt," the leader said. "This is so you won't see the entrance to the hideout."

Patti continued to argue and struggle as they blindfolded her.

Mark thought it was a little too dramatic but decided not to fight them. He wanted to get this over with, since the box was painfully heavy in his arms.

Then the Israelites spun Mark and Patti around several times to make sure they couldn't track where they were being taken.

As they quietly marched through the woods, Mark listened carefully. Natural noises seemed amplified—the padding of their feet on the leaves, birds singing, a distant voice of a mother calling her child. And the smells were familiar—a dark woodsy odor, green pine, and damp leaves.

Eventually the sounds and smells gave way to something new: fresh air and distant traffic. They were near an opening to the woods. But Mark had no way of guessing where they might be.

Then they stopped again.

"Here," a voice said.

He shifted the box's weight from one arm to the other. He heard brushing noises, as if someone were sweeping a wooden floor. Then it sounded as if a latch were being lifted on a large door. A creak and a groan followed when the door—if it was a door—opened.

"Watch the steps," someone else said.

"How can I watch the steps with this stupid blindfold on?" Patti asked. Her voice sounded distant when she spoke.

Mark was led forward and then down a stairway. Outside noises were swallowed up by hollow nothingness. Their footsteps squeaked and clicked as they walked. Mark thought they might be in an underground tunnel. A door closed behind them with a heavy iron clang.

We're in a dungeon, Mark imagined. *A cobwebbed castle with shackles and chains, musty smells, mildewed walls and instruments of torture.* The thought didn't faze him. By now, his arms ached from carrying the box. He could endure anything, if only they would let him set it down.

They stopped again, and another door opened. They were led into another place where the air was fresher, the mustiness gone. But it was still very quiet.

"Sit down," a voice ordered. "You can put the box by your feet."

Mark gladly obliged, reaching back to make sure there was a place to sit. He felt the rugged texture of a wooden bench and sat on it. Patti sat next to him.

"Can we take these blindfolds off now?" Patti asked. "This whole thing is really dumb."

"In a minute," came the reply.

Mark and Patti sat patiently. Mark wondered what was supposed to happen next. All was quiet.

Too quiet, Mark thought.

"Hello?" he called.

No answer.

"Anybody here?" he asked.

No answer again.

He reached up and slowly pushed up his blindfold. It took a moment for his eyes to adjust. He blinked a few times. The room was obviously some sort of basement, but the Israelites had slipped away.

"They're gone," Mark whispered to Patti.

They both took off their blindfolds.

Mark blinked again. The room came into focus. It was obviously a workroom cluttered with tools, gadgets, and strange parts. A large machine sat in the center of the floor.

"Where are we?" Patti asked. "Look at this place!"

"I don't know," Mark replied. He couldn't take his eyes off the machine. Inside it, lights twinkled like a Christmas tree through the deep-brown colored glass.

"What is that thing?" Patti asked, mouth hanging open with awe.

A low, resonant voice answered, "It's the Imagination Station."

Chapter
Eight

JOHN AVERY WHITTAKER STOOD at the door, a broad smile on his face. "Do you like it?"

Mark's eyes locked on the machine as he walked slowly toward it. *So this is the Imagination Station! This is how to get things back to the way they used to be.* Mark circled it, taking in every detail.

"You brought the part," Whit said, stooping to retrieve the box from the floor. "Thank you."

"Hey, Whit," Patti began, "what's with those kids who brought us here? The . . . what do you call them?"

"The Israelites," Whit said. "You took so long getting back with the part, I decided to send them out to look for you."

"Yeah, but the Israelites? I never heard of a gang called the Israelites," Patti said.

"It's make-believe," Whit answered, pulling the contents from Tom Riley's box. "They pretend they're a band of King David's men. Sometimes they battle the forces of wicked King Saul; other times they're off fighting the Amalekites. It's fun, and they get to learn the Bible in the process."

"Oh," Patti remarked with an easy acceptance.

Whit turned to Mark. "What do you think of my little invention?"

The question startled Mark. He was deep in thought about the machine and didn't realize Whit was standing next to him. "It looks great," Mark replied. "Does it work?"

"Not yet. I hope it will after I put this power source in and make a few more adjustments."

Whit flipped a panel switch on the side of the Imagination Station, and the station went dark. Then he began to unscrew bolts that held a small metal plate attached to the back of the machine.

Mark watched carefully. "Can I help?" he finally asked.

Whit handed the metal plate to Mark. "You can hold this while I get the new part hooked up."

Mark held the plate while Whit went to work. He undid a bolt here, attached a wire there, fastened a clip to this side, adjusted a screw to that side. He moved quickly, with the confidence of a man who knew exactly what he was doing.

"It's kind of cute," Patti observed.

Mark groaned inwardly. *A machine this powerful isn't cute*, he thought. He wished she would go home.

"We're almost there," Whit said softly as he continued working.

Mark's mind wandered. He pictured himself climbing into the machine, pushing the buttons, and riding back in time to the day his dad left. It was real. He could do it!

"Mark?" Whit's eyebrow was cocked. His arms were outstretched for the metal plate Mark was holding.

"Sorry," Mark mumbled as he handed it over.

"Daydreaming?" Whit asked, bolting the plate back to the machine.

Mark shuffled. "Yeah, I guess."

"About what?"

Mark looked at Whit and wondered how much he should say.

Finally he shrugged. "I was imagining what it would be like to go back in time."

"Ah, that depends on where you want to go," Whit said.

Patti jumped into the conversation. "I want to go back to . . . to . . ." She screwed up her face, realizing she had started to speak without knowing what she wanted to say. "I could go anywhere," she concluded.

"It also depends on why you want to go," Whit added.

Mark looked deeply into Whit's face. Did this kind old man know more about people and what they were thinking than he ever let on?

"What do you mean, why? Why not? I think it would be fun," Patti said.

"Fun, yes. A way to learn, too. But sometimes people want to go back in time for other reasons." Whit turned to his workbench and fiddled with one of the gadgets.

Mark felt uneasy. He had a strange feeling Whit was referring to him.

"Why would you want to go back in time, Mark?" Whit asked casually.

Mark swallowed and said, "I . . . I thought I'd like to go back to . . . to see my dad. That's all."

Whit turned slightly and asked, "Go back to see your dad? Why can't you see him now?"

"It's not the same now," Mark answered. "Everything's different. He's different."

Mark's heart pounded, and his voice shook. He didn't want to talk about this. Not to Whit. Not to anybody. He just wanted to get in the Imagination Station and go back.

"I don't know that going back in time will help," Whit said quietly. "Unless you think you're going back to change things."

Whit now faced Mark full-on. His eyes seemed to search Mark's. But Mark couldn't speak.

Whit spoke firmly. "Changing the past will never really bring present happiness, you know."

Their gazes locked. The statement hung between them on an invisible string.

No, you're wrong! Mark wanted to scream. *It has to make us happy again. Don't you see? It's all my fault my parents broke up. If I could go back, I could change it. I will change it!*

But Mark didn't say any of those things. He stared at his shoes instead.

Whit sighed deeply. "The Imagination Station isn't ready for operation anyway, not until I make those adjustments. I guess it doesn't make a whole lot of difference. Let's go on upstairs and forget about it."

"Yeah, let's go," Patti agreed.

Chapter
Nine

MARK SPENT THE REST OF THE DAY doing errands around Whit's End. Patti stayed on even though she wasn't needed anymore, but she didn't seem to care. At dinnertime, they went their separate ways.

On his way home, Mark plotted how he could get to the Imagination Station. Whit was wrong, Mark felt. He could go back in time and change things. He had to.

At home, while he and his mom were eating dinner, she asked him about his day. Then she talked about all the nice people she had met shopping that afternoon and the ones who had known Mark's grandmother. Mark's mind drifted away.

He helped his mom clean up the dishes, and then excused himself to go to his bedroom. He turned on the light, sat at the small rolltop desk, and carefully opened the crumpled letter he had written to his father. Had it only been this morning that he had met Patti and ruined the letter when he pulled her off Joe? The time between then and now seemed longer than any one day should be.

Mark double-checked the letter spread out before him. His handwriting was as neat as he could make it; he wanted everything to be perfect.

Dear Dad,

Hi. It's me, Mark. How are you? I'm fine. I don't like Odyssey very much, even though I haven't seen all of it yet. But I know I won't like it because you aren't here. Will you come to visit? You said if I asked you to come, you would. Please come for the Fourth of July weekend. We can do fireworks like we always used to.

Dad, I figured out that it was my fault you went away. I'm sorry. If you come back, I promise to clean my room and put my clothes away and not leave my sneakers in the middle of the living room floor for you to trip over when you come home. I'll do anything you want me to, if you come back.

But come for the Fourth of July anyway.

Love,

Mark

P.S. I really mean it.

Mark carefully wrote out his father's name and address on a clean envelope. His mom had given it to him earlier, along with a curious look. Mark wondered how she would respond if she knew what he had written.

The phone rang, making him jump enough to mess up the zip code. "Oh, no," he moaned.

Now he would have to get another clean envelope from his mother. He tossed the pen on the desk and frowned. "I can't even write a stupid zip code," he said to himself.

Downstairs, he heard his mother in the kitchen on the phone. *It's probably one of the women she met shopping today*, he figured.

He walked quickly through the dining room, slowing only when he heard his mom's tone of voice.

"No!" she said in a harsh whisper. "You will not put that

responsibility on me. If you want him to know, tell him yourself."

Mark heard the squeaking of her rubber soles as she paced across the kitchen floor.

He stood near the doorway and listened.

"It's one thing for you to take the coward's way out with me. It's another thing to do it with him. He deserves better. You hold on, and I'll get him." His mother paused. "Yes, now, Richard."

She put the phone down as Mark moved away from the doorway. He tried to act as if he had just walked into the room.

"Mark!" his mother called. Then spotting him in the dining room, she said, "Oh, there you are."

"Hi," Mark replied nervously. "I was looking for a new envelope."

She moved close to him and touched him lightly on the shoulder. Her voice was like a soft blanket, so different from the one he had heard her use on the phone.

"Your . . . your father is on the phone," she said. "He wants to talk to you."

Mark's heart raced. *This isn't good news*, he thought as he walked to the kitchen phone. *Something's wrong.*

He looked for some assurance from his mother. She was gone. It was just like the morning his dad left, when Mark had stood outside on the steps of his house in Washington, D.C., and looked back at the front door. He had wanted to see his mother's smile. Something that said it would be all right. But she had closed the door. Only this time, he heard her feet padding up the stairs. Was it his imagination, or did he hear a sob?

When Mark picked up the receiver, the phone line seemed to hiss like a charmed snake. "Hello?"

"Hello, son," Richard Prescott said cheerfully. "How are you?"

"I'm okay, Dad," Mark answered. "I'm mailing you a letter. I was going to mail it today, but it got scrunched up in my back pocket when I—"

"Mark," his dad interrupted, his voice sounding tight. "I want to hear about the letter. But I have to tell you something. Okay?"

Mark felt his cheeks flush. "Yeah, okay."

The pause seemed endless.

Then his father said, "Son . . ."

Mark held his breath.

"Son, I've been doing a lot of thinking. And, well, your mother and I have been talking a lot about it." The line crackled.

Whatever his father was about to say, Mark knew he didn't want to hear it. "Dad, listen, you got to come for the Fourth of July weekend, okay? I want you to see Odyssey and Grandma's house and my bedroom. I keep my bedroom really clean, Dad. You'll be proud. I don't even leave my shoes in the middle of the floor. So you have to come and—"

"Mark," his dad interjected, "my separation from your mother was a way to see if . . . if we could work it out or . . . or make it more permanent."

"Dad, listen—"

"No, Mark, you have to understand what I'm saying. I can't come for the Fourth of July." His father's voice sounded strained, full of tears. "See, your mother and I are going to proceed with the divorce. We won't . . . can't live together anymore."

Mark felt cold and heartsick. His father continued talking as Mark put down the receiver. Mark didn't want to know what he was saying. He didn't care. He only knew that his father wasn't coming for the Fourth of July. His father wasn't coming home for anything ever again.

The thought was enormous, larger than anything Mark had

ever tried to fit into his brain. It was so big, in fact, that scalding tears slid down his cheeks.

Mark walked to the front door and quietly stepped out into the warm summer night. He knew what he had to do.

Chapter
Ten

MARK WIPED THE TEARS FROM HIS face and looked across the street. Whit's End looked like a dark giant that was fast asleep. Mark glanced around for oncoming cars and then stepped from the curb.

He should have been afraid of what he planned to do. He wasn't. His fear was numbed by the news from his father.

Mark examined his watch in the dim street light. It was 9:38 P.M. Whit's End had closed at nine. Would Whit lock the front door of his shop in such a small, trustworthy town?

Probably, Mark guessed. *No town is that trustworthy.*

He silently made his way around to the side of the large building. He crept along like a shadow on the wall, searching for a way to get inside.

The basement has a window, he recalled. *Maybe it's unlocked.*

He ran toward it and then slowed down, approaching cautiously. *Whit might be working late*, he thought.

He carefully peered in the window. A small light, near the workbench, sent a colorful pool of warmth throughout the basement. No one was around. All was silent and still. The Imagination Station sat waiting.

Mark's heart quickened. He pushed on the window frame, but it didn't budge. He knelt and searched for the latch, finally spotting it near the top of the sill. It was in the locked position. Mark stood and leaned against the wall. He didn't know what to do.

"Hey! What are you doing?" someone shouted.

Mark jumped up and looked around to see who it was. Beneath the pale street light, he saw a police car. A large policeman stood nearby.

"Don't move!" the officer said, turning on the squad car spotlight and adjusting it toward Whit's End.

Everything in Mark's being told him to run as fast as he could, so he did.

"Hey!" the policeman shouted. "Come back here!"

Mark wasn't sure where he was going in the darkness. He thought he remembered a grove of trees somewhere behind Whit's End and a wide-open park beyond them.

"Stop!" the policeman yelled, taking up the chase.

Mark wondered if Odyssey policemen shot at their suspects.

The grove of trees appeared in the summer moonlight. Mark dove into the shadows, tripping over logs and leaves, feeling the sting of an odd branch lashing at his face.

The policeman was closing in.

Mark scrambled behind a fallen oak. A large root caught his foot and sent him sailing through the air. He landed in a pile of leaves. The fall knocked the wind out of him. He couldn't moan. He couldn't speak. He couldn't breathe. In fact he couldn't do anything but lie there gasping, trying to take in some air.

The officer stopped at the edge of the woods and turned his flashlight on. The beam bounced off the trees, scanning in all directions. For a moment the light rested near Mark; then it moved away again.

"Come on, kid. I know you're here somewhere," the policeman called out.

Do Odyssey policemen throw boys in jail? Mark wondered. *If they do, is it for the rest of their lives?*

He imagined his arrest. They would take his picture and make him hold one of those little cards with a number on it. His mother would be ashamed. His father would refuse to speak to him. The newspapers would say he was another product of a broken home. And Whit would never ever let him near the Imagination Station again.

Mark prepared himself for the worst.

But the policeman didn't come into the woods. He let the flashlight beam do the searching for him. It spotted trees and leaves and a fat old owl that hooted and flew away. Finally muttering something Mark couldn't hear, the policeman turned and walked back toward Whit's End. The night was quiet again except for the ongoing sound of crickets.

Mark sat up. What was he going to do now? If he went back to Whit's End, the police might be waiting. And if he went home, he would have to wait for another time to get to the Imagination Station. But would there ever be another time?

Mark's feelings told him there wouldn't be. What he had to do, he had to do this very minute.

When he started to push himself up off the ground, his hands slipped, and he felt something cold and hard. He jerked up and slid away from the spot.

When he felt convinced that the thing wouldn't hurt him, Mark crawled closer to see if he could make out what it was. He reached down to touch it again. It was metallic like the side of a car. He felt rivets along a straight edge.

What is this thing? he questioned as he scurried around it.

He brushed the leaves away with his hand, wishing he had a broom. A broom! Then he remembered the brushing sound he had heard when the Israelites led him and Patti back to Whit's End. They had brushed the leaves away and opened a door. A door to Whit's End!

As he was clearing off the leaves and dirt, his hand banged against a latch. Mark smiled with satisfaction. It was the way in!

Mark looked around to make sure the policeman was gone. He didn't want to risk getting caught now. All remained quiet.

Sweat mingled with the dirt on his hands as Mark grabbed the handle. The latch groaned and clicked but didn't release the door.

Mark adjusted his stance, planting his feet firmly on the ground. Then he yanked up on the latch until the door gave way. It wasn't as heavy as it looked. The hinges creaked in protest as Mark swung the door over and gently placed it on the ground. Pleased with himself, he looked down at a large, black, square hole.

Now what should he do? Mark's brain clicked over the details. What else had he heard when the Israelites led him this way? They went down a few stairs and then followed a long tunnel. Stairs and a tunnel.

Mark looked across the yard to Whit's End. It seemed like a distant fortress now. Even so, the tunnel must go underground from this point all the way to Whit's End—in complete darkness. Mark gulped hard.

Did Odyssey have rats? Large spiders? Snakes? Mark felt a chill trickle down his spine as he wondered what might be waiting for him in the black hole.

Taking a deep breath, he tried to decide if the journey was worth it. He thought of his mother and father, his home in Washington, D.C., his happiness.

Mark wished the large black hole would give some hint of friendship. It didn't. He braced himself and stepped into it anyway.

He made it to the bottom step before he expected to and nearly fell. Reaching out to steady himself, he felt the walls, which were rough and cool. His eyes started to adjust to the darkness, but he saw only more darkness. He moved forward slowly.

He began to sing tuneless "la, la's" and "da, da's." It was something he had learned to do to help fight his fears, to keep monsters away in the closet. He couldn't remember where he had learned the rule, but it had always proven true: Make music, and you'll feel safe.

Mark didn't really believe in monsters, though. But he sang anyway. No sense taking any chances.

A sudden thought stopped him. *Do rats and spiders and snakes understand the rule?* He hoped so.

Mark wasn't sure where he was now. Somewhere under the backyard of Whit's End, of course, but where? How far did he have to go? He thought he heard a noise behind him.

Is someone else in the passageway? Maybe Whit has someone or something down here to keep guard.

Mark's stomach tangled up into a hundred knots. He wanted to get out of this hole. He wanted to scream. He wanted the policeman to come and save him.

He gasped, thinking he heard a low pounding nearby. Or was it his heart? Maybe he should turn back. Maybe he was crazy to do this in the first place.

He looked behind him. The small amount of light that had

spilled into the doorway was gone. Up ahead, Mark could see a tiny dot of yellow. He prayed it was the door into Whit's End.

Something brushed against his leg. A scream caught in his throat, unable to come out. He pressed hard against the wall, and whatever it was brushed against his leg again. Mark kicked out wildly, but his foot didn't strike anything. He felt frozen with fear and stood as still as he could.

Then came a sound like a violin string being scratched. "Meow!"

Mark gave a startled jump. "A cat! A stupid cat!" he muttered to himself.

It meowed again and started its purring motor. The creature, unaware of Mark's terror, rubbed against his leg once more. Mark relaxed. He wasn't sure if he loved the cat for not being a monster or hated it for scaring him so badly.

When Mark's rubbery legs decided they could move again, he continued moving forward. The cat went ahead of him in the darkness, meowing, as if it were guiding him along. Mark willingly followed; he was less afraid now. Having the cat nearby made it all right.

The tiny yellow glow grew larger as he got closer. It was a night-light outside a door. Mark assumed it was the door leading into the basement of Whit's End. He sighed with relief.

The cat brushed against his leg and meowed again before running off in the opposite direction. *Poor cat*, Mark thought. *It must have gotten locked in the tunnel somehow.*

Locked! Mark groaned. *What if the door is locked?*

Mark hadn't even thought of that possibility. It seemed logical to him that if the secret door to the tunnel was unlocked, the secret door to Whit's End would be unlocked, too. Right? Surely he hadn't come all this way to get stopped by a locked door.

Mark reached out and seized the door handle, turning it quickly. The door opened silently on greased hinges. Mark's eyes widened as the room came into focus. It was exactly as they had left it that afternoon. He stared at the cluttered workbench, the orange glow, and the Imagination Station.

Mark made sure no one was lurking about when he stepped into the room. His throat was painfully dry, and his breathing was heavy. He circled the machine that remained at the center of his hopes, reaching the panel where Whit had turned off the Imagination Station. Mark looked around once more to make sure he was alone and then reached up and flipped on the silver switch.

At first he wasn't sure it was working. Nothing happened. Then he heard a low hum. Through the smoky glass, he could see the lights on the control panel blinking happily. When Mark opened the door, it made a whooshing sound. He smiled nervously and climbed inside the Imagination Station. It was like climbing into his dad's sports car, small and comfortable.

Fortunately Whit had clearly marked the buttons and switches on the control panel. There was also a small, square message panel in green letters, suggesting that he close the door.

Mark's fingers trembled as he pushed the labeled button. The door shut with another whoosh, followed by a gentle bump.

The message panel displayed a question: *When?* It also indicated a series of numbers beside another label marked: *Day, Date,* and *Time of Day.*

Mark turned the knob and twisted the stem of a small clock to provide the information. He thought it was easy. It was so easy, in fact, he was afraid that he might be doing something wrong.

Now the panel displayed the question: *Address, City, Country?* A small keyboard lit up. Mark guessed he was supposed to spell everything out. Since Mark didn't know how to type, he carefully pushed the letters in order. He gave the machine his home address in Washington, D.C., and finished with U.S.A.

"There," he said to himself proudly.

Next, the panel said: *Push the Red Button to Proceed.*

Mark reached for the red button. It blinked invitingly. Then he paused.

This is the right thing to do, he assured himself. He had to get his parents back together. He had to prove to his dad that he could be the son he should be. He had to go back to that day and make everything better, to make everything the way it was.

Mark pushed the blinking red button.

Instantly, a recording of Whit's soothing voice surrounded him, saying, "Welcome to the Imagination Station."

Chapter
Eleven

THE PANEL LIGHTS AND MESSAGE and even the orange glow outside the tinted-glass window vanished. Mark was in total darkness. He wondered if he had blown a fuse or broken the machine. Then suddenly it got very cold.

"I better get out of here," he said aloud. Reaching forward, he tried to find the button to open the door. But instead of the metal and plastic panel, Mark felt something wooden. It was long and shaped like a pole.

"Something's wrong here," he muttered. He felt around, hoping to find a door handle. When Mark found one, he gave it a tug, and the door slid back easily with a hollow crash.

Bright morning light and crisp, frosty air poured in. Mark blinked several times. He had expected to be taken back to his room in Washington, D.C., but the Imagination Station wasn't as precise as that. It wasn't precise at all.

Outside, he saw a trimmed lawn and the back of a house; on the inside, he noticed a rake, lawn mower, and folded patio furniture. As best as Mark could figure, the Imagination Station had put him into an outdoor shed. Even worse than that, it wasn't the Prescotts' shed.

"Mark? Mark Prescott? Is that you?"

Mark cupped a hand over his eyes to block the sunlight; he couldn't see who was calling him.

Mr. Moorhead, the old man who lived across the street from the Prescotts, had a large plastic garbage bag in his hand. He was dressed in a bathrobe and slippers.

"What are you doing in there?" he asked angrily, dropping the bag into the garbage can and moving across the lawn toward Mark.

Mark shuffled out of the shed, speechless.

Mr. Moorhead persisted, "You're trying to play hooky by hiding in my shed? Shame on you!"

"No, sir. See, I was—"

"Don't give me any foolish excuses. What would your parents say if they heard about this?" Mr. Moorhead interrupted.

Mark tried to explain, "I wasn't trying to—"

"I'm very disappointed in you," Mr. Moorhead went on. "I thought you were above this sort of behavior."

"But, I . . ." Mark sputtered, thinking he should make a run for it.

Before he could, Mr. Moorhead grabbed his arm. "Come on with me. I'm taking you back across the street to let your parents deal with you!" He started across the lawn, pulling Mark alongside of him.

Mark considered this a mixed blessing. On one hand, he would get back to his dad. On the other hand, his dad wouldn't be very happy with him. How would Mark explain it?

"See, Dad, I was in the Imagination Station trying to get back to my bedroom, but it put me in Mr. Moorhead's shed instead."

"Sure, Mark," his dad would say. "Make up another story."

Mr. Moorhead rounded his house and crossed the front lawn with Mark in tow.

"I'm sorry to do this to you, son," Mr. Moorhead explained.

"But if parents don't nip this sort of behavior in the bud right away, you'll be out driving fast cars and killing yourself with drugs."

Mark looked across the street at his house. *Home! This is it. I made it!*

The familiarity overwhelmed him. He felt a lump form in his throat and grow into a small softball. He was home again. He wanted to cry, a feeling he hadn't expected.

Mark also didn't expect to see his mother pull out of their driveway in her car.

"Hey, Mrs. Prescott!" Mr. Moorhead shouted.

"Mom!" Mark cried out.

She didn't hear their calls. The windows were up, and her back was to them. The car screeched away to their right, stopped at the corner, turned left, and disappeared.

A new panic rose in Mark's mind. What time was it? Had the Imagination Station dropped him off at the wrong time, just like it had dropped him in the wrong place? Maybe his dad had already left!

"Well, what do you know about that?" Mr. Moorhead said, scratching his head.

"What time is it?" Mark asked.

"Time for you to be in school!"

My father might be home, Mark thought. *If I could get to the house, it might not be too late.*

He was about to mention this to Mr. Moorhead when he heard the familiar sound of squealing brakes off to their left. Mr. Moorhead and Mark turned at the same time.

It was Mark's school bus. It had pulled up to the stop sign and was ready to turn onto Mark's street.

Mr. Moorhead smiled pleasantly. "Well, well. Guess it's not too late for you to catch the bus, at least."

He pulled Mark to the edge of the curb and began to wave for the long, yellow vehicle to stop. Mark looked up at the windows filled with the half-awake faces he knew so well.

"No." Mark squirmed. "You don't understand."

"What's the matter, Mark? Do you have a test you don't want to take?" Mr. Moorhead's grip tightened.

"I have to go home, Mr. Moorhead. Please, let me go home," Mark begged.

"Are you sick?"

"No, but—"

"Then you're getting on that bus," Mr. Moorhead said with finality.

And that's exactly what Mark did. The bus driver gave him a disapproving look, pulled the lever to close the doors, and put the bus in gear. Mr. Moorhead watched with satisfaction. It was his good deed for the day.

Mark turned to the busload of kids. They giggled and smirked at him.

"What happened to you?" Joe Hirschman asked. "How come you had to get escorted to the bus?"

The other kids giggled.

"Sit down!" the bus driver barked.

Mark walked down the aisle to find a seat. His mind raced. What was he going to do? The bus was taking him to school! He would miss his dad! He peered longingly out the side window as they passed his house. Mark collapsed on a seat next to Kenny Ellis.

"What's the matter with you?" Kenny asked. "You look like you're in some kind of trouble."

Mark didn't like Kenny much; he was considered a trouble-maker. But seeing his uncombed hair and the gap in his front teeth made Mark realize that he had missed the boy. Mark was filled with the desire to tell Kenny that he had moved away to a place called Odyssey. He wanted to confess about breaking into Whit's End to get to the Imagination Station.

I came back in time, Mark wanted to say. *My dad is going to leave, and I'm trying to stop him.* But he didn't say any of those things.

Instead, he whispered urgently, "I have to get off this bus."

"Don't we all," Kenny chuckled.

"I have to get home to see my dad. It's an emergency." Mark's eyes filled with tears.

No, I don't want to cry in front of all these kids, he thought. *I can't cry.*

Kenny looked concerned. "Tell the bus driver to let you off."

"He won't let me, you know that. He'll tell me to go to the school office and call my parents." Mark swallowed back the softball still growing in his throat. "Then it'll be too late."

Kenny frowned and said, "It's that important, huh?"

"Yeah," Mark said.

Kenny stared thoughtfully out the window. "All right, you owe me your lunch money." He smiled and then climbed over Mark to get into the bus aisle.

"Huh?"

"I'm going to act like I'm hurt. When the bus driver stops, you ditch out the emergency exit in the back." Kenny pressed his face close to Mark's. "This is an emergency, right?"

"Yeah, but won't the alarm go off?" Mark asked, suddenly afraid of the scene it might cause.

Kenny rolled his eyes impatiently. "Do you want off the bus or not?"

"Yes, I do."

"Then get moving," Kenny said as he dropped onto the aisle floor. He clutched his leg and cried like a dying cow in a hailstorm.

The bus driver looked up into his large rearview mirror. "What's going on?"

"Stop the bus! Something's wrong with Kenny!" yelled Karen Sizer.

Chapter Twelve

WHEN THE BUS PULLED OVER TO STOP, Mark yanked the latch on the emergency door, swung it open, and jumped out. An alarm honked again and again. The bus driver shouted at Mark, but he kept running without looking back.

I can't be too late, I can't be too late, Mark thought, puffing as he ran. Through side streets and backyards, he pushed himself faster than he had ever gone before.

I'll tell Dad I'm sorry. I'll promise to keep my room clean. I'll keep the television turned down low. I'll stay out of his way when he has work to do. I'll be the perfect son. It's all my fault. All my fault. I'll make it up to him somehow. Somehow.

On and on Mark ran, feeling the morning chill. He was dressed for an Odyssey June, not a cold February in Washington, D.C., but it didn't matter to him. As long as his father was home.

Please, be home, Mark begged silently.

He skidded around the corner of the Taylors' house next door to his own and then suddenly pulled back. Mr. Moorhead was setting his garbage cans out at the end of the driveway.

Does he spend his entire day with trash? Mark wondered.

Mark crouched down, sneaking behind the Taylors' car. He moved behind the bushes lining their front porch and then behind the tree at the edge of the house. He couldn't go any farther without being seen. He waited and silently prayed for something to draw Mr. Moorhead's attention away.

Nothing happened. Mr. Moorhead continued to fiddle with his garbage cans. Unable to stand the wait anymore, Mark prepared to make a dash for it just as Mrs. Moorhead appeared at the front door. She told Mr. Moorhead he had a telephone call.

When he turned toward his house, Mark seized the moment and sprinted to the porch, his very own porch, and ran up the stairs. Finally! He opened the storm door, slipped in, and quickly turned the knob on their large front door. It was locked.

Locked! Mark nearly screamed. *Why did they lock the front door?*

What if he had an emergency at school, like he cut himself or something and had to come home all of a sudden? He couldn't get it! He would have to sit on the front porch and bleed to death.

Suddenly he remembered the key his parents kept under the doormat for emergencies. He felt silly.

Watching carefully for Mr. Moorhead or any other nosy neighbor, Mark dashed down the porch stairs and scrambled to the rear of the house. He rounded the corner and barely missed colliding with some trash cans, only to rush headlong into a stack of firewood.

"Stupid, stupid, stupid," Mark said to himself as he pushed the logs away and got to his feet.

How could he forget so quickly? He climbed the stairs to the brown rubber doormat and knelt down. Breathless, he tossed the mat aside.

It revealed an exact square of the mat, two dead worms, and no key. Mark looked again. One of the worms wasn't dead, but the key was still gone.

"No," Mark moaned.

This can't be happening. Is this a dream or a nightmare? I didn't come all this way to have everything go wrong.

He tried to think of how he could get in. He could pound on the door. He could try all the windows. If his dad was home, he would come running, right?

Mark began to argue with himself. What if his dad was upstairs, out of earshot? What if he was in the shower? What if someone else heard, like Mr. Moorhead, and called the police? What if . . . what if his dad wasn't home?

Had Mark seen the car out front? He couldn't remember. Even if it wasn't parked on the street, sometimes his dad kept it in the garage. What should Mark do? Was it enough of an emergency to justify throwing one of the logs through the back window? Probably not. Then . . . what?

Lost for an answer and tired from all the running, Mark slumped against the door—and fell face-first onto the kitchen floor. His arms and legs sprawled out like a spider's on ice. For the first time ever, he noticed the big balls of fuzz under the refrigerator.

He rolled over and sat up. Everything looked so friendly and familiar: the table, pale blue kitchen counters, appliances, and the clock radio.

The glowing joy of being home struck him. He pulled himself up to the kitchen table, his eye catching his mother's note placed carefully in the center. It said:

Richard,
     I don't want to be here when you leave. It hurts too much.
     I pray to God you know what you're doing.
     Julie

Mark thought, *So that's why Mom left.*

For a moment, Mark tried to imagine his mother's pain, but he couldn't. He knew what he had been feeling but had never bothered to wonder how she felt. In that moment, Mark was ashamed of himself.

But only for a moment. What Mark had come to do still needed to be done. And if he succeeded, his mother wouldn't be hurt at all.

The grandfather clock ticked loudly when Mark passed through the living room to the stairs. The house was clean and so very still. Was this what homes were like when kids were at school? It seemed unnatural to Mark.

He jogged up the stairs, listening intently for any sound, any movement that might let him know his father was home.

A nagging fear whispered in his ear, *You missed him. He's long gone.*

His heart pounded out a drumbeat of growing panic as he headed down the hallway toward his parents' room. On his right, he passed the doorway to his own room. He paused.

His room was exactly as he had left it that morning. The closet was half open with games, toys, and scattered clothes threatening to fall out. His bed was carelessly made. His small desk had piles of endless clutter stacked on it, old school papers, and gum wrappers. Drawers hung recklessly from his dresser. It was a mess.

No wonder his father had left. No wonder he couldn't stand to live with Mark anymore.

He turned away from the awful disarray and walked more quickly to his parents' room. The door was slightly ajar. Mark peeked in. Everything looked normal. The bed was neatly made, the floor clean, all drawers and doors were closed.

Mark ran to the closet and threw open the door. Hangers were hanging empty and loose. *Richard Prescott no longer lives here*, they announced.

"No!" Mark exclaimed.

But Mark got the same message from the dresser drawers and the medicine cabinet in the bathroom. *Richard Prescott is gone.* The emptiness howled like a Halloween wind. *You missed him. You didn't make it in time. He's gone, gone, gone.*

Mark stood in the middle of the room. The silence screamed at him. For months he had longed for this moment. In the hours since he met Mr. Whittaker, he believed it could really happen. But he hadn't made it in time. It was his one chance, and he had blown it.

Mark sat on the edge of his parents' bed and did the only thing that made sense. He put his face in his hands and began to cry.

Chapter
Thirteen

MARK WAS LOST IN HIS TEARS WHEN the door downstairs slammed. His ears heard it, his brain made note of it, but Mark couldn't accept the possibility. Then the front storm door slammed again. Mark sprinted to the stairs and took them two at a time to the bottom floor, where he slipped, recovered, and then rounded the corner to the front hallway. No one was there.

But someone had been there! The large oak door stood open. Two suitcases sat on the floor next to the storm door. His dad's suitcases! Maybe Mark hadn't missed him.

He was just about to hurry outside when a figure appeared in the window of the storm door. It grew larger as it came up the front steps and then turned into a blur through the frosty glass. The door opened, and the figure stepped inside and reached for the suitcases.

Mark froze in place. He was unable to move or speak. "Dad," Mark finally said, letting out a breath of air.

Richard Prescott turned and stood up straight. He looked surprised. No, he looked shocked. "Mark? What are you doing here? Why aren't you in school?"

Mark remained frozen, silent. The sudden reality of his father standing before him was more than he could take in.

"Son? Are you all right?" Richard Prescott took a step toward Mark, glancing back at his suitcases self-consciously. "Look, you weren't supposed to be here when this happened. I thought you went to school."

Mark's throat was dry when he spoke. "Dad?"

"I was planning on talking to you later, calling or writing. I didn't know how to tell you," his dad said, shoving his hands in the pockets of his winter coat, the coat Mark and his mom had given him for Christmas.

"Don't leave, Dad," Mark croaked.

"Mark." His dad's voice was low and full of sadness. He took a couple of steps closer to Mark and knelt.

Mark began to speak slowly at first, and then his words sped up and ran into each other. "I figured it out, Dad. You don't have to leave. I know what's wrong. I know how to make it better. I'll keep my room clean. I'll pick up after myself. I'll leave you alone when you have to work. I'll be good, Dad. You don't have to leave. I know it's all my fault, but I'll make it better. I promise, I will. I'll make it better, please, Dad, I promise."

The words dissolved into tears, and Mark threw himself into his father's arms.

Richard Prescott held his son tightly. His unshaven face pressed against Mark's, scratching it. "Mark . . . Mark, listen to me. This isn't your fault. None of it is your fault. Your mother and I . . ."

A gentle hand stroked Mark's hair. His dad continued, "It's my fault. Something's wrong with me. I'm confused. I don't know what's right and wrong anymore, so I'm going away to try to figure it out. It's not your fault. Do you understand?"

Mark sniffled and tried to make sense of it. He wasn't sure he could, but his dad made him want to.

"It's not your room or your messes or . . . or anything about you." His dad began to cry. "There's nothing you can do to change this, Mark. This is something I have to work out. You can't change this."

Mark stepped back from his dad. They looked into each other's red-rimmed, water-filled eyes. Mark believed him.

"I love you," said his dad. "I love you."

When they hugged again, Mark believed that, too. The tears came once more, and Mark buried his face in his father's chest.

"Don't go, Dad. Don't go," he whispered. "Don't go." His words sounded muffled and strange to his own ears, but Mark kept saying it anyway. "Don't go."

"I'm not going anywhere, Mark."

A different voice now spoke, yet it was full of the same deep love as his father's. Mark pulled away and looked up.

His mother, her cheeks flushed and stained from crying, was looking down at her son.

Chapter Fourteen

HAD IT BEEN A DREAM? Had it been some kind of fantasy?

Mark was back in Whit's basement; his mother was holding him in her arms. The Imagination Station hummed quietly only a few feet away. Whit and a policeman were watching the scene quietly.

"Oh, honey," Julie said as she brushed Mark's cheek, "are you all right?"

Mark sighed, "Yeah, I think so."

"I went up to your room to find you and found this instead." She held up the letter Mark had written to his father. "I wish I knew you were feeling these things. We could have talked about it."

Mark shrugged. Why hadn't he talked to his mother? He could have. He should have. Maybe he had thought he knew what she would say. Maybe he had thought she wouldn't understand. As he looked into his mother's face, he knew he was wrong.

"I'm sorry, Mom," he said quietly. That softball was forming in his throat again.

Whit knelt next to them. "I had a feeling that's why you were so interested in the Imagination Station. But, Mark," Whit said, pausing to make sure Mark was listening, "the Imagination Station wasn't created to change the past—only to learn from it."

Mark nodded.

Whit continued warmly, "Things change, Mark. It's as true as the sun rises and falls. And change isn't good or bad, it just is. Sometimes we can control change through the decisions we make, other times we can't. What's important is how we react to change."

Mark glanced at his mother. She smiled gently in agreement.

Whit reached over and rested his hand lightly on Mark's shoulder. "We can try to run away. We can try to change what has already happened, but most of the time it only makes everything worse. The best thing we can do is face up to the changes in our lives and have faith that God is watching over those changes. That's the challenge for all of us."

Mark nodded and looked deep into Whit's eyes. They were alive with the meaning of his words.

"I believe," Whit said, "that the greatest adventure is the one I'm having right now. It may not be like yesterday's adventure or even like tomorrow's, but it's the one I'm having now, and that's all that matters." Whit patted Mark's shoulder affectionately.

Then Whit turned to the waiting policeman and said, "I won't be pressing charges, officer. Thank you for all you've done."

"Yes, thank you," Mark's mother said.

"You were very smart to realize the boy you chased into the woods might be the same one Julie reported missing," Whit added.

"Just trying to do my job." The policeman smiled.

"And you've done it well," Whit said.

The officer paused at the door. His voice sounded amazed as he gestured to the Imagination Station. "You mean to say that machine actually works?"

Whit chuckled, pulling the door closed behind them.

Julie searched Mark's face. "Come home, Mark. We have a lot to talk about."

Mark sniffled and nodded.

They hugged long and hard one more time before they left. The Imagination Station hummed happily beside them.

Mark watched the maze of people at the town carnival. It was the Fourth of July weekend, and Odyssey was exploding with the celebration. On Main Street an endless parade of floats, bands, baton twirlers, and costumed characters was passing by. The night sky lit up with the red, white, and blues of the fireworks.

Mark sat on a bench near the cotton-candy seller, taking in all the excitement. He could see Whit at the Whit's End Charity Booth. He had invented a variety of games and inventions to raise money for the homeless. Mark had worked on some of them. As part of his punishment for breaking into the Imagination Station, he had to work for Mr. Whittaker for a week without pay. Mark didn't mind. Whit's End was always fun.

Suddenly Mark saw something, someone out of the corner of his eye. He watched closely, a warm rush flowing over him. It was a man who looked a lot like his father. The man turned to kiss his wife while reaching for a little girl's small hand. A soft ache touched Mark's heart.

He turned away and strolled to another part of the carnival. He found his mother trying to hit a bull's-eye with a ball that would knock a clown into a large container of water. Her aim was so poor, the clown finally jumped into the water himself.

His mother laughed hard. Mark thought she seemed happy, even though the two of them had shared a lot of tears since Mark's trip to the past. His dad's leaving wasn't easy for either of them. He understood that now.

She saw Mark and waved. He waved back and then shoved his hands in his pockets and walked on.

Change, he thought. *Like the sun rises and falls, Mr. Whittaker said. Things change. They'll change again.*

Another burst of fireworks added multi-colored stars to the sky, and Mark smiled.

High Flyer with a Flat Tire

Chapter One

"MARK! HEY, MARK!"

Mark Prescott looked up expectantly. He had been watching a group of boys play basketball in McAlister Park. Like most Saturday mornings since arriving in Odyssey, he had waited an hour for someone to ask him to join the game. He thought the moment had arrived.

"Mark!" Patti Eldridge called across the green expanse of park.

Mark cringed. Patti and a girl he didn't know were riding their bikes toward him. A few weeks ago when he met Patti, she had decided she was going to be his best friend. Mark wasn't happy about the idea. He liked Patti well enough, but it was embarrassing for boys to have girls as friends—even if she did a lot of boy-type things. As if to prove the point, Patti let out a wild yell, pulled the front of her bike into the air, and did a wheelie down the path.

"We're going to Whit's End. You want to go?" Patti asked breathlessly as she and her friend stopped alongside Mark. "Oh, uh, Mark," Patti said, "this is Rachel Morse. Rachel, this is Mark Prescott. He's the one I told you about."

"Nice to meet you," Rachel said, hardly above a whisper. She glanced away shyly.

Mark nodded. Rachel was a chubby girl with large blue eyes and freckles dotting her round cheeks.

"So, let's go!" Patti urged.

Mark looked back at the boys and their basketball game. "Okay," he said with a shrug.

Together, they started walking across the park. Patti stopped for a moment and pushed her loose sandy hair up under her baseball cap. Mark's eye caught sight of a tiny red dot near her temple.

Patti must have noticed Mark's glance because she suddenly turned her face away. "Don't look at it! It's like a volcano!"

"What?" Mark asked innocently.

"You saw it. You know. It's a zit," Patti mumbled.

She turned to Rachel. "You said nobody would notice. I told you they would."

"A zit?" Mark wasn't sure what the fuss was about. "You mean a pimple?"

"Yes, what other kind is there?" she shouted.

"I . . . I don't know." Mark felt awkward. Patti had never yelled at him like this. "What's the big deal?"

"You're a boy," Patti added. "You wouldn't understand."

Mark had to agree; he didn't want to know about Patti's pimples.

"Oh no, look who's coming," Patti moaned. "Just what I don't need."

Like cowboys on wild horses, Joe Devlin and his gang rode toward them, stirring a cloud of dust as they weaved their bicycles across each other's paths.

"Let's just walk on," Mark whispered to Patti. "Maybe they'll ride past us."

"Ha!" said Patti.

Joe and his gang surrounded Mark, Patti, and Rachel.

"Well, well, well, look who's out for a Saturday morning stroll," Joe said with a sneer.

"Yeah, look who it is!" Joe's younger brother Alan piped in.

"Shut up, Alan, or I'll make you go home," Joe snapped.

Alan hung his head and closed his mouth.

Joe turned to Patti. "Where are you headed, Patti? Is it playtime at Whit's End?"

"None of your business, Joe," Patti said. "Just leave us alone."

Joe stuck his bottom lip out in a mock pout. "Aw, can't we come play with you?"

"Whit's End is open to everybody. Go on if you want," Patti replied with an air of formality.

"But we want to go with you," Joe pleaded in a whiny voice, getting a laugh from his gang.

"Get out of our way!" Patti shouted, shoving past him. She caught Joe off guard and sent his bike crashing to the ground.

Mark took a sharp, deep breath and braced himself. Rachel watched wide-eyed.

Joe quickly picked up his bike and examined it. "You're in for it now, Patti. If you hurt my new bike, I'm going to do some major damage to you."

"New bike! Is that a new bike?" Mark asked brightly.

"Yeah. A ten-speed High Flyer!" Joe announced. "It can outrun any bike in town. And there better not be any scratches on it."

"Who cares?" Patti returned. She gestured for Mark and Rachel to follow. "Come on, guys."

Joe grabbed Patti's arm and said, "I didn't give you permission to leave."

Patti tried to pull her arm away, but Joe held firm.

"Ow!" Patti cried. "Let go."

Joe laughed. "I told you I didn't give you permission to leave. Ask for it!"

Patti struggled to get free, but Joe twisted her arm to keep his hold. Mark was about to jump into the tug-of-war when a loud, commanding voice shouted, "Let go of her!"

Startled, everyone turned to the unlikely source of the outburst. Rachel put a hand over her mouth and blushed.

Joe gave Patti a shove as he let go of her arm.

Then he glared at Rachel in a mocking way and asked, "Did you say something to me, fatso? Did a voice really come out of that barrel of blubber?"

Mark stiffened. He could think of few things more insulting than picking on someone's weight problem. Rachel lowered her head.

"Be quiet, Joe. That's no way to talk," Mark said as he stepped between Joe and Rachel.

"Stay out of this, Press-snot," Joe snorted. "El blubbo can get on her bike and ride off anytime she wants, if her bike can hold all that weight. You got special shock absorbers, Rachel?"

"Shut up, Joe!" Mark shouted.

"Don't listen to this ignoramus," Patti said to Rachel.

"I'd rather be an ignoramus than a fat-oramus," Joe snickered.

"You're a jerk, Joe!" Patti said, clenching her teeth.

Mark turned to Rachel and said, "Let's go."

It was too late. Rachel's face was turning red as she strained to keep from crying. Then large tears formed in her eyes and rolled down her cheeks. When she climbed onto her bike, she started sobbing.

"Rachel," Patti said, stepping toward her, but Rachel pushed her bike forward and took off pedaling up the path.

"Rachel!" Patti called.

Right before Rachel disappeared around the bend, Mark spotted an unfamiliar blond-haired boy on his bike. He came from behind a tree and called Rachel's name, but she didn't stop. He darted an angry look in their direction and then rode after her.

"Can't take a joke," Joe chuckled.

"You creep!" Patti roared and threw a punch at Joe. He quickly stepped back, but tripped over his brother's feet and fell. Patti moved toward him with her fists clenched.

"Patti! Stop!" Mark yelled, grabbing her arm.

Her eyes ablaze, she turned; for a moment, Mark thought she was going to take a swing at him, too.

Joe sat on the grass and shouted a stream of bad names at Patti. Alan extended a hand to help him up, but Joe slapped it away.

"Get lost!" he spat and got up by himself. "Just stay out of my way."

Patti shook a finger at Joe. "Don't you ever talk to Rachel like that again."

"Why don't you try something now when I'm ready for you? Come on, tomboy. Try to fight me now."

"Don't do it," Mark said.

"That's right," Joe jeered. "Listen to your boyfriend."

"Shut up!" Patti yelled.

"Don't pay attention to him," Mark said to Patti. "My dad says that sooner or later guys like him get what they deserve."

"Guys like who?" Joe jibed.

"Guys like you who go around and start trouble for no reason," Mark returned.

Joe smiled sarcastically. "What does your dad know about anything? He's not even around. Right? That's why you and your mom came to Odyssey. I've heard all about it. Your dad doesn't like you, so he left you."

Mark threw a wild punch that grazed the side of Joe's face.

"You're going to be sorry for that," Joe shouted, tackling Mark. They fell into the dirt, tossing up a cloud of dust as they rolled over each other, struggling to pin the other one underneath. Mark swung his arms furiously, his elbow connecting with Joe's mouth. This dazed Joe enough for Mark to climb on top.

"It's the police!" someone shouted. "Police! Let's get out of here!"

Mark looked up. Joe threw Mark off his chest and gave him a blow to his cheek.

"Joe, police!" Alan cried out, pulling at his brother.

Patti grabbed Mark. "Give it up, Mark!"

Breathless, dirty, and sweaty, Mark and Joe strained against the arms that held them.

"You jerk! You better hope we're never alone to finish this fight," Joe yelled. His lower lip was split and bleeding.

Mark shouted back, "Anytime, Joe! You'll get what you deserve! You'll see!"

Joe and his gang jumped on their bikes and rode off. Mark glanced around for the policeman who had scared everyone away. Across the park he saw Officer Hank Snow watching them. His arms were folded, and his expression was one of silent rebuke.

"He should arrest those guys," Patti said.

Mark tried to dust himself off and then shoved his shirttail back into his jeans without much care.

"Do you still want to go to Whit's End?" Patti asked as she picked up her bike.

"No," Mark answered. "I better go home."

He took one last look at Joe, wreaking confusion among Odyssey's Main Street traffic. He was cycling recklessly between the cars. Mark wished someone would get Joe and get him good.

✦ ✦ ✦

"Ouch!"

Mark Prescott dropped the washcloth into the bathroom sink and then stretched upward to get a better look at his face in the mirror. The red lump next to his right eye seemed to be growing.

"Oh, great," he moaned to himself, noticing the small bruise on his left cheek. "Mom's going to kill me."

He picked up the damp washcloth again, dabbed it on the sore spots, and groaned from the sharp, jabbing pain. Then he ran his fingers through his dark brown hair and checked himself in the mirror one last time.

"The red lump doesn't look too bad," he assured himself.

The scratch could easily be explained to his mother. It wouldn't be an outright lie to say he had fallen, would it? He considered telling her the whole story, but he was afraid it would upset her. She had enough on her mind without worrying about Mark getting into fights. And it would hurt her if she knew the kids were saying things about Mark's dad and their separation.

Mark decided he couldn't tell her the truth. They were still the new people in town, and his mother was nervous about making a good impression. Getting in a fight, no matter whose fault it was, rarely ever left people with good impressions. Besides, Mark didn't want to get punished.

He threw the washcloth into the hamper, went to his room, and put on a clean shirt and a favorite pair of jeans.

Just like new, he thought as he walked down the stairs.

Jumping the bottom two steps, he could see his mother through the living room doorway. She was sitting on the love seat, her hands knotted in her lap. Her glance caught Mark's.

"Come in here, son," she called with a worried tone that Mark knew well.

As he stepped through the doorway into the living room, he saw why. A stern-looking woman was sitting on the couch, holding a slashed bicycle tire that looked like chopped black licorice.

Joe Devlin was sitting next to her.

Chapter Two

MRS. DEVLIN'S FACE WAS PINCHED into lines of disapproval. She waved her hand accusingly at Mark. "If you don't believe me, just take a look at your son's face. He was in a fight with my Joseph, Mrs. Prescott. One look at his face proves it."

Mark glanced at Joe. A large scrape went down the side of his face, and his lower lip was swollen. Mark felt a moment's satisfaction that Joe looked like he had gotten the worst of the fight.

"Mark, were you and Joe in a fight today?" Mrs. Prescott asked.

"Yeah, Mom, but—"

Mrs. Devlin interrupted. "No 'buts' about it, young man. Simply answer the question."

"Yes, ma'am. We were in a fight today."

Mrs. Prescott frowned. "Who started it?" she asked.

"Mark did," Mrs. Devlin answered, as if she had seen the fight herself.

"What?" Mark shouted with disbelief.

"According to my Joseph," Mrs. Devlin said, glaring at Mark, "you picked a fight while he and his friends were riding their bikes through McAlister Park."

"My new bike," Joe added sadly.

"Your Joseph is lying!" Mark blurted out.

"Mark!" his mother warned.

"But it's true, Mom. Patti and Rachel and I were going to Whit's End and—"

"Yes and that Patti. I don't know what to make of a girl who goes around beating up boys," Mrs. Devlin said.

"She didn't beat me up, Mom," Joe quickly corrected her. "She just tried to."

Mark anxiously rocked from one foot to the other. "Joe started it! He always starts it!"

"Liar!" Joe screamed, leaning forward as if he were going to leap off the couch. Mrs. Devlin put a restraining hand on his arm.

"He picked on Patti and called Rachel names, and then he said—" Mark stopped himself. He didn't want to repeat what Joe had said about his father, not in front of his mother.

"What else did he say, Mark?" Mrs. Prescott asked.

"Nothing," Mark looked down at the floor. The room was heavy with silence for a moment.

Finally, Mrs. Prescott spoke. "Regardless of who started it, Mark, I think you should apologize to Joe for fighting with him. You know better than to behave like that."

"But, Mom—" Mark looked at her helplessly.

She was resolute. "Go on, son."

Mark mustered his strength to keep from saying what he really wanted to say. Then he muttered, "I'm sorry, Joe."

Joe looked at him with a smug expression of victory.

"And now," Mrs. Devlin began, "there is a financial matter to take care of."

Mark and his mother exchanged uneasy glances.

Mrs. Devlin held up the slashed tire. "I expect Mark to pay for a new tire for my son's bike."

Mark's mouth fell open.

Mrs. Prescott stammered, "Why. . . why should Mark pay for the tire?"

"Because he is obviously the one who cut it to pieces!" Mrs. Devlin announced grandly, like a detective who had just solved a murder case.

"I didn't do it! I don't know anything about his tire!" declared Mark.

Mrs. Devlin looked at Mark with strained patience. "Please, young man, you'll only make things worse by lying more than you already have. Everyone at the park heard you say you would get back at my Joseph. Clearly you followed him to Whit's End after he beat you in the fight and slashed his tire while he was inside. It's an open-and-shut case of revenge."

"It's not true!" Mark exclaimed, turning to his mom. "I came home after the fight—ask Patti."

"Asking Patti won't do any good. Naturally she'll side with Mark. They're best friends," reasoned Mrs. Devlin.

"Boyfriend and girlfriend," Joe added.

"She was probably in on the whole thing," Mrs. Devlin concluded.

"No!" Mark protested. "I came straight home! You were here, Mom. You know."

Mrs. Prescott shook her head. Of course, Mark realized, she *didn't* know. He had sneaked in the house so she wouldn't see his marks from the fight. Mark slumped despondently.

"Well?" Mrs. Devlin prodded.

"I think we'll have to discuss it, Mrs. Devlin," Julie Prescott said, rising from the chair.

Mrs. Devlin took the hint and stood as well. "Discuss it?

Discuss it as much as you like, just as long as we get our money for the tire. I would hate to involve the police."

Joe smirked at Mark.

"I'm sure we'll get this all worked out," Julie said.

Mrs. Devlin agreed that they most certainly would.

Mark's mom walked Mrs. Devlin and Joe to the front door while Mark waited in the living room. They left the slashed tire on the floor.

When his mother returned, she gestured for Mark to sit down on the couch. "Now, do you want to tell me what really happened?"

Mark told her everything, from watching the basketball game that morning through to his fight with Joe. He left out Joe's comments about his father, though. He made it sound like he got in the fight to protect Patti and Rachel, which was partly true.

Julie took Mark's face in her hands. "Why didn't you tell me about this as soon as you got home?"

Mark tried to look away, but his mom's grip was firm. "I didn't want you to get upset," he said.

She caressed his cheek, lightly touching the scratch and examining the red lump next to his eye. "Oh, Mark."

Mark felt sorry for causing so much trouble. He should have told his mom everything when he got home. Why hadn't he talked to her?

"What are we going to do about the tire?" his mother asked softly.

Mark wondered the same thing and shrugged. They could pay for it, but that would be the same as admitting guilt. Then Mark would have a reputation as a vandal. He didn't want that. But what could he do? How could he prove he didn't do it?

He thought about it and then suddenly smiled at his mother.

Kicking at the tire next to his feet, he said, "I know, Mom! It'll be easy."

His mother looked at him skeptically.

His eyes were alight with the flame of a good idea. "All I have to do is find out who really *did* slash the tire!"

Chapter Three

MARK WAS REACHING FOR THE FRONT doorknob to Whit's End when someone called his name. He turned to see a couple of boys coming toward him on the sidewalk. He remembered them from somewhere, Whit's End probably, but he had no idea who they were.

"I heard how you whipped Joe," the first boy said.

"Yeah?" Mark said vaguely. He didn't want another fight if these were two of Joe's friends.

"Yeah," the second boy said. "Good job. Joe's been needing it for a long time."

"Yeah, cool," the first boy said.

Mark barely masked his surprise. "Well . . . ah . . . thanks," he said.

"You didn't have to slash the tire on his new bike, though," the second kid said.

"Yeah, uncool," the first boy added.

Before Mark could deny it, the two boys turned and walked away.

Is this how it's going to be? Mark wondered. How could he be a hero and a villain? He sighed and walked into Whit's End.

The sound of kids at play immediately gave Mark reassurance. He liked coming to Whit's End. Better still, he liked the friendly old inventor named John Avery Whittaker, or Whit, as he liked to be called.

He owned the place and was popular with everyone in town, especially the kids. It was easy to understand why. Whit was the kind of grown-up that let kids act like kids, but he talked and listened to them as if they were grown-ups. He made them feel important. Mark had figured this out for himself during the two weeks he worked for Whit as an errand boy.

Whit was behind the ice cream counter, talking with Patti. Mark guessed by her dramatic gestures and facial expressions that she was retelling the events of that morning. Whit, a pleasant-looking man with unruly white hair and mustache, seemed to be listening with fascination. At times he smiled. Other times he frowned. In any case his face beamed with deep interest.

As Mark approached the counter, Whit and Patti turned to him. Patti smiled in a way that made Mark feel uncomfortable. It was the kind of smile people made when looking at a litter of kittens.

"Hi, Mark," she gushed.

"Hi," Mark mumbled.

"There's a red lump next to your eye," she said proudly.

"I know," he answered with annoyance. *Good grief*, he thought.

"Sounds like you had a pretty tough morning," Whit said, his voice a rich, deep bass.

Mark nodded. "Yeah, I guess."

"You went home and changed clothes," Patti said.

Mark wondered why she was stating the obvious.

"So did I," she added.

Mark felt as if she were waiting for him to say something, but he wasn't sure what. "Oh," he finally said.

She frowned indignantly. "Don't you like it?"

Mark was puzzled. He looked to Whit for help. Whit, sensing the need, gestured to his shirt. Why his shirt? Mark was perplexed.

Whit tilted his head toward Patti's blouse.

Mark still didn't understand and finally gave up. "Like what?"

Whit put his hands over his face.

"My new blouse!" Patti sounded hurt. "You didn't notice."

"Oh that . . . ah, you know . . . I . . ." Mark groaned.

Girls! he thought. *Doesn't she realize I have more important things to think about than a new blouse?*

Whit rescued the moment by changing the subject. "I guess you know we had a little mishap outside Whit's End today."

"Joe's slashed tire," Patti said.

"I didn't do it," Mark announced right away. "I went straight home after the fight. I didn't slash Joe's tire. Honest!"

Whit scrubbed his chin. "Hmm. Joe and his parents are convinced that you're the culprit."

"I don't care," Mark snapped. "I didn't do it."

"Then who did?" Whit asked.

"That's what I have to find out."

Patti was delighted. "We're going to solve a mystery!"

"We? Who said 'we'?" Mark challenged.

Patti was taken aback by his tone and stared at him, speechless.

"Now, Mark, every great detective needs an assistant," Whit said, his expression a mild rebuke.

Because it was Whit, Mark gave in. "Oh, all right."

Patti grinned.

"How are you going to start your investigation?" Whit asked.

Mark shrugged. "That's what I came to ask you. Where should I start?"

"Well, if you really want my help, I'd like to have a look at that tire. Do you have it?"

"Joe's mom left it at my house. But why?"

Whit shrugged. "Looking at the tire might tell us a few things, give us some clues."

"Okay, I'll bring it in. But what should I do?" Mark asked.

"What should *we* do?" Patti corrected him.

"What do you think you should do?" questioned Whit.

Mark thought for a moment and then exclaimed, "The scene of the crime! We should look for evidence outside at the bike rack. That's where it must have happened, right?"

Mark turned to go, but Patti stopped him. "Wait, Mark. The bike rack's no good."

"Why not?"

"Because everyone parks there. What kind of clues would you find after all this time?"

Mark grimaced. "Oh, that's right."

"Unless," Whit observed, "Joe didn't park his new bike at the bike rack."

Mark could tell Whit knew something. "What do you mean?"

"Maybe Joe is like a lot of people who get new cars. They don't park in the normal places. They park further away so their cars won't get bumped or scratched."

"Yeah?"

Whit grinned as he continued, "And maybe I took the trash out earlier today and noticed that Joe's new bike was parked under the large oak tree away from the rest of the bikes."

"Maybe?" Mark smiled.

"Maybe."

Mark and Patti searched under the large oak behind Whit's End. The shade was surprisingly cool, considering the heat of the summer day.

Patti disappeared around the side of the tree. "See anything?"

"No, do you?"

"Nope." Patti reappeared. "Can you give me a hint about what we're looking for?"

"Clues!" Mark responded crossly.

"Don't talk to me like that," Patti snarled. "What kind of clues?"

"I don't know. Anything."

There was a soft thud against the side of the tree, and a pebble fell at Mark's feet. Joe stood a few yards away.

"I'm a good shot, and I could have hit you just as easily as I hit that tree," he said with a smirk.

Mark and Patti didn't answer but watched him silently.

"Looking for my bike so you can slash the other tire?"

"I didn't slash your tire," Mark said.

"Uh-huh," Joe answered with obvious disbelief. "Well, you better consider yourself warned, Mark-ee. I'm going to get you for what you did. Understand? Just watch yourself."

Joe kicked the dirt and walked away.

Patti started to go after him, but Mark took hold of her arm. "Don't, Patti."

Patti looked down at her arm and then up at Mark's face. She blushed. Mark pulled his hand away quickly.

"Come on," he said. "We aren't going to find anything around here."

Patti nodded and then suddenly looked down. "Wait," she

said, kneeling. She picked up a small bracelet from the grass. "Do you think it's a clue?"

"I don't know. It might be," Mark said.

Patti held it up for both of them to see. The bracelet was made of two small chains with a wooden heart attaching them together. "It's kind of funny-looking, kind of like it was homemade."

Mark reached out for the bracelet. "Let me see."

In the middle of the wooden heart, written in an attempt at fancy script, was the name *Rachel*.

"Rachel!" Patti gasped.

"That's what it says." Mark shrugged. "Do you think it's your friend's?"

"There aren't a lot of Rachels in Odyssey. At least, not many who would lose a bracelet near Whit's End," she said, stopping to think about it a moment. "This is a weird place to lose a bracelet. I mean, it's not like people play around this tree very much."

Mark agreed. And he couldn't help but wonder if the same Rachel who had been picked on by Joe that morning had dropped the bracelet while she was slashing Joe's tire. Rachel seemed so nice, though.

Patti looked at Mark with concern. She must have guessed what Mark was thinking. "You don't think my friend, Rachel, slashed the tire, do you?"

Mark stared at the bracelet and said, "There's only one way to find out."

Chapter
Four

As Mark and Patti walked to Rachel's house, he thought about the bracelet and the questions it raised. If the bracelet were Rachel's, what was it doing under the tree? Had she dropped it while she was slashing Joe's tire? Was Rachel the kind of girl who would even slash a tire?

Mark turned to Patti and asked her if Rachel would do something like that.

Patti considered it for a moment and said, "I don't think so. We've been friends for a long time, and I've never seen her act like that. She's quiet. If she's mad or upset, she goes home and eats ice cream."

Mark recalled the surprising way Rachel shouted during the argument with Joe. "She sure yelled this morning," Mark said.

"So what? There's a big difference between yelling and slashing tires," Patti replied irritably.

"Then what was the bracelet doing there?" Mark asked.

"Maybe it's a coincidence." Patti grew more defensive. "Maybe it doesn't have anything to do with Joe's stupid bike!" She shoved her hands into her jeans pockets and stared at the sidewalk.

Mark didn't say anything else. *What's wrong with her?* he wondered. *Why is she being so moody?*

They arrived at Rachel's house not long after that. She was sitting on the top step of her front porch, eating ice cream. Mark noticed that her eyes looked red and puffy.

"How are you doing?" Patti asked when they reached her.

"I'm okay." Rachel shrugged.

"Joe's a jerk, Rachel. You know that," Patti offered.

"Yeah, I know."

"Mark and Joe got in a fight after you left. It was a whopper, too," Patti said proudly.

"Uh-huh," Rachel said and scooped a spoonful of vanilla ice cream into her mouth. Mark was getting hungry watching her.

Patti shuffled uncomfortably for a moment. When she spoke, she sounded stiff, as if she were trying to sound casual. "Um, have you . . . ah, you know . . . lost anything lately?"

Rachel looked up at Patti self-consciously. "You mean, weight?"

"No!" Patti said quickly. "I mean, like, jewelry or something like that."

Rachel thought about it and then shook her head no. "Not that I know of."

Patti continued, "I mean, like a necklace or bracelet maybe?"

Mark wished Patti would come right out and show Rachel the bracelet.

"I haven't lost anything, Patti. Why?" Rachel asked.

"Well . . . ah . . ." Patti pulled the bracelet from her jeans pocket. "We found this today and figured it was yours. See? It has your name on it."

Rachel looked at the bracelet. For a second Mark thought her eyes widened. She quickly looked down and mumbled, "Nope. It's not mine."

Mark and Patti exchanged glances. Patti's expression seemed to ask, *What now?*

Mark sat on the step beneath Rachel's feet. "Are you sure?"

"I'm sure. I would know my own bracelet, wouldn't I?"

Mark nodded.

"Why? Is something wrong?" asked Rachel.

Patti looked to Mark. He explained what had happened since the morning: the fight, the slashed tire, his being accused, and finding the bracelet where Joe parked his bike.

Rachel turned to Patti. "You thought the bracelet was mine, so you figured I slashed the tire! Is that why you're here? Thanks a lot, friend."

"It's not like that," Patti said apologetically. "We're just checking clues. Really."

"Oh, you're checking clues. So you're playing detectives now, huh? And I guess you automatically suspected the fat girl. They always do in the movies."

Mark tried to remember if the fat girls were always accused in the movies he had seen. He gave up when he couldn't think of any movies with fat girls in them. The ones in movies always seemed to be too thin and kept the hero from doing his job—kind of like Patti.

"Go pick on somebody else!" Rachel cried out. "I didn't slash Joe's tires. But I'm glad somebody did! Sometimes I wish he would move away or get in big trouble with the police, so they would arrest him or something." Her voice trailed to a mumble. Then, as an afterthought, she shrugged and added, "I don't even have a knife to slash his tires with."

Of course, Mark thought. *Why didn't I think of that before? Whoever slashed the tire must have been carrying a knife! Or if they weren't carrying one, they had to get one from somewhere. But where? Whit's End? Did the villain steal one of Whit's kitchen knives to do the job?*

"If you didn't slash the tire, who did? Who would want to?" Mark asked.

Rachel shrugged again. "Anybody who's ever been bugged by Joe. And that's most of the kids in Odyssey. He's a disgusting bully. He deserves to have more than his tire slashed."

"You got that right," Patti agreed. Shoving the bracelet back into her pocket, she said jokingly, "Maybe I did it, Mark."

Mark frowned at her. "Don't be stupid."

He turned his attention to Rachel again. "Can you think of someone else who would want to hurt Joe, someone Joe hurt recently? I can't talk to all the kids in Odyssey."

Rachel's expression made Mark suspect that she had thought of someone right away, but she didn't say it. She waited a moment and then reluctantly answered, "Well, there might be one person."

She paused dramatically. Growing more impatient, Mark began to gnaw at the inside of his lip.

"Chad Cox," she finally said.

"Chad!" Patti exclaimed. "Why would he want to hurt Joe? They're friends. He's been in the gang forever."

Rachel shook her head. "Not anymore. Something happened, and Chad got thrown out of the gang."

"What happened?" Mark asked.

"I don't know. Just . . . something happened." She stood slowly.

"But . . . but . . ." Mark stammered. "If you know he got thrown out of the gang, you have to have some clue."

"You two are the hotshot detectives with all the clues," Rachel replied. "I have to go inside. Lunch is almost ready. See you guys later."

Once they were beyond Rachel's yard, Mark said, "Let's go back to my house and get the tire for Whit."

"Okay," Patti responded. She nonchalantly pulled the bracelet out of her pocket again and sighed. "Did you see it?"

"See what?"

"The way she looked when I asked if the bracelet was hers and she said 'no.'"

"What do you mean? What was I supposed to see?" Mark asked.

Patti held out the bracelet. "She was lying. This bracelet is hers."

Chapter
Five

MARK AND PATTI WERE A BLOCK away from Mark's house when Patti suddenly gasped, "There's Chad Cox."

Mark looked ahead and saw a blond-haired boy in overalls sitting on the curb. He was concentrating on something at his feet.

It was Mark's turn to be surprised. Chad Cox was the same blond-haired boy he had seen on the bike in the park, the one who had ridden after Rachel.

"I saw him at the park," Mark whispered.

"What?"

Mark signaled that he would tell her later. As they approached, Chad picked up the object at his feet. It was a small, half-finished wooden replica of a train engine. Chad pulled out a pocketknife and began whittling at the engine.

"He's got a pocketknife!" Patti whispered.

Mark nudged her to be quiet.

Chad slowly turned his head and looked up at them. He didn't acknowledge them in any way but went back to his whittling.

"Hi, Chad," Patti said, as she sat down next to him. "Do you know Mark?"

"I've seen him around," Chad replied. He spoke slowly in a soft monotone voice.

"Hi," Mark said, kneeling next to him on the other side. "That's a great-looking engine. Did you make it yourself?"

"Yep."

"You're pretty handy with a knife, huh? I guess you would have to be to make it look so real," Mark said, hoping to draw Chad out.

"I guess so," Chad responded.

"Where did you learn to whittle?" Patti asked.

"My daddy taught me."

They fell silent while Chad continued to work. Every once in a while he would stop to push his stringy, blond hair out of his face. Mark thought he could be good-looking if he scrubbed some of the dirt off his cheeks and wore some clothes without so many stains and holes.

"You and Joe are friends, aren't you?" Patti asked.

"Used to be."

"You're not anymore?" Patti pretended to be surprised.

"Guess you could say that."

"Boy, that's weird. How come you're not friends?"

Chad shrugged. "Just aren't, I guess."

Mark gritted his teeth. *This could take all day*, he thought.

"Did you hear about what happened to Joe's new bike?" questioned Patti.

"Somebody slashed the tire," Chad answered as he examined his engine. He blew the wood dust off it and examined it closely again.

"Somebody thinks Mark did it," Patti explained, "and we're trying to prove he didn't."

"Uh-huh." Chad started whittling around the engine's smokestack.

"We thought you could help us," Patti went on.

Chad stopped whittling. For the first time, he looked full into Patti's and Mark's faces. "What makes you think I can help you?"

Mark said, "Because you had a falling out with Joe."

"So? Does that make me a tire slasher?"

"No, but—"

"But you think I did it."

Mark eyed Chad more carefully. "Why did you and Joe stop being friends?"

"It's none of your business."

"Then how will we know you didn't slash the tire?" Patti reasoned. "You can tell us. Please, Chad? Anything you know might help crack this case."

Chad half-smiled, "Crack this case? You sound like one of those private whatevers on TV."

"All we want to do is find out who slashed the tire so Mark won't have to pay for it," Patti pleaded.

Mark was touched by her earnestness.

"I didn't slash anybody's tire," Chad said firmly.

"Okay, but why did you and Joe stop being friends?" Mark asked.

"I can't tell you," Chad responded, tightly gripping the engine. He knocked a sliver of wood away with his knife. "You'll laugh just like they did."

"We wouldn't laugh at you," Patti said assuringly.

"Yes, you would. You would laugh because you don't understand."

"Understand what?" Mark asked.

Chad looked at Mark and held the knife up like it was a finger. "You ever like a girl, Mark?"

Mark was taken aback. Like a girl? Did he mean like ooshy-gooshy holding hands or did he mean like a girl as a friend?

"Huh?" he replied.

"You know, have you ever liked a girl?"

Mark blushed slightly. It was the kind of question boys asked each other only when they were good friends, only when they were talking seriously away from girls. Patti was staring at him with intense interest.

"What's that got to do with it?" asked Mark.

"It might have plenty to do with it," Chad said. "Well?"

Mark remembered a girl named Debbie back in Washington, D.C. He thought he liked her, but when she wrote a note to Karen saying she liked a boy named Bob more than Mark, he decided he didn't like her after all. "I might have . . . once," Mark answered.

Patti smiled.

"I might have liked a girl once, too," Chad started to say and then fell into a thoughtful silence.

Mark and Patti waited. Mark felt sure Chad would open up and explain.

Chad took a deep breath and looked as if he might go back to whittling again. Then he put the engine on the pavement. "I didn't tell anybody I liked her. It was my own secret. I didn't even tell her for a long time. Then I told Joe because I thought we were friends. He laughed at me and told the rest of the gang. They wouldn't quit teasing me, so I left. I don't know why I ever hung out with them in the first place."

"Who did you like, Chad?" Patti asked quickly.

Chad was on guard again. "I told you enough." He picked up his wooden engine and carefully started carving again.

There wasn't a good reason to stay after that, so Mark and Patti said good-bye and walked on toward Mark's house.

"Okay, let's sort this out," Mark said. "There's this mysterious bracelet with Rachel's name on it that we found at the scene of the crime. And we know Rachel could have slashed the tire because Joe humiliated her this morning."

"And," Patti added, "even though she says the bracelet isn't hers, I think she might be lying."

"Why would she lie to us?"

"I don't know, but she is. I can tell."

"How can you tell?" Mark asked.

Patti glanced shyly at Mark and said, "Call it girl's intuition."

"We don't know where Rachel got the knife," Mark said, ignoring her comment. "Which brings us to Chad. He carries a knife. And he might have used it on Joe's tire because Joe laughed at him for liking a girl."

"But what girl?" Patti asked curiously.

"Rachel," Mark answered confidently.

"What?" Patti stopped and stared at Mark.

He was pleased. This reminded him of some of the detective stories he had read. He felt like Sherlock Holmes, with Patti as Dr. Watson.

"Are you nuts? You think Chad liked Rachel?"

"Not liked, he likes her."

I'm working into the role nicely, Mark thought.

"You're out of your mind," Patti scoffed.

Then Mark explained how he had seen a blond-haired boy on a bike at the park—Chad, in fact—follow Rachel after Joe teased her.

"A boy acts like that when he likes a girl," Mark said.

"Wow!" Patti's mouth gaped open.

"And that makes Chad a greater suspect," Mark added.

"It does?"

"Sure! If Chad has a crush on Rachel and saw how Joe picked on her, he might have slashed Joe's tire to get revenge for her."

Patti stared at Mark with amazement. "How did you figure this all out?"

"Elementary, my dear Patti," he smiled. "Elementary."

Chapter
Six

MARK AND PATTI PICKED UP THE slashed tire at his house and gave his mom an update on the case. She said they were doing a wonderful job, but Mark had the feeling she was only humoring them. He didn't understand why mothers didn't take such things more seriously.

"It's getting near suppertime," she said as they were leaving. "Be home soon. I may have a surprise for you."

Probably pizza, Mark guessed.

Back at Whit's End, Mark showed the tire to Mr. Whittaker. "What do you think?"

Whit turned the tire this way and that, examining the inside and outside of it before he answered. "It's a slashed tire all right."

"Yeah, but can you figure out any clues from it?" Mark tried to sound detective-like. Even though his reputation was at stake, he was beginning to enjoy the mystery.

"I'll need to do a few tests," Whit determined. "That's the only way to find out anything for sure. How is the rest of the case coming?"

Mark started to speak, but Patti interrupted and told Whit everything they had discovered. This annoyed Mark and made him wish Patti would go away. Dr. Watson should never interrupt Sherlock Holmes.

Whit stroked his chin again. He seemed particularly interested in the news about Chad and Rachel. "From what I saw on Friday," he said, "I don't think they are friends at all."

"Friday? What happened Friday?" Mark asked.

Whit brushed his finger lightly along his mustache. "Friday afternoon Chad was hanging around but not really doing anything. He acted like he was waiting for something or someone. When Rachel came in a little later, he was shy and nervous. Eventually, he talked to her, and they sat down together."

"You were right, Mark. It *is* Rachel he likes!" Patti exclaimed.

"Of course," Mark said.

Whit continued his account. "Chad and Rachel were in that booth," he said, gesturing toward one of them. "He had a soda, and she had a sundae. I thought it was nice that a boy and a girl can be friends, like you two," he smiled.

Patti blushed, and Mark rolled his eyes.

Whit continued, "Then it seemed like they were having a disagreement. She was looking very uncomfortable, and he was acting upset. She got up and walked out. A moment later, he followed her."

Mark put on his best thoughtful expression. "Hmm, curious."

"It concerns me when kids fight like that in my shop, so I walked outside to make sure everything was all right. I found them around the back by the oak tree. I didn't hear what was said, but I got there in time to see her throw something small at Chad and storm off. Chad saw me, became embarrassed, and left in another direction. So much for boys and girls being friends, I thought." Whit smiled. "Well, Inspector? What do you make of it?"

Mark's voice was low and serious when he answered, "This

makes it look worse for Chad. He's good with a knife and would have wanted to get revenge because Joe picked on Rachel. It's pretty simple."

"The bracelet!" Patti suddenly blurted. "That's why the bracelet was under the tree!"

Mark was confused. After playing the detective so well, he was ashamed to ask her why.

Whit asked instead. "Why was it there?"

"Because," Patti said proudly, "that's what you saw Rachel throw at Chad!" Patti dug in her pocket and held up the bracelet. "See the small wooden heart in the middle! I'll bet Chad made it for Rachel. He could have whittled it. And when they had a fight, she threw it at him!"

"Well done, Patti!" Whit exclaimed.

Mark reluctantly admitted, "You might be on to something."

"Might be! You know I'm right, Mark Prescott, and you're afraid to admit it," Patti scolded.

Mark scowled. "Okay, if you're so smart, tell me what they were fighting about."

She thought about it a moment and then shrugged it off. "It doesn't matter. Now we know why the bracelet was at the scene of the crime. Rachel didn't slash the tire."

"She still might have," Mark insisted.

"It's only circum . . . circum . . ." Patti got stuck on the word and then said, "You know, that kind of evidence."

"If you mean it's only evidence that appears to be true because of the circumstances, but may not be true in fact, you mean 'circumstantial evidence,'" Whit explained.

"Thank you. It's only cir-cum-stantial evidence," Patti finished.

"But why did she lie about the bracelet?" Mark demanded.

"Where would she get a knife to slash a tire?" Patti countered.

Whit held up his hands. "All right, you two. That's enough. Some of these questions may be answered when I get a good look at this tire." Whit looked at his watch. "Your parents are probably wondering where you are. Go home for dinner, and we'll continue this later."

Walking through McAlister Park, Patti suddenly announced to Mark that she was going to walk him home. "I don't think you should go alone," she said.

Mark turned to her and asked, "Why not?"

"Because of Joe and his gang."

"What about them?" Mark asked.

"Joe said earlier he would get you for slashing his tire. He might be waiting around. I'm . . . I'm worried that he'll hurt you. I'll walk you home," she offered.

"I'm not going to have a girl walk me home. You think I can't handle Joe myself? He's after you, too, you know. I'll walk you home." Then Mark mumbled under his breath, "Dumb girl."

He noticed Patti smiling, and he wondered what she thought was so funny. Nearer to Patti's house, they began talking about Chad's crush on Rachel. Mark was wondering why, if Chad liked Rachel, he would get in a fight with her under the oak tree.

"Mark, you said you once liked a girl," Patti said. "Did you really?"

"Yeah, I did," he answered. He felt his cheeks turn warm.

"A lot?"

Mark growled, "Drop it, Patti. I don't want to talk about it."

"But . . . I think it's kind of cute."

"Cute!" Mark felt like his face had turned bright red.

"Yeah."

She had that same funny look again. It made Mark nervous. He tried to pick up their pace.

"Mark?" Patti ventured when they reached her front porch.

"What?"

"Did you ever . . . you know." Patti looked down at her feet shyly. "Did you ever kiss the girl you liked?"

"Are you crazy?" He looked around self-consciously, wondering if anyone else in the neighborhood heard the question.

"You mean, you liked her, but you never kissed her?"

Mark swallowed hard. "I . . . I have to go home, Patti."

"You could kiss me if you wanted to," Patti suddenly blurted.

"No way!" he replied, louder than he meant to.

Patti looked wounded. Her voice snapped back to its normal volume. "I wouldn't want you to kiss me anyway!"

With that, she turned and marched into the house. She slammed the door hard enough to make the front window rattle. Convinced that everyone in the neighborhood had gathered on their porches to see what the commotion was all about, Mark hurried off to the woods across the street.

The woods were dark. The thick leaves of the trees blocked what little light was given off by the slow summer dusk falling over Odyssey. Mark was doing his best to decide what in the world was wrong with Patti.

Why is she acting so strange? he wondered.

He pondered the question until he was deep in the woods, until he heard the crunching of leaves. His thoughts suddenly shifted from Patti to Joe.

Then Mark heard the sharp snapping sounds of branches breaking.

He spun around. The sounds suddenly stopped, but he couldn't see anything.

It's nothing, he thought.

The strange quiet told him otherwise, and he shuddered. He

wished Patti hadn't reminded him of Joe's threats. It was like hearing a horrifying monster story before going to bed.

Swish . . . swish . . . swish. It was the unmistakable rhythm of feet moving through the leaves. Mark's heart began to pound. He jerked his head suddenly to the right, sure he saw something out of the corner of his eye.

"Is somebody there?" he called out feebly.

No one answered.

Frankly he wasn't sure he wanted an answer. What if it wasn't Joe? What if someone else were following him? What would Sherlock Holmes do? Would he run? Would he reason with the beast? Would he try to outwit it? Mark didn't know, and he didn't care to wait around for an answer. The shadows came alive, the sound of snapping branches and crunching leaves seemed close behind him. Mark started to run.

He thought he heard someone laugh. Or was it a cough? A growl? He ran faster, without looking back, following the path closely. He was racing as fast as his sneakers would take him. But the noises seemed to be keeping pace.

At last he reached the edge of the woods and broke into the brighter, though fading, sunlight. He wished he felt safer. His nerves wouldn't let him. If Joe or some sort of creature wanted to get him, it would be just as easy to get him in the street. Mark kept running, even though his legs were beginning to feel like two loose rubber bands.

He raced across his yard and went to the door closest to him, the one on the side of the garage. He pushed it open, his chest heaving from effort. He slammed the door and collapsed against it. Clutching his aching side, he closed his eyes for a moment.

Slowly he reached up to the pane of glass in the door. Pushing the curtain aside, he peeked out to see if anything had followed him. Everything looked normal, even peaceful. He pressed his head against the glass to look down to the woods.

There, on the barely shadowed edge, Mark saw something move. It was a dark figure. Mark blinked and looked again. He could see it. It wasn't a trick of his imagination. Something was moving down there, watching, waiting—then suddenly it was gone.

Mark felt as though he would throw up and swallowed a couple of times to try and relax. He was home now and safe, he assured himself. Whatever was after him was down by the woods. It wouldn't dare come up here after him. No way. It wouldn't dare. Mark took a deep breath. It wouldn't dare.

Then he was grabbed from behind.

Chapter Seven

MARK TRIED TO SCREAM, but he couldn't get a sound past the hand over his mouth. He struggled, but the strength of his captor was too great. Then he heard a gentle chuckle in his ear, very low, soft, and familiar.

"That's for all those times you used to scare me when I was working in the garage," Richard Prescott said as he let go of his son.

"Dad!" Mark shrieked, leaping into his father's arms. They hugged for a moment that felt like forever.

Julie Prescott appeared at the doorway leading into the house and smiled as she watched them. "Did you find the box you were looking for, Richard?"

"I found more than that!" he answered and hugged Mark again.

"I told you there might be a surprise for dinner," Mark's mom said.

Mark laughed. "I thought we were going to have pizza."

"I hope this is a little better than pizza. I drove all the way from Chicago to see you," his dad said as they walked into the kitchen.

"What are you doing here?" Mark asked, hoping this visit was a good sign of some sort.

His dad smiled. "I'm going to California on business, but before

I go, I decided to come here. Only for the weekend, though."

Mark tried to disguise his disappointment. They hadn't seen each other for months, not since the family split up in the spring. Mark and his mother had moved to Odyssey and his father had stayed behind.

The marriage wasn't working out, Julie had told Mark. His parents needed time apart. He didn't understand then, and he wasn't sure he understood any better now. But he was glad to see his dad, if only for a weekend.

"Your mom's been telling me about Odyssey," his dad said. "You've been having some interesting adventures. You want to tell me about them?"

Mark grinned. In a flood of words, he unleashed all the facts and stories he had collected since arriving in Odyssey: Mr. Whittaker, Whit's End, Joe Devlin, and the slashed tire.

Mark talked all the way through supper, ignoring the amused looks his mother and father exchanged. It took Mark back to the days when they were together and happy. He finished his Odyssey adventures with his race through the woods to get away from the mysterious pursuer.

Mark's father looked concerned. "Did you know about this, Julie?"

Mark's mom looked wide-eyed. "It's the first I've heard about it. It's not like Odyssey has a high incidence of crime. I haven't read of a single mugging or robbery since we moved here."

She turned to Mark. "Do you think it was Joe Devlin?"

Mark nodded. "It had to be. He said he was going to get me. Who else would chase me through the woods?"

"Maybe we should have a word with the Devlins," Julie suggested.

Richard Prescott pondered this a moment. "Maybe we

should," he said. Then he tossed his napkin on the table and smiled. "Well, I want you and your mom to give me a full tour of Odyssey tomorrow, okay?"

Mark looked to his mom for approval.

"After church," she said.

"Yeah!" Mark shouted.

Richard Prescott reached for his wife's hand, but she moved it away self-consciously.

"Mark," his mother said softly, "your father and I want you to know that . . . that . . ." It was as much as she could say. Her eyes filled with tears, and she put her head down.

A tight grip of fear seized Mark's stomach. *What now?* he wondered. *Are they getting a divorce? Is this the big announcement?*

He stared intently into his father's face. It was set in a determined expression, but the eyes were sad.

His father cleared his throat nervously. "Son, I know this separation has been hard for you. It's tough to understand what's going on. We don't want to make things worse than they've been. But we don't want to give you any false hope."

False hope? Mark wondered what he meant.

His dad's eyes were teary, causing Mark's to water. "I've been an idiot. I . . . I'm not sure what I was thinking. I'm not sure how we're going to do it, but . . ." Mark's father took his mother's hand again, and this time she wrapped it in hers. "But your mother and I want to get help. We want to see if we can give our marriage another try. I want to be part of the family again."

Mark's mouth fell open.

"Do you think you can forgive me enough to let me do that?" his father asked as large tears rolled down his ruddy cheeks.

Mark fell into his dad's arms and cried. Julie joined in, the three of them hugging and crying at the dining room table. It was the only answer Mark could give.

Then the phone rang, once, twice, and several more times before his mother pulled herself away to get it.

"It won't be easy," his dad said, stroking Mark's hair. "We have a lot of things to work out, a lot of things to decide. But we'll get counseling. Your mother thinks the pastor can help us." He kissed Mark on the top of his head. "I don't know how I thought I could live without you."

Julie returned to the dining room. She was visibly shaken.

"Julie? Is everything all right?" Richard asked, rising from his chair.

She dabbed at her eyes with a tissue. "That was Mrs. Devlin, Joe's mother."

Mark looked up and cried out, "We can't pay her until I find out who really did it! Why is she bugging us?"

Julie shook her head. "That wasn't why she called. Apparently Joe got beat up in the woods on his way home this evening. She says she's going to call the police if we don't come right over."

"Joe was attacked in the woods!" Mark said with surprise. "But what does it have to do with me?"

"Mark," his mother said, "Mrs. Devlin thinks you did it."

Chapter
Eight

THE DEVLINS' HOUSE WAS A SPRAWLING, run-down Victorian on the south end of Main Street, right where the shops and office buildings ended and a residential section began. An electric red-and-white pole with a barber sign was on the street. A small stairwell led to the basement of the house, where Mr. Devlin had his barbershop.

The Prescott family walked past the pole and the stairwell to the front porch steps. Mrs. Devlin was waiting at the door. Her expression was stern and unyielding.

She led them to the living room where Joe sat on the couch, his head tilted back to balance the ice pack on his eye. Alan, Joe's younger brother, stood nearby and seemed fascinated by all the fuss. He flitted around nervously until Mrs. Devlin told him to sit down and be still. They were all informed that Mr. Devlin was in the basement with a late-evening customer.

"I didn't call the police," Mrs. Devlin said. "I thought we could work this out ourselves as civil and mature adults. I know you must feel terrible having a juvenile delinquent for a son."

Richard Prescott protested, "Excuse me, Mrs. Devlin, but I'm not sure we have enough facts to know that Mark did this to Joe."

Mrs. Devlin looked surprised. "What do we need? Mark has been terrorizing my Joe all day. First the fight, then the tire, now this!" She folded her arms. "Maybe I should have called the police. I didn't believe you would have the nerve to come here and deny it!"

Mark's father spoke calmly. "Why don't we hear Joe's story? Then we'll see whether you should call the police. Joe? Can you tell us what happened?"

Joe leaned forward, letting the ice pack drop into his hand. His left eye was a deep red and was turning black and blue. Apart from that, he looked like he always did—angry.

"I took a shortcut through the woods to get home," he explained. "Somebody jumped me and gave me this black eye."

"Not somebody," Mrs. Devlin corrected him. "Mark. Didn't you say it was Mark who did it? Remember when you came home?"

Joe looked up at Mr. and Mrs. Prescott, his resolve floundering. "Well, no. *You* said it was Mark, Mom. You said it couldn't be anybody else."

"You didn't actually see who jumped you?" Mark's father asked.

"No, I got jumped from behind. If it was face-to-face, I wouldn't have this black eye. I would have won. I always win in a fair fight," Joe insisted.

"How long ago did this happen?" asked Julie Prescott.

"About a half hour ago," Joe answered.

Mr. Prescott held up his hands. "Well, Mark couldn't have done it then."

Mrs. Devlin looked at them suspiciously. "Why not?"

"Because he's been home with us for the past hour," Mark's father replied.

Mrs. Devlin sneered. "That's exactly what I would expect you to say—anything to cover for your son."

Richard Prescott looked intently into her face. "Mrs. Devlin, I don't think you know us well enough to judge whether we would lie for our son or not."

"All parents lie for their children," she said.

"Do you?"

"Well . . ." Mrs. Devlin stopped, realizing the trap she had fallen into.

Mr. Prescott went on, "If Mark has done something wrong, he'll be punished. But, in this case, I promise you that he was home with us when Joe was attacked. In fact, he was afraid someone was following him in the woods, too."

"So he was in the woods!" Mrs. Devlin exclaimed. "And so was my Joe."

"Yes, but that was an hour ago," Mr. Prescott answered. "Maybe the same person who chased after Mark also hurt Joe."

As Mark looked at Joe, he came to an unexpected realization.

"How long were you in the woods?" Mark asked.

"I told you; it happened half an hour ago. I was taking a shortcut home," Joe snapped back.

"A shortcut home from where?" Mark asked.

"What are you, some kind of lawyer? I was coming home from—" He paused for a second and then said, "Whit's End."

"You took a shortcut through the woods from Whit's End? But it's shorter through the park. You would have to go out of your way to go through the woods."

"I don't know," Joe stammered. "I'm . . . I'm confused. Maybe I was coming from somewhere else. I don't remember."

"It was only a half hour ago, Joe. You must remember where you where," Mr. Prescott said.

"Mom, tell them to quit asking so many questions. My eye hurts!" Joe cried.

"That's enough," Mrs. Devlin said, rushing to her son's side. "He's the victim, not the culprit. You won't turn this on him!"

Joe laid his head back, and his mother placed the ice pack on his eye.

"You were the one who chased me in the woods, weren't you?" Mark asked Joe. "That's why you were coming home through the woods. It's a shortcut from *my* house, not Whit's End."

Joe jerked himself up, yanked the ice pack from his eye, and shouted, "I told you what happened! I was taking a shortcut home from Whit's End when someone jumped me from behind. We wrestled in the dark, and then *she* hit me!"

"She?" Julie asked.

Joe stumbled over his words. "She. He. It. Whatever it was. I couldn't tell. But that's how it happened! If you don't believe me, that's your tough luck."

Mrs. Devlin urged Joe to sit back down and then whispered, "It's all right, Joseph. Calm down."

She put the ice pack on his eye again and turned to the Prescotts. "See what you've done? You've upset him."

Sitting there with his frail face, black eye, and ice pack, Joe looked weak.

He's not so tough, Mark thought. *He's a scared kid just like me.*

Mr. Prescott gestured for Mark to come along and then addressed Mrs. Devlin. "You can call the police if you want, Mrs. Devlin. I don't think they'll be able to help you, though."

The Prescotts let themselves out into the warm summer night. On the front porch, Mark could hear Mrs. Devlin in the living room. "How could you be so stupid!" she screamed at Joe. "You're going through the woods. You're coming from Whit's

End. Why don't you get your story straight? You humiliate me! We'll see if your father has something to say about this—with a razor strap! Now, go to your room!"

"Ow, Ma. Don't! Let go of my arm!" Joe protested.

Mark could also hear Alan laughing and wondered if he would do the same if he had an older brother who got in trouble. For the first time, Mark felt sorry for Joe.

Chapter
Nine

MARK FOUND IT HARD TO CONCENTRATE on the sermon in church.

For one thing, he was excited that his father was with them. For the other, he was trying to piece together the clues surrounding Joe's slashed tire and the black eye someone had given him in the woods.

Considering all the enemies Joe seemed to have, it could have been anyone. Rachel? She had her own reason to want to hurt Joe. Her bracelet had been found at the scene of the crime, but could she have given Joe a black eye? It didn't seem possible.

Chad had the motive, and he had a knife. He could have easily been in the woods and attacked Joe. Maybe there was someone else Mark didn't know about, someone who had it in for Joe? Mark slumped in the pew. If that were true, then he might never find out who did it. One way or another, Mark had to discover who was doing these things to Joe Devlin. Otherwise he would be stuck with the blame and have to pay for the tire.

After the church service ended, Mark looked for Whit so he could introduce his father. He also wanted to tell Whit the latest news about what had happened to Joe Devlin in the woods. But Whit had already left.

"You two should have some time alone," his mother said to Mark and his dad after they returned home and changed clothes. "I've fixed some sandwiches for a picnic. Why don't you go up to Trickle Lake for a while?"

She gave Mark's dad an awkward kiss before they left. Until then, Mark had forgotten how long it had been since he had seen them show any affection.

Mark and his father climbed into Mr. Prescott's rental car and drove through the picturesque mountain roads to one of the most beautiful spots in the area: Trickle Lake. On one end, it offered a view of the town of Odyssey. On the other end, it was surrounded by paths leading into the adjoining hills and mountains. The people of Odyssey treasured it for its clean water, good fishing, and general quietness.

Mark and his father ate and then threw a baseball around for a while. Then they hiked along the shadowed paths of the forest. Mark knew them because of Patti; they had wandered there together a few times. He pointed out the Great Tree, supposedly the tallest tree in the county. It was said that whoever could climb to the top of the tree would see cities in three surrounding counties. Neither Mark nor his father was in the mood to find out if it were true.

"Patti said she climbed the tree once," Mark said, "but I'm not sure I believe her."

His father chuckled. "I've been meaning to ask you about this Patti you keep talking about. Does my son have a girlfriend?"

"No!" Mark thundered. "She just likes to hang around me, that's all."

"Come on, Mark. This is your dad you're talking to. You can tell me man-to-man."

"Cut it out, Dad!"

"Maybe one of these trees has your initials, huh?" He laughed and moved to the side of the path, where several trees were scarred with a variety of carvings. Outlined by the brown bark, the hearts with arrows through them, initials, and names were a lighter tan. At the base of one tree, a small sign said that it was the Lover's Tree and noted that many of the carvings went as far back as the middle 1800s, when Odyssey was first established.

Mark frowned and tugged at his dad's sleeve. "Come on, Dad. Let's go."

His dad waved for him to wait. "I want to look at some of these older inscriptions. Maybe it'll give me inspiration for your mom."

Mark shuffled his feet and glanced at the tree-trunk carvings: Billy Loves Suzie. Rocko & Delores. J.D. + P.J.

Pretty stupid stuff, Mark thought. Then he did a double take when his eye caught one particular carving. He moved closer to make sure it said what he thought it did. To his horror, it read: Patti & Mark 4 Ever. It was in the middle of a perfectly rounded heart. Mark groaned.

Mark's dad was at his shoulder now. "Well, well, well," he said. "What do we have here? Ah, it looks fresh. And it's so artistically done."

Mark walked away. *Patti!* he fumed to himself. *Why did she do such a thing? I never said I liked her! Now everyone in Odyssey will think we're boyfriend and girlfriend!*

He kicked a small stone that spun into the woods and muttered aloud, "I never want to talk to her again!"

"Are you sure there isn't more to your relationship with Patti than you've told me?" his dad teased.

"She's really weird, Dad," Mark responded. "She started following me around when we first moved here. Everyone teased me. I mean, I didn't want a girl for a friend anyway, but . . . but she kept coming around."

"I think it's good for boys to have girls as friends," his dad observed.

Mark recalled that Mr. Whittaker had said the same thing, but it didn't make him feel any better.

"Everything was okay," Mark continued. "When we did things together, I kind of forgot she was a girl because she's good at sports and knows how to play army and . . . well, she's fun. But lately she's been acting funny."

"What do you mean by funny?"

Mark screwed up his face as he tried to explain. "She got all upset because she woke up with a pimple yesterday morning. Then she kept looking at me with this goofy expression. And she got mad because I didn't say how nice her clothes were."

Mr. Prescott began to chuckle.

"And . . . and . . . she asked me to kiss her!"

Mark's dad laughed heartily. He pulled his son closer and gave him a hug. "What a terrible thing to suffer through."

"You're telling me! I don't know what her problem is," Mark cried out.

"Patti's problem, if it's a problem at all, is simple," his dad explained. "She's becoming a young woman."

Mark grimaced. "Oh, brother."

His father shrugged. "It happens eventually. Didn't we have this little talk before?"

"You mean about the birds and the bees and the storks and stuff?"

"Well, yes."

"I think this whole thing is disgusting," Mark said. "And if

Patti is starting to get like that, she's going to have to find a new friend. I'm not interested."

"Son, don't lose a good friend over something like this. Friends are to be valued like family whether they're boys or girls. Just be patient while she goes through these changes."

Mark wasn't sure he agreed, but he nodded anyway.

"Besides," his father added, "she may grow up and make a lot of money as a woodworking artist."

Mark didn't know what he meant.

His father pointed to the tree. "Look at the way she carved your names into this tree. She shows a lot of dexterity with a knife."

"Dexterity?" Mark asked.

"Dexterity means 'skill,'" Mr. Prescott explained. "It means she's good at using a knife."

Mark looked at the carving and had to agree. It was well-done, certainly not like the other scrawls. But Patti had never told Mark she was good with a knife. Why hadn't she?

By the time he and his father returned to Odyssey, Mark had new suspicions about who might have slashed Joe's tire.

Chapter
Ten

ON THE WAY HOME FROM TRICKLE LAKE, Mark took his father to Whit's End. He hoped Mr. Whittaker might be around, even though it was closed Sundays. Whit wasn't to be found, and Mark was disappointed.

"I'll have to meet your Mr. Whittaker friend next time," his dad said.

Mark was pleased to hear there would be a next time. Any mention of his parents' future together helped him believe they really could be a family again.

Back home, Julie informed Richard that she had talked to the pastor about counseling. The pastor said he could meet with them for a short time in the afternoon. Mark sensed that his mother and father needed to be alone for a while, so he decided to go visit Patti. This was his chance to ask her a few new questions about the slashed tire.

He took the shortcut through the woods again. In the daylight Mark wondered why he had let himself become as frightened as he had. Then he remembered the dark figure on the edge of the woods.

He hurried to the Eldridges' house and waited on the veranda while Patti's mother went to get her. Even though it was late in the afternoon, the day was still bright and alive. Mark closed his eyes and listened to a distant lawn mower, the neighbor children laughing, a passing bike with a card in the spokes, and a slamming door that announced Patti's arrival.

Mark looked up as Patti sat down next to him. She was wearing a delicate pink dress Mark assumed she had left on from church. She kept her gaze away from his, looking ahead to the front lawn or down at her tightly clenched hands. A knuckle on her right hand was scraped. Her hello was awkward and her manner distant.

This wasn't the Patti Eldridge Mark had become friends with over the summer. This was the Patti with a new dress and a pimple on her forehead, who had asked him to kiss her the evening before. This was the Patti who had carved a heart and two names in a tree at Trickle Lake.

Do I really know her? Mark questioned. *No, I don't.*

Yet this was the same Patti who could have slashed Joe's tire. Exactly why, Mark wasn't sure. He wished he had stayed home. He didn't want to be with this new Patti. He didn't know how to talk to her. What would Sherlock Holmes do?

"My dad's here to visit," Mark said. Sherlock Holmes probably wouldn't talk about his dad, but it was the only thing Mark could think to say.

"Yeah, I know. I saw him in church this morning," replied Patti.

A moment of silence passed between them.

Then Mark asked, "Did you hear about Joe getting punched?"

Patti shook her head. "No, what happened?"

"He said he was walking through the woods on his way home last night and somebody jumped him from behind. His mother thought I did it and called us up. We went over to their house, and Joe was sitting on the couch with an ice pack on his face. He looked terrible."

Patti smiled slightly. "Really?"

"Yeah!" Mark said. "He had the biggest fat lip I've ever seen. It was funny looking."

Patti looked perplexed. "You mean black eye."

A bird screeched and flew from the roof above them. Mark spoke softly. "I thought you didn't know about it."

"I didn't," she said.

"Then how did you know it was his eye instead of his lip?" Mark asked. He thought it was a trick worthy of Sherlock Holmes, but he didn't feel good about it. It was like catching Dr. Watson stealing money from his desk.

Patti's cheeks reddened. "You . . . you said it was his eye."

"No, I didn't."

"Yes, you—" Patti stopped. Her face suddenly went very tight and Mark thought she might cry. She tugged at her dress and turned away. "You're right. I punched Joe."

"Why?"

She turned to face him again. "Because!" she snapped. "I know Joe better than you do. He's been picking on me for years. He said he was going to hurt you, and I figured he would try it when you were walking home last night. After you left my house, I followed you through the woods."

"That was you? You were the one who scared me half to death?"

"No, you idiot! That was Joe!" she shouted. "I told you he would do it. But you wouldn't listen to me, so I followed you, and I saw Joe, Alan, Lance, and a few others. I saw them chase you in the woods. It made me mad. After you ran into your garage, I followed them back to see what they were going to do next. Joe and

Alan got in a fight, and Joe made him go home. Then the rest of the gang sat around and laughed at you. I was really mad, so when they split up, I followed Joe and jumped on him."

Now Mark understood why Joe had accidentally said "she" when he told his side of the story. That's why he hadn't confessed. He was too ashamed to admit a girl had given him a black eye.

Patti sighed deeply. "Are you going to tell?"

"No," Mark said, pausing to think about it. "But *you* should. Right?"

She looked sadly at Mark and nodded in agreement. Then she began to cry. Slowly, at first, with a slight quiver of her bottom lip and a film of water over her eyes. Then the telltale sniffles came, quickly followed by tears sliding onto her cheeks.

Mark didn't know what to do. Something inside told him to put his arm around her, but it was broad daylight. They were on the front porch, after all. What should he do? Patti settled it by springing up and running inside.

Mark walked home feeling like a jerk. He hated to make a girl cry.

But he still puzzled over the most important question. Since she had punched Joe, had she slashed his tire, too?

Mark reached his front lawn and saw his mother and father standing in the driveway. They were next to the rental car, talking intensely, oblivious of Mark. Then they hugged each other. His father was leaving.

"Dad!" Mark called out as he ran to them. "Where are you going?"

"Work. I've been waiting for you," his dad said, pulling his son close. "I thought you were going to make me miss my plane."

"But you can't go! I thought you were leaving tomorrow."

"I'm going to California tomorrow, but I have to drive back to

Chicago tonight. I'm glad you got here in time. I promised myself I would never leave you again without saying good-bye first," he said, giving Mark a squeeze.

"But you can't go," Mark said weakly.

Richard Prescott held his son at arm's length and looked him square in the eye. "I'll be back, Mark. I promise."

They hugged again; then he hugged Mark's mom, climbed into the car, and drove away. They watched until the car reached the end of the street. His dad tapped the horn and disappeared around the corner. Now it was Mark's turn to cry.

Chapter
Eleven

MONDAY MORNING, WHIT DIDN'T even have time to turn around the Whit's End Open sign before Mark arrived. Whit listened with great interest as Mark told him about his dad's visit and his parents' counseling and about Joe's black eye and Patti's confession. He also explained his latest suspicions. When Mark finished, Whit gestured for him to follow him to the basement.

Whit's workroom, a room Mark knew well, was cluttered with odd-shaped gadgets and half-finished inventions. The Imagination Station sat in the center, a large and imposing machine. Mark touched it affectionately as he walked past it to the workbench. Joe's slashed tire and a large microscope were sitting on the bench. The tire looked more mangled than before.

"I checked the tire for clues," Whit said with flourish. "Climb up on this stool and look through the microscope. I have a piece of the tire under there."

Mark pressed his eyes against the double lens and focused the microscope. A black mass of tire came into view.

Whit guided him along. "You see the tire?" he asked. "Notice the edge of it on the right side there. What do you see?"

Mark could make out the bumps of the tread, which were

mountainous through the magnifier. He then noticed the inter-
ruption where the clean edge of the slash had been made.

"All I see is a slashed tire," Mark confessed.

Whit chuckled. "But take a good close look at that slash and
I'll show you something else. Don't move."

Mark watched through the lens as Whit removed the piece of
tire. Bright light replaced it for a moment, and then Whit slid
what looked like the same piece back under the lens.

"I tried a little experiment with a tire of the same make,"
Whit said. "Do you see a difference?"

Mark could see the bumps of tread beside the slash mark. But
this time the slash mark was ragged and frayed. It wasn't sharp
and straight like the first one.

"This is different!" Mark exclaimed.

Whit patted Mark's shoulder. "Good. Because the second tire
was slashed with a regular pocketknife with a normal blade. It's
the kind of knife Chad would use to whittle with or Patti might
use to carve initials in a tree. Even a kitchen knife makes a similar kind of slash."

Mark felt embarrassed. "I don't get it," he admitted.

"It means that Chad or Patti would have had to use a much
sharper knife to slash Joe's tire. A knife requiring a very special
kind of blade."

Mark stared at Whit, puzzled.

"I think we should call all the suspects and have them meet
us here," Whit said with a smile. "I think we've reached the end
of this case."

Chapter Twelve

WHEN MARK AND WHIT ENTERED Whit's office, everyone involved in the case was waiting for them. Patti was sitting off by herself, tugging uncomfortably at her blue-and-white patterned dress. Chad was standing nearby, his hands shoved deep into his overalls. He had the same blank expression he always seemed to have. Rachel was sitting by the opposite wall.

Mrs. Devlin, Joe, and Alan were sitting together on the visitor's couch. Joe's eye had turned a light shade of bluish-red. Alan couldn't seem to sit still, so Mrs. Devlin pinched him.

"Too much boyish energy," she said to Whit.

Mark wished Mrs. Devlin hadn't come. But when Whit called, she had taken the phone from Joe and insisted that she be there.

"Well?" Mrs. Devlin said impatiently. "What's this big secret you're keeping? I can't wait to see how Mark has weaseled his way out of this one."

"I didn't weasel my—" Mark began.

Whit touched Mark's arm to silence him and moved to the center of the group. "Since we're not the police or lawful authorities," he said calmly, "I thought it would be best to settle this case quietly among those involved. I didn't see any sense in making a big fuss out of it."

Mrs. Devlin scoffed, "Oh, that's right. Protect the guilty one! Well, I'll be the one to say whether the police will be involved or not." She glared at Mark.

Whit gestured to Mark and said, "It's all yours, Inspector."

Whit sat down behind his desk as Mark stepped forward nervously and cleared his throat. "Thanks, Mr. Whittaker. I know you've all been wondering about this case since you're involved in it one way or another. It's taken a few twists and turns since the beginning and—"

"Get on with it!" Joe growled. "You think this is a movie or something?"

Mark stopped, stammered a little, and then continued in a detective-like tone. "Okay. Let's go through it one step at a time. Somebody slashed the tire on Joe's new bike. A few people thought it was me because Joe and I had a fight earlier. It so happens that I wasn't the only one who had a run-in with Joe. Lots of people in Odyssey seemed to have a reason to slash Joe's tire. I've narrowed it down to a handful. The fact is, it was someone in this room."

Everyone looked around suspiciously.

"You think I did it?" Patti asked, injured. "Thanks a lot!"

"You could have, Patti," Mark stated. "You and Joe do a lot of fighting. But that wasn't the only reason you were a suspect. I also saw some of the carving you did on a tree at Trickle Lake." Mark gritted his teeth as he mentioned it.

Patti blushed. "So? I was just playing around. It was a joke."

"But it showed me you can be real handy with a knife. Slashing Joe's tire would have been easy for you. You had enough motives. You could have slashed Joe's tire because he picks on you or because he picked on Rachel that morning or for other reasons. We know you and Joe had a fight Saturday night."

"What?" Joe bellowed.

"In the woods, Joe," Mark said. "You know as well as I do that it was Patti who punched you in the eye. You knew it all along. You didn't say so because you didn't want anyone to know a girl gave you a black eye."

Alan made a snorting sound.

Patti rose to her defense. "I did it because Joe and his gang scared you in the woods, and it made me mad. He deserved a black eye."

"Is that true?" Mrs. Devlin shouted at Joe.

Joe sank further into the couch's cushions. "Yeah, but that was to get back at Prescott. We were just having fun."

"And you let this girl give you a black eye?" Mrs. Devlin demanded. "Wait until your father hears about this!"

"Aw, Ma," Joe whined.

Mrs. Devlin turned to Patti. "Then you slashed my son's tire."

"No!" Patti cried out. She faced Mark. "Did you think I would let you take the blame for slashing Joe's tire if I did it? I . . . I thought we were friends."

"We are, Patti," Mark said.

"Aw, isn't that sweet," Joe mocked.

"Patti didn't do it, Mrs. Devlin," Mark stated.

"Oh, yes. I'm going to believe you after that little love scene? If she didn't, who did?" Mrs. Devlin gestured to Chad, who was leaning passively against the wall. "Was it Mr. Overalls over there? He's always walking around whittling things with that pocketknife of his."

Chad looked self-consciously at his pocketknife.

"I wondered the same thing," Mark said, resuming his detective-like tone. "He certainly had the right kind of weapon, and his motive was even better. Revenge."

Chad straightened his shoulders. "This isn't anybody's business."

Mark pleaded, "Do you want everyone to think you did it?"

Chad thought about it and then slumped against the wall again. "I don't care. It doesn't matter much anymore."

"What's all this nonsense? What are you talking about?" Mrs. Devlin snarled.

Mark paced slowly in front of a large bookcase. "When Patti and I first checked the scene of the crime—"

"Come on, Prescott, stop trying to be so tough. What scene of the crime?" Joe taunted.

"The tree where you parked your bike," Mark returned. "We found a small bracelet there. It had a wooden heart and the name *Rachel* carved on it. We thought Rachel had dropped it. But she later denied it was hers. It didn't make sense. Why would she lie about her bracelet?" Stabbing the air with his finger, he said, "Unless Rachel slashed the tire and dropped the bracelet by accident."

Rachel turned to Mark, her eyes wide with horror.

Mrs. Devlin frowned. "Rachel? Why in the world would she want to do that?"

"Because Joe teased her that morning about being . . ." Mark tried to find the right word and then said, "a little overweight."

"Fat! She's fat! Why don't you just say it?" Joe shouted.

Rachel lowered her head.

Mrs. Devlin pinched his arm. "Shut up, Joe! You're in enough trouble as it is."

"But Rachel didn't do it," Mark explained. "For one thing, she's not the sort of person who would hurt Joe or his tire. For another thing, the bracelet really wasn't hers."

Patti looked surprised. "It wasn't?"

Mark shook his head. "Nope."

"Then whose was it?" asked Patti.

Mark paused for full effect. "Chad's."

All eyes turned to Chad, whose face turned red.

Mark kept talking. "Chad made it for Rachel because he liked her. You knew about that, Joe. That's why Chad left the gang."

"You can't like girls and be in my gang," Joe said simply. "Especially not girls like—"

Joe squealed when Mrs. Devlin pinched him again.

"Finish your story, Prescott," she said.

"Chad tried to give the bracelet to Rachel under the oak tree. But she didn't feel the same way about Chad and told him so. Chad got mad. Maybe he said a few things he didn't mean to say. He told her to keep the bracelet, but she didn't want it. Rachel threw the bracelet at him and walked away. He left it on the ground. On Saturday, Joe parked his bike under the same tree. And the bracelet was still there when his tire was slashed. Isn't that right, Chad?"

Chad shrugged. "You're the detective."

"And my guess," Mark continued, "is that Chad was trying to find Rachel in the park Saturday morning to apologize. That's when Joe teased her so much she went home crying. Chad saw what happened, and he was steamed about it. That's why I thought he'd slashed the tire."

Mrs. Devlin turned to Chad. "Okay, Mr. Overalls, I think you owe us some money."

Chad opened his mouth to speak, but Mark interrupted. "That would be true, Mrs. Devlin, if it were Chad. But it wasn't."

"Good grief," Mrs. Devlin groaned. "Are you going to give us the life story of everyone in Odyssey before you get to the bottom of this? I'm still not convinced you're innocent, you know. And if you're guilty, I might just make you pay me for all this time you're wasting."

Mark moved back toward Whit. "Just one more thing, Mrs. Devlin. Whit examined the tire and discovered that it wasn't slashed with an ordinary pocketknife or even a kitchen knife. It was slashed with a special kind of blade."

Mrs. Devlin shook her head impatiently. "Why should I care what kind of blade slashed the tire?"

"Because you might recognize it," Whit said, leaning forward in his chair. He held up the object Mark had seen on the workbench.

"A straight razor?" Mrs. Devlin blinked.

"This was my father's," Whit said as he carefully pulled the stainless steel blade from its cover. "He used to shave with it every morning. It's extremely sharp. Of course, most men don't shave with straight razors anymore. They use the disposable kind. These days you'll usually find straight razors being used in one place."

Whit paused, and everyone remained quiet as they waited for him to tell them where. Mrs. Devlin already knew and had turned pale.

"A barbershop," Whit said.

"Just like Mr. Devlin's barbershop," Patti gasped.

Mrs. Devlin's tone of voice turned to a vicious growl. "What are you saying, Mr. Whittaker? You think my husband slashed my son's tire?"

"Of course not," replied Whit.

"I didn't do it!" Joe cried out.

"I certainly didn't," snapped Mrs. Devlin.

Rachel asked quietly, "Then who did?"

Mark and Whit both looked at the culprit. One by one, the rest of the group did the same.

"Alan?" Patti cried out.

Alan's eyes darted back and forth as he curled up on the couch. It seemed as if he wanted to shrink into the fabric itself.

"Alan!" Mrs. Devlin screamed.

"I . . . I . . ." Alan stuttered.

"Did you slash Joe's tire?" Mrs. Devlin asked, pressing her face closer to Alan's.

His mouth moved without forming any words; then he scrunched his face into a frown. "Joe yells at me in front of the gang and makes me feel stupid. And you got him a new bike and wouldn't get me one. And I hate him! He's the worst brother in the world!"

With an indignant roar, Mrs. Devlin was on her feet in an instant. Her face was a patchwork of reds, purples, and violets. She grabbed one of Alan's ears and one of Joe's. "Home! This minute! Both of you! I've never been so . . . so just wait until your father . . . you're going to regret the . . ."

Chad opened the door for them, and she stormed out with her boys yelping all the way down the stairs. They could be heard muttering and screaming all the way through Whit's End and out onto the sidewalk in front.

"Whew!" Mark sighed.

"It's heartbreaking," Whit observed. "It's bad enough when strangers try to hurt each other. Somehow it seems worse when it happens between brothers."

Everyone nodded silently.

Whit stood and said, "Maybe they'll learn something from this. Maybe we all will."

Mark recalled how it had felt to be at the Devlins' the night he was accused. He remembered Mrs. Devlin yelling at Joe. Then

Mark thought about the time Joe had yelled at Alan. One person bullying another person who bullies yet another. Mark wondered how a home could become so full of anger and jealousy.

"You can go now, if you want," Whit announced, "or you can stick around for some free ice cream. It seems the least I can do after all this."

Chad declined the offer and moved toward the door.

Mark caught him before he could go. "I'm sorry, Chad," Mark said. "I hope you're not mad at me."

Chad shrugged. "Nah, you great detectives have to get your cases solved, don't you."

Chad turned and strolled out of the office.

Rachel said to Whit, "I would have some ice cream, but I just had some."

As she hurried out the door, Mark thought he heard her call Chad's name.

"Well done, detective Prescott!" Whit said proudly, thumping Mark on the back.

"You were the one who solved it," Mark responded.

"Not at all. You and Patti put together most of the pieces." Whit gave Mark's shoulder a gentle squeeze and walked over to Patti, who was still in her chair. "It was nice of you to dress up for the occasion, Patti. Doesn't she look lovely in that dress, Mark?"

Patti looked up at Mark expectantly.

"Yeah," he said. "It's pretty, I guess. But will it be any good when I ask her to play catch with me?"

"You were going to ask me to play catch?" Patti asked.

Mark nodded.

Patti stood and moved toward Mark, wagging her finger. "You think I'm going out and throwing a ball with you, Mark Prescott? After all that's happened? After you almost accused me of slashing Joe's tire? After you nearly got me in trouble for punching Joe? Is that what you think? Huh?"

"Well," Mark said sheepishly as he looked from Patti to Whit and then back to Patti again. "Yeah."

Patti smiled. "Okay. Let me go home and change first."

She laughed and Whit did, too, long and heartily.

Maybe things will get back to normal again, Mark thought.

Book Three

The Secret Cave of Robinwood

Chapter
One

SPLASH!

Mark Prescott let out a yelp, withdrew his spear from the cool mountain water, and stood poised to make another thrust at his prey. For today, he wasn't Mark at all. He was Robin Hood dressed in woolen green hose that were soaked up to his leather britches. His matching, open-necked tunic was damp from all the splashing. Robin was fishing for dinner in LeMonde's River.

"I'm growing terribly hungry, sweet Robin," said Patti Eldridge, who wasn't Patti at all. She was Maid Marian resting on the riverbank and watching Robin with an amusement she could barely contain. He had been trying to catch a fish for the better part of an hour.

"Do you doubt me, gentle one?" Robin asked.

Marian smiled as she tilted her face toward the afternoon sun and stretched out her legs, buried beneath several layers of her ruffled dress. "Never, but are you sure this is the best way to catch fish?"

Robin turned to her and said, "Have I spent the entire summer surviving in the forest with the men of Sherwood without knowing how to fish properly?"

"Dear, dear Robin," Marian sighed pleasantly.

"I suppose you know a better way," Robin said as he lunged forward with his spear. "Blast!" he yelled, holding up his empty spear.

Marian giggled.

"It is for your sake that I soak myself to the bone, my lady," Robin said as his eyes carefully scanned the water. "Couldn't you bring me words of encouragement while I seek supper?"

"Breakfast, you mean," she jibed. "Why not let me try?"

"What? A fair and gentle woman?" Robin protested. "I cannot permit you to fish like a common gamekeeper."

"But I know the ways of the forest as well. Why can't you allow me to use what I know?"

"You can when you need to, my heart. But I am here, and I will do it. Ah!" he cried as he flung himself forward.

It was a faulty move. He overextended his reach, fell off balance, and with an enormous splash, spun headlong into the river.

Marian laughed loudly and fell helplessly back into the grass. "Maybe we should have gone out for hamburgers."

Robin sat in the water and blinked twice. With a dunking like that, he couldn't sustain his imaginary game any longer. He instantly returned to being Mark Prescott, a dark-haired kid in jeans and sneakers.

"Good grief," he sputtered.

Patti Eldridge—no longer a fair maiden in ruffles but a freckle-faced, blue-eyed young lady in a baseball cap, shorts, and a T-shirt—rushed to the edge of the water.

"My hero!" she said, giggling.

Mark frowned. "It's not funny. I'll bet the real Robin Hood had his off days."

Patti held out her hand. "I think Robin Hood would have found a better way to catch fish."

"If you know so much about fishing, why don't you come in and catch a few?"

Mark reached for Patti's hand, grabbed hold of her wrist, and pulled.

"Hey!" she screamed as she tumbled into the water.

"Oops," he said with a snicker.

"No fair." Patti wiped her face and splashed Mark.

He laughed and splashed her back, inciting a water battle. They finally called it quits when they began to cough from laughing so hard. Mark pushed away from her, half crawling, half swimming to the grassy bank. He climbed out and rolled onto his back.

"What about our fish?" Patti called.

"If you're so good, you catch them," he challenged, propping himself on his elbows to see what she would do.

"Okay," she said.

"You're crazy. You don't even have a spear."

"I don't need one." Her eyes moved quickly around the water. She froze in one position and said, "There's one."

He couldn't imagine what she thought she could do. Was she going to try and catch it with her hand? Mark sat up to watch.

In one swift motion, Patti snatched off her baseball cap, circled her arm through the air, scooped the cap into the water like a net, and brought it out again. It was all done so gracefully Mark thought he could have been watching a ballet dancer.

"Ta-dah!" Patti smiled proudly. A small fish flapped about in her cap.

Mark instantly felt hurt because he had been shown up by a girl. But this wasn't just any girl, and he didn't want to spoil such a good day by getting mad. Besides, it was a wonderful trick, so he applauded.

Patti bowed grandly once and then again. The third time, she swung her cap back into the water, allowing the squirming fish to escape.

Mark stood. "Let's go to Whit's End and get something real to eat."

Patti sloshed her way to the river's edge. "Okay. Maybe we'll be dry by the time we get there."

Mark held his hand out to her. She gripped it firmly, and he pulled her to the bank.

"Thanks," she said, smiling.

This time, without the mischief, the touch of their hands gave Mark a peculiar sensation. He suddenly realized that there was a time when he wouldn't have enjoyed such a simple afternoon of fun. Patti was a girl, after all. And girls shouldn't be good friends with boys—should they?

The answer to that question had been very slow in coming for Mark. But now, on this perfect August day as her hand slid from his, he knew they could. He didn't even care if some of the kids called them "boyfriend and girlfriend." Odyssey was a small town, and the others could have small thoughts if they wanted, Mark reasoned. Patti was as good a friend as any boy Mark had known.

All these thoughts flashed through Mark's mind in the few seconds his hand touched hers. He looked at Patti's eyes, half expecting them to show that she felt something similar. But her eyes were their usual blue and gave no hint that she had experienced the same feelings.

"I want you to tell me more about Robin Hood and his gang," Patti said. "I only saw the movie version."

As they strolled under a rich green canopy, Mark told her

everything he knew about Robin Hood and the men of Sherwood Forest.

Patti idly kicked at a broken branch in their path. "They had hiding places in the woods?" she asked with more than a casual amount of interest.

"Yeah," Mark answered, noting her tone. "Why?"

"No reason. Have you ever had a hiding place?"

"I built a tree fort with Tommy Smith when I lived in Washington, D.C.," Mark said. "What about you?"

"My bedroom at home has kind of been my hiding place. That's where I used to go to get away from everyone. But . . . it isn't the same as when I was little. I was going to fix it up before school started. My parents did it that sissy-looking pink."

"Pink's the right color for a girl," observed Mark.

"Not this girl! I want my room to be green like these woods. This is where I like to run. It's where I like to hide. My parents keep saying we'll repaint my room one of these days, but they put me off when I say I want to do it myself." She paused, glancing at Mark out of the corner of her eye. "I came up with a better place anyway."

"A better place?"

Patti's eyes widened with excitement. "Yeah! One in the woods, just like Robin Hood. In fact, that's what I named it, Robinwood. Neat, huh? But I haven't told anybody about it."

"Where is it? Can you show me?"

"Maybe," Patti said, suddenly playing it cool. "But you have to promise not to tell anyone. Ever! Do you promise?"

"Sure," Mark said.

"Then follow me."

Chapter
Two

PATTI LED MARK TO WHERE THE river fed into Trickle Lake. The warm sun had begun to dry their clothes by the time they had started up the mountainside. After they had hiked awhile, Patti suggested they stop on the pathway to take in the view of lush pines and sparkling water below.

The lake glinted like an open bag of diamonds. Mark had never seen the lake at this angle before. This trail was uncharted territory for Mark, like many parts of Odyssey. *It's beautiful*, he thought. When he turned to say this to Patti, she had disappeared. Surprised, Mark spun around.

"Patti?" he called out.

How did she vanish like that? he wondered. *Is she hiding behind one of the trees? Maybe she hiked up the steeper side of the grade.*

"Patti!" he yelled again.

She giggled.

Mark turned to see where the sound was coming from. Her voice seemed to be everywhere at once, but he still couldn't see Patti anywhere.

Patti laughed and said, "I'll bet Robin Hood didn't have a hiding place this good."

Again Mark turned around, now feeling foolish because he knew he must look foolish. He could feel his cheeks turning crimson.

"All right," he said. "Where are you?"

"Over here," she called.

Mark heard a rustling of branches.

Then, as if appearing out of thin air, Patti emerged from her hiding place. The illusion surprised Mark so much he blinked a few times to make sure he was seeing correctly. One moment he saw a wall of green foliage, the next moment Patti appeared in front of it.

"Neat, huh?" Patti said proudly, bowing like a magician.

Mark looked harder to see where Patti had disappeared. The scattered light, dense forest, heavy brush, and ivy had played a trick on his eyes. On closer inspection, he could see that a lush green curtain was camouflaging the hillside.

Mark stared in wonder. A casual passerby would never have seen it. "What is it?" he asked.

"Come on," Patti said, spreading the green curtain aside and stepping into the darkness. "This is my hiding place."

She struck a match and lit a small candle stuck in the top of a soda bottle.

"I'll get a lantern later on," she added.

When Mark's eyes adjusted to the light, he could see that they were in a cave the size of a small room, with plenty of space to walk around. Patti had placed a couple of wooden crates in the center to use as seats. Otherwise the cave was barren rock and dirt. Toward the rear, it continued on in darkness.

"What's back there?" Mark asked.

"I don't know. I didn't want to go back there alone."

Mark was going to tease her for being a chicken, but he thought better of it. He wouldn't want to go back into the yawning blackness by himself, either.

"Patti, this is a terrific hideout!" he exclaimed. "How did you find it?"

"Last weekend when your dad was visiting I got bored playing by myself and decided to look around the lake. While I was up here, I started to think about pirates. You know, like the ones you told me about in . . . in . . ." She furrowed her brow, trying to remember the name of the book.

"*Treasure Island*?" Mark offered.

"Yeah, that one. Anyway, I got to thinking about how they hid things in caves and wondered if maybe there was a cave around here somewhere."

"Pirates hid their treasures in caves near the sea, Patti," Mark said, correcting her. "This is just a lake."

"I know. I was just pretending," she answered defensively. "I kept thinking, where would I hide my treasure if I were a pirate? When I saw the bushes and ivy, I thought it would be neat if a cave was behind them. And it was!"

Mark was amazed as he looked around the cave. Maybe it had been here for thousands of years, and they were the first humans to set foot in it. Or maybe early settlers used it as a shelter. Or maybe it was the hideout for a notorious gang. Or maybe . . . .

"I'm going to fix it up," Patti announced, interrupting Mark's flight of imagination. "I'm going to bring my own treasures up here."

"What kind of treasures?"

"My special private stuff. You know, my keepsakes and dolls and diaries."

Mark shivered. How could she use such a terrific hiding place to store dolls? It seemed like a waste to him. *This cave should be the scene of great adventures,* he thought. *A place to meet, to escape, to share secrets.*

"I think you could do better things than that with this cave," Mark suggested.

Patti frowned and shook her finger at him, "Oh, no you don't. This is my secret hideout. I'll share it with you, but you can't take it over."

Mark spread out his arms and shrugged innocently.

Patti put her hands on her hips. "I mean it, Mark Prescott!"

"I know, I know," Mark said.

Later, when Mark and Patti hiked back to Odyssey through the woods, they walked in silence. Mark's mind buzzed with ideas for Patti's hideout. Oh, the things he could do with it. He imagined drilling a hole through the roof and installing a periscope, so they could see Trickle Lake. They could hang hammocks to sleep in and get a table to eat on and real chests to store their treasures in and lanterns to see with. And maybe they could rig up a portable heater to use in the wintertime.

Mark shared some of his ideas with Patti. She seemed excited, too. She even helped him scheme how they might save money to buy such things.

In the midst of their brainstorming, Mark heard some loud talking in a section of the woods not far from their path. Mark slowed his pace and signaled Patti to be quiet.

"What's wrong?" she whispered.

"Don't you hear the kids talking?" Mark asked.

"So?"

"I think something's going on. Let's go see," Mark said.

He made his way as quietly as he could through the fallen leaves; Patti followed a few steps behind. They reached the edge of a clearing and hid behind a tree. Only a few yards away a dozen boys were sitting in a small circle. It looked like they were having an Indian powwow.

"It's only the Israelites," Patti said, her voice full of disappointment.

Mark felt just the opposite. He had heard things about the Israelites and even had a brief encounter with them at the beginning of summer, shortly after he had moved to Odyssey. They were a gang of boys that often hung around Whit's End, the popular soda shop and discovery emporium run by John Avery Whittaker. It was rumored that they did different kinds of errands for Mr. Whittaker. Some of the kids in town claimed the Israelites performed good deeds for people in need.

Mark asked Mr. Whittaker about them once, but Whit dismissed them as a bunch of kids simply playing Old Testament characters. They dressed in leather vests and carried shields, spears, and bows and arrows. Mr. Whittaker thought it was healthier than pretending to be aliens from another planet or tortured heroes from the comic books.

The gang members had names like Jonathan, Ezer, Obadiah, and Attai. Those weren't their real names, of course, but it allowed the kids to pretend while learning about the Bible. At least, that's how Mr. Whittaker had explained it.

As Mark watched the Israelites talk, he knew something more was going on, and he wanted to know what it was.

"I don't know why you're so interested in these guys," Patti whispered. She sat in the leaves and leaned against the tree.

"Just listen," Mark said, trying to hear what the Israelites were discussing.

He couldn't make out entire sentences. The tone of their

voices was sharp, on edge. Whatever they were talking about, it sounded like they were having a serious disagreement.

He desperately wanted to hear the inner workings of this secret gang. Maybe he could find out who they really were and what they were up to. He crouched beside the tree, preparing to creep forward.

He glanced at Patti and started to gesture for her to stay still, but her expression quickly changed his mind. Her gaze was fixed on something behind him. Before he could turn around, a hand suddenly grabbed Mark's shoulder.

Chapter
Three

"WHY WERE YOU SPYING ON US?" demanded the leader of the Israelites.

Mark and Patti had been moved to the center of the clearing and were now surrounded by the gang.

Mark wanted to play it cool. He shrugged and said, "Just curious."

"You guys are always so overdramatic," Patti said scornfully. "Why would anybody want to spy on you? It's not like you have anything interesting to say."

"Don't be so rude, Patti," Mark said with a frown.

Patti glared at Mark, folded her arms, and gnawed at her lip.

Mark looked back at the leader, who was called Jonathan, and said, "I've been interested in you guys ever since that time you took me to Whit's End. Remember?"

Jonathan nodded, so Mark continued, "I've heard a lot of good things about you."

"We've been hearing about you, too," Jonathan replied. He swatted at a fly buzzing around his curly, chestnut-colored hair. "All the kids know how you and Patti put Joe Devlin in his place and solved the mystery of the flat tire. We were impressed with that, weren't we?"

The other Israelites muttered their agreement, except one of them.

A boy with brown hair and a round, pudgy face grimaced. "I wasn't that impressed," he said.

Jonathan turned to him and replied, "Nothing impresses you, Attai."

"So?" Attai looked at Mark with half-closed eyes as if he were bored.

Jonathan returned his attention to Mark and Patti. "We were so impressed with your attitudes that we were thinking of asking you to join our gang. You would be our first girl member, Patti."

"You want us to join the Israelites?" Mark asked with surprise.

"I'm asking you to consider it," Jonathan answered. "There's a process for actually becoming a member."

Mark couldn't hide his enthusiasm. "Yeah! We'll do it!"

"No," Patti said simply.

Everyone turned and stared at her.

Is she crazy? Mark wondered. *They don't ask just anybody to be in the gang. This is an honor.*

"Patti!" Mark cried out. "What's the matter with you?"

Patti stood. "Look, I don't want to talk about this, and I don't want to hang around here anymore. Are you coming with me or not?"

Mark couldn't believe she was acting this way. "Patti, wait a minute. Think about it. Why don't you want to join the Israelites?"

"Why should I?" Patti countered. "It's just a silly gang. Why do we need to join a silly gang?"

"Because . . ." Mark searched for an answer but couldn't find one. "Because!" he insisted.

Patti thrust her jaw out defiantly. "I'm not interested. It's a dumb idea."

She whirled on her heels and broke out of the circle of Israelites, walking away from them without looking back.

Mark jumped to his feet. "Can you wait?" he asked Jonathan as he started away. "I mean, can we still consider it? I'll . . . let me talk to Patti, and I'll tell you later." And then he stumbled over a small log, gathered himself up, and ran to catch up with Patti.

"What's wrong with you?" Mark demanded when he reached her.

"There's nothing wrong with me," Patti replied. "I just don't want to join their stupid gang, that's all."

"But why not?"

"Because I don't want to. That's why."

"I don't get it," Mark said with a growl.

Patti halted in her tracks. "Why do you want to join them? What will the Israelites give you that we don't already have? It's been a great summer. We're having fun, so why do we need them?"

Patti didn't wait for an answer; she continued to walk.

After a second or two, Mark called after her, "Because they're a special kind of gang. Haven't you heard?"

"Hah!" Patti shouted over her shoulder.

Mark jogged to catch up to her. He was beginning to get angry. "Look, Patti. What will it hurt? Let's join and see what adventures we can have like Robin Hood and . . . and the three Musketeers."

Patti maintained her quick stride. "We've been having plenty of adventures without the Israelites, Mark. Just the two of us. Why do we have to have a gang?"

"We don't have to have a gang. Why do you keep asking me questions like that? I just think it would be lots of fun. It would be neat to be part of a gang like that."

Patti paused momentarily and scowled. "Then I feel sorry for you. I think it's good enough for the two of us to be friends and have fun. And I don't know why you have to spoil everything."

She started to move quickly down the path again.

"Where are you going?" asked Mark.

"Home!"

"But—but can't we talk about this?" implored Mark.

"No!" she replied curtly.

Mark frowned as he watched her hurry away.

"Girls!" he groaned to no one in particular.

Mark walked on alone to Whit's End. John Avery Whittaker, Whit as he preferred to be called, was behind the counter. He was experimenting with what appeared to be an ice cream dispenser. His white hair seemed to accent the bobbing of his head as he peered into the machine, looked into another section, and then checked the top of it again.

They exchanged hellos, and then Whit said, "If it doesn't work this time, I may have to scrap it and start over again."

"How does it work?" Mark asked.

Whit gestured with a screwdriver toward various mechanisms. "These scoops are supposed to dip the ice cream out of the containers and transfer it to the bowl over there."

Whit pointed to a small platform with a glass bowl on it. He turned back to the machinery and continued to calibrate and adjust different parts.

"But why do you need this? Are you getting tired of scooping the ice cream yourself?"

"My word, no!" A small spot of grease marred Whit's thick white mustache.

"Then why?" Mark asked, giving Whit an inquisitive look.

"For the fun of inventing something. Good grief, Mark,

inventions don't have to make life easier or do jobs I don't want to do. Sometimes they don't even have to work."

"Why bother?" Mark asked.

Whit smiled. "I find inventions to be worthwhile just for the experience of inventing them. Haven't you ever done something just for the experience of it?"

Mark thought about it for a moment. "Yeah, in fact, just today Patti and I got into a fight because I wanted to do something for the fun of it, and she didn't."

"And what was it that you wanted to do and Patti didn't?" Whit asked, tapping the screwdriver against something metallic on the inside of the ice cream dispenser.

Strangely enough, Mark had a feeling Whit knew the answer to his own question. Whit was like that.

"Join the Israelites," Mark said.

"Oh? And why doesn't Patti want to join?" Whit asked, continuing to tinker.

"I don't know," Mark said. "She kept saying she thought it was dumb, and we don't need to join because we're having a lot of fun by ourselves and . . . and . . . that kind of thing. I can't figure her out sometimes."

Whit peered over the machine at Mark. "Really," he said. "Do you think she's afraid the Israelites will wreck your friendship?"

The question surprised Mark. "What? Wreck our friendship? Why would she think that?"

"Oh, because it took you a long time to be her friend, and now that you are, she might be afraid of losing you," Whit said, disappearing behind the machine again.

"It's not going to wreck any friendship," Mark muttered.

Whit fastened a remaining bolt and then moved to the front

of the ice cream dispenser. "If you're sure of that," he said, "you might want to tell Patti."

That's the problem with having girls as friends, Mark thought. *You have to explain everything to them. Boys don't care. Boys just do things together. But girls always have to be assured.*

"Let's see if this thing works," Whit announced, rubbing his hands together. He flipped a switch on the side of the machine. The dispenser hummed. Then a mechanical arm reached over to the small container of ice cream, dipped into it like a bird going after bread crumbs, and reappeared with a scoop of vanilla.

"So far so good," Whit said proudly.

The mechanical arm moved upward and then turned toward the glass bowl. Suddenly the machine popped and whined. The arm lurched backward and then sprung forward, propelling the scoop of ice cream at the glass bowl. It was a direct hit. The bowl shattered on the floor.

Whit sighed, "Back to the old drawing board."

"Maybe you could use it for a catapult. The kids would like it for target practice," Mark offered.

Whit considered the suggestion. "You may have a good idea, Mark."

A few minutes later, while Whit was cleaning up the mess, he handed Mark a small note. Whit's eyes sparkled as if he were thinking of a joke he wanted to tell someone.

"I was asked to give this to you," Whit said.

Mark unfolded the note. On a plain piece of paper, these words were scribbled in blue ink:

If you still want to join . . . The gazebo in McAlister Park. Nine tonight.

Chapter
Four

BACK HOME MARK WALKED INTO the kitchen just as Julie Prescott slammed down the receiver. His mother slumped into one of the dinette chairs and put her hands over her face.

"Mom?" Mark asked cautiously.

"He makes me so mad, I could . . ." she said with a low growl.

Mark's heart sank; he knew she had been talking to his dad. When his parents had separated earlier that year, Mark was sure they would get a divorce. But over the past month, his parents had decided to try and work out their differences. They wanted to save their marriage, they had assured Mark. They wanted to be a family again. Mark had been living on the edge of that hope.

It was taking longer than Mark had thought it would. His parents squeezed in counseling sessions with the pastor when his dad could visit. They spent hours on the phone, sometimes talking softly, other times arguing like they were now.

What makes adults so weird? Mark wondered.

"You're not going to cry, are you?" he asked awkwardly.

"No," his mother said, her cheeks flushed with anger.

"Were you fighting again?"

She eyed her son curiously. "No, Mark, not really. Sometimes your father doesn't realize what he's saying. He has his own way of looking at things and can be very stubborn. It makes me mad."

"Are you still trying to get back together?" asked Mark anxiously.

"Yes, honey," she said, reaching out and pulling Mark close. "Don't let our little spats worry you. We're still trying to sort out our differences. We have to resolve certain things before we can live together again."

"But what's the problem?" he asked. "Why can't you guys just kiss and make up?"

His mother smiled sadly. "I wished it were that easy. You see, your father and I hurt each other. We said things we didn't mean. Our marriage didn't fall apart in one night—no marriage ever does. It was a slow breakdown, and the healing process is slow, too. It takes time to restore trust, and it takes work to rebuild love. Do you understand?"

"I'm trying to," he replied.

They were both quiet for a moment. Then his mother asked brightly, "So what have you been doing today?"

Glad for the change of subject, Mark told his mother all about playing in the woods with Patti—leaving out the secret cave because he promised he would—and about meeting the Israelites and being asked to join their gang.

"A gang?" questioned his mother warily.

"A *good* gang, Mom. Nobody knows for sure, but we think Mr. Whittaker has something to do with it. The Israelites sometimes run errands for him."

His mother tapped the table thoughtfully. "Well, if Whit is involved, I'm sure it's all right."

"He gave me this note from them." Mark took the crumpled piece of paper out of his back pocket and handed it to her.

"Nine o'clock is awfully late to meet with a bunch of kids," she observed.

"It's not so late in the summer, Mom. The sun's barely gone down by then. Please, let me go. Please?"

She handed the note back to Mark and said, "I'm going to call Whit about this gang. I want to know what they're up to."

The conversation with Whit didn't last long; it consisted mostly of his mother saying, "Hmm" and "I see." She asked a question or two and then hung up. Mark's curiosity was chewing him up, but he didn't want to nag his mother with too many questions. All he knew was she had agreed to let him meet with the Israelites at nine o'clock that night, and that was good enough for him.

For the rest of the afternoon, Mark prowled around the house nervously. He couldn't concentrate on anything or keep interested in the activities he usually enjoyed.

His mother finally suggested, "If you're so bored, you could clean your room."

"I'm not that kind of bored," he explained.

Finally he settled on the idea of writing a letter to his father. He sat at his desk, pushed away the clutter, and started writing quickly. He put in the usual how-are-you-I-am-fine beginning; then he told his dad about the Israelites.

As Mark wrote, it dawned on him that he had discovered the answer to Patti's earlier question about why he wanted to be an Israelite. Becoming a member of the gang would give him a sense of belonging in Odyssey, and he wouldn't feel like an outsider anymore.

"Mark," his mother called from downstairs, "Patti's here."

Mark glanced at his watch. It was seven o'clock, just two hours before meeting the gang. He called back to have Patti come upstairs.

Patti entered silently, paced around the room, casually picked up one of Mark's model cars, and then flipped through the pages of a book.

"What are you doing?" she asked with strained casualness.

"Writing to my dad."

"What about?"

"Stuff," he said offhandedly. "What are you doing?"

Patti sat on the edge of Mark's bed. "I was thinking about going to the movies. You want to go?"

"I . . . I can't," he said.

"You're doing something with your mom?"

"No."

Patti's eyes narrowed. "Then why can't you go?"

Mark shifted from foot to foot uncomfortably and glanced away from her gaze. "I just can't, all right?"

"You're going to join the Israelites," she said flatly.

Mark didn't respond.

"You are," Patti continued. "I got one of those notes, too. They taped it to my mailbox."

Mark looked at her hopefully. "Are you going?"

"No," she snapped. "We don't need to join a gang. They'll ruin everything."

"Why do you keep saying that? What will they ruin?"

"Us," she said.

Mr. Whittaker was right, Mark thought. *Mr. Whittaker is always right when it comes to these things.*

"No they won't," Mark insisted.

"Yes they will. You'll get all wrapped up with them, and we won't do things together anymore." Patti's tone was despondent.

"That's not true. If you join, we'll do things together all the time."

"With them," she said.

"So?"

"So, I don't want to run around with a gang. We're having fun by ourselves. I thought we were friends."

Mark bit his lip. Why did they even have to have this conversation?

"We are friends, Patti. Why does everything have to be such a big deal with you?"

"It's not a big deal!" shouted Patti. "If we're friends, then let's go to the movies tonight."

Mark didn't know what to do. Slowly he moved to his window and looked out onto the stretch of green grass below. A cat crept along the fence, its eye on something Mark couldn't see.

His back to her, he said, "I can't. I want to meet with the Israelites."

Mark's bed gave a gentle squeak as Patti stood. She stomped across the room and slammed the door as she left.

Chapter Five

WHY DID HE HAVE TO MAKE A CHOICE? Mark wondered as he sat on the gazebo steps in McAlister Park. What was so wrong with wanting new friends? Couldn't he be friends with Patti and be an Israelite, too? She wasn't being fair.

Mark was so lost in his thoughts that he didn't hear the Israelites until they were almost behind him. Mark stood and looked expectantly at the group. They were all dressed in dark-colored clothes. Three of them were carrying bulging burlap sacks, but Mark couldn't tell what was in them.

"I told you he wouldn't be dressed right," complained Attai.

Mark glanced self-consciously at his white T-shirt.

"I didn't tell him," Jonathan said. "It's all right."

Then he turned to Mark and asked, "Are you sure you want to do this?"

"Uh-huh," Mark replied.

"Let's go." Jonathan waved for everyone to follow.

They moved with such purpose that Mark felt intimidated. He was the outsider here, as usual. He followed Jonathan closely, wondering if it would be dumb to ask where they were going.

They walked along silently. As they neared Fulton Street, Jonathan held up his hand. Mark heard a low rumble; then he saw headlight beams. The car went by without any hint that the driver had seen them.

"Okay," Jonathan said. "Obadiah, check it out."

The one called Obadiah ran across the street, looked around, and then gestured for them to follow. They moved quickly. Mark imagined how it would look to a passerby to see a gang of boys wearing dark clothes.

"Where are we going?" whispered Mark, finally mustering the courage to ask.

"Quiet. We're not supposed to talk," Attai hissed.

Mark felt rebuked and lowered his head.

The Israelites followed LeMonde Street for a few blocks; then they turned onto Chatham Boulevard. Numerous trees and no street lights made it dark enough for them to move along without being noticed. The sounds of crickets and an occasional barking dog filled the night. Lights winked at them from the windows in warm, bright yellows and pale-blue television flashes.

Mark pictured the families behind those windows going about their usual summer night's business, totally unaware that a gang of boys was slipping past on a secret mission.

A wave of nervousness rolled through Mark. What were they doing, anyhow? What if they were doing something they shouldn't? Mark tried to calm himself by remembering that Whit was somehow involved.

The houses were spread farther apart now; the older homes were on farm-like tracts of land. Jonathan signaled the boys to stop again. He walked over to an antique mailbox stuck in the dirt near the driveway. *Douglas* was written in an artistic cursive on the side of the box.

Jonathan started to jog down the driveway, motioning the

boys to follow. Mark noticed that the modest white house was completely dark in the moonlight. He wondered if the people who lived there were away or if they were in bed already.

The Israelites moved quietly past the house toward the garage at the end of the driveway. Beyond the garage, there was a large garden, where the boys spread out in a circle. Jonathan gave a signal, and the burlap bags were set down. Mark heard a distinct rattling.

Tools? he guessed. *Why do they need tools?*

The bags were opened and flashlights were distributed to everyone. Mark still had no clue what the boys were going to do. He glanced back at the dark house. Were they going to break in?

Everyone moved about with determination, as if they had done this before. Several small garden trowels, weeders, and cultivators had been laid out on the burlap bags. Mark shone his flashlight on the garden itself. Part of it was dedicated to flowers, but the majority seemed to contain vegetable plants.

"Weeds," Jonathan whispered in Mark's ear.

"Huh?"

Jonathan directed his flashlight beam to the dirt between the plants. It was filled with thick patches of weeds.

"The weeds are destroying the garden." Jonathan handed Mark a pair of work gloves. "Emma Douglas has been too sick to take care of it. She's also too proud to ask for help, so we're going to do it for her. It'll be a nice gift."

"We came here to weed?" Mark asked with surprise.

"Sure. What did you think we came to do?"

Embarrassed, Mark shrugged.

"All right, gentlemen," Jonathan said in a loud whisper. "Let's get to work. We don't have much time. Whatever you do, be quiet. Don't talk unless you have to, and don't bang your tools around. Attai, I want you and Mark to go to the garage and get the spades, shovels and hoes."

"Won't it be locked?" asked Attai.

"Whit came to visit Emma earlier. He said he made sure it was unlocked for us," explained Jonathan.

Mark was relieved to hear that Whit really was part of this plan.

Attai tugged at Mark's sleeve. "Let's go."

The side door to the garage was unlocked. Mark and Attai had to navigate around Emma's car to reach for the tools they needed. Mark spotted a shovel hanging on the wall next to a small workbench.

"Shh!" Attai hissed. "Don't talk."

Attai's tone was unnecessarily harsh, Mark thought. He wondered what he had done to make Attai unfriendly.

Mark saw the spade, rake, and hoe hanging near the shovel. He was going to tell Attai but still felt the sting of his last rebuke.

Attai can look around in the wrong places if he wants to, Mark thought. *I'm going to get these tools myself.*

Mark put his flashlight on the workbench and carefully unhooked the shovel from its wall holder. He lowered it by the handle, resting it in the crook of his arm. Then he took down the rake.

From the other side of the garage, Attai saw what Mark had found. "Wait, I'll help you."

"Don't talk," Mark said in a vindictive tone.

"Don't be stupid," Attai replied.

Mark reached up for the hoe, but it was caught on the lip of the hook. With the rake and shovel still in the crook of his arm, he grabbed the hoe's handle with both hands and shoved upward.

"Don't!" Attai whispered loudly.

Mark was determined to show Attai that he didn't need help, so he pulled down hard on the hoe's handle. This time the hook gave way. The hoe banged against a spade on the wall, making a loud "*ching!*"

Mark tried to catch the hoe, but as he lurched forward, he stumbled. And all the tools went crashing to the floor.

The sound echoed through the garage and into the quiet night like harsh clanging cymbals. Mark regained his balance and stood still as if the horrifying clatter had frozen him in place.

Attai groaned, ran to the side window, and looked out. "They heard you out at the garden," he said. "Let's just hope Emma Douglas was sleeping on her good ear."

Mark, his heart thumping, joined Attai just in time to see a light go on in an upstairs window. Mark gasped with the realization of what he had done.

"Now you did it! You woke her up," Attai said, scrambling toward the open garage door.

Mark remained where he was, still stunned by his own stupidity.

"Come on," Attai called out coarsely. "We have to get out of here!"

Chapter Six

MARK'S EYES WERE STILL BURNING when the morning light spread across his room. He lay in his bed remembering every detail of the night before. He felt the same hot humiliation as he recalled the falling tools, the crashing sound, and Attai's expression when Emma Douglas's light went on. Scalding embarrassment had washed over him when Jonathan sent them all home. Jonathan had stayed behind to explain to Emma. He didn't want her to be frightened or think she had a prowler.

The last thing Mark remembered seeing was Jonathan standing on the porch, waiting for Emma to answer the door.

Walking home, Attai had lectured Mark about the blunder. "The Israelites are a special group," he said at one point, "and we only accept special people as members."

Mark's mother was still awake and reading in bed when he arrived home. When she asked him how it went, Mark bravely told her everything that had happened, holding back the tears as he explained how he had tried to show off and ruined the mission.

His mother hugged him. "I'm sure they'll still let you join. They wouldn't hold one little mistake against you."

"Yes, they will," Mark argued. "They want members who will move quickly and quietly. They don't want some clumsy oaf."

"I think you're wrong," his mother said gently.

That's what Mark had expected her to say. Mothers didn't really know about things like gangs and how they operate. The decision would rest with Jonathan, Attai, and the other Israelites. Mark doubted that even Whit could do anything to help him.

Mark had crawled into bed and stared at the ceiling. He wasn't sure if he had slept, but suddenly it was nine o'clock the next morning, and the phone was ringing in another part of the house.

Moments later, his mother tapped lightly on the door, opened it, and peeked in. "Mark?" she said softly.

"Yeah?"

Her tone was hopeful. "That was Whit on the phone. He would like you to come to the shop as soon as you can."

When Mark arrived at Whit's End, the place was already alive with kids moving every which way. Some were browsing in the library. Others were sitting in the restaurant booths talking across the tables. Still other kids were excitedly playing a variety of brightly lit games in the far corner of the house. Mark expected that the county's largest train set, as the banner proclaimed, was in full operation on the second floor. A distant whistle confirmed it.

The sounds merged into a single hum of activity, proclaiming the joy of having fun, of being children. It was a joy that John Avery Whittaker seemed to spread to everyone he met.

But Mark's heart was heavy and refused to be lifted by the spirit of celebration at Whit's End. For the first time, Mark was honestly afraid to see Whit. Mark was sure the Israelites had already told Whit about Mark's goof-up. What would Whit say? How would he break the news that the Israelites had rejected Mark? How would Whit express his own disappointment with Mark?

Mark walked slowly around the counter to where Whit had

been working on his ice cream dispenser the day before. The dispenser was gone, however, and Whit was nowhere to be seen.

Maybe he's in his workroom in the basement, Mark thought.

Rounding the corner to the stairwell that led down to the workroom, Mark nearly collided with Whit.

Whit laughed and said, "Fancy running into you here."

"Mom said you wanted me to come."

"I certainly did!" Whit looked around to see if anyone was listening. Then he leaned forward and said quietly, "I heard about what happened last night, and I want you to know that everything has been taken care of. It worked out rather nicely, in fact. A near miracle."

"A miracle?" Mark asked with astonishment.

"When Jonathan explained to Emma Douglas what you boys were up to, she was so touched she said the Israelites could come back any day to finish the job. And if you knew Emma, you would know how much her pride keeps her from asking for help."

Whit smiled and clapped Mark on the shoulder. "See, your little mishap was a blessing in disguise."

Mark frowned. "It doesn't feel like it."

At that moment Mark heard the rumbling of voices in the workroom below. It sounded like an argument.

"I think it's all right to tell you—the Israelites are borrowing my workroom for a meeting," Whit explained. "They're arguing about where to find new secret headquarters."

"New headquarters?"

"Their old tree fort was torn down when the bulldozers cleared the land for a housing development." Whit gestured to the workroom and sighed as the loud voices continued below. "The Israelites do a lot of good things together, but they still argue like a bunch of kids."

Mark tried to figure out what this information should mean to him.

Whit drew Mark closer and said, "What happened to you last night could have happened to anyone. Jonathan knows that. That's why he's the leader."

"But Attai said—"

"Attai can be a bit hotheaded at times. That's why he's not in charge," Whit remarked, pushing Mark along. "Go down to the workroom, and tell them I told you to join the meeting. They haven't voted you in or out yet. It might help if they can talk to you . . . that is, if you still want to be a member."

Mark's face brightened with this new hope. "Are you kidding?"

Whit chuckled. "Go on, then."

Mark thanked him and crept down the stairs. The workroom door was closed, but Mark could hear the Israelites clearly. Jonathan was suggesting they build a new tree fort in another part of town. Attai was arguing about doing all that work again.

"There must be a better place to put a secret hideout," he insisted.

When Mark opened the door, all heads turned toward him. He felt himself blush and started to back out again.

"What do you want?" Attai snarled as he leaned forward in his chair, his black eyes blazing.

"Mr. Whittaker told me to come in," Mark said, barely above a whisper.

Attai sat back and replied, "Oh, then I guess our meeting's over."

Jonathan shot Attai a reproving look. "Don't be so rude, Attai."

"What's the point of a meeting about secret headquarters if anybody can come in and listen?" stated Attai. "He's not a member."

"Even more reason for you not to be rude," Jonathan said.

Attai folded his arms defiantly. "Okay, fine. Let's tell the whole world. Maybe Prescott can even suggest a place for us."

Attai turned to Mark and threw the challenge to him. "Can you? I would feel better about you being a member. Maybe you are better at finding hideouts than getting garden tools."

Anger and embarrassment welled up inside Mark. Every instinct in his body wanted to prove Attai wrong. Mark would show him.

"I know a place," Mark began.

All eyes were fixed on him now.

"You do?" Jonathan asked. "A place for us to meet?"

Mark nodded. His heart was pounding. He had to be accepted by the Israelites. At the moment it was all the mattered.

"It's up by Trickle Lake," he continued. "A hidden cave."

This caused a buzz among the members. Attai's face looked stricken.

"I don't believe you. Where is it?" Attai demanded.

This was what Mark needed. He was in control now. He spoke confidently. "I'll have to show you. Meet me at the Great Tree at two this afternoon."

Mark was in a cold sweat by the time he reached Patti's house. He had to talk to her. He had thought about it the whole walk over; he had to persuade her to join the Israelites. If he could, then maybe—just maybe—she wouldn't be so mad that he had broken his promise to her. Maybe she would understand. He was panic-stricken that she wouldn't.

Mrs. Eldridge greeted him with a smile and showed him to Patti's room. The furniture had been rearranged since he had been there a few days ago. Patti stood in the middle of the room, hands on hips, pondering the walls.

"I think I might paint my room even though I have the other you-know-what to put things in. You want to help me?" she asked without even saying hello.

"I can't right now," Mark muttered. He felt like his thoughts were swimming in his head. What was he going to say to her? How could he talk to her about the cave?

Patti misunderstood his tone. "You're mad at me, aren't you?"

The question caught Mark off guard.

"You are," she said, "and I don't blame you. I talked to my mom about it, and she said I was being childish. I shouldn't have been so . . . so jealous. I guess that's what it was. If you joined the Israelites, I figured we would never have time to do things together anymore."

Patti sat on her vanity chair and then asked, "Did you meet with them last night?"

"Yeah, I did," said Mark. This was his chance to get her to join the Israelites. If she joined, he could get her to let them use the cave.

"Patti, why don't you join the Israelites with me?" he blurted.

She looked at him curiously.

"They do some really neat things and . . . and we would still have fun together. Just think about it."

"No thanks, Mark."

"Why not?"

"I told you before, I don't want to. I don't care about belonging to a gang. Some of the kids say they're a bunch of snobs, sneaking around, calling each other by those weird names."

Mark pleaded, "It's not like that. They do good things for people. They just keep it a secret, so the people they help won't be embarrassed."

Patti shrugged. "So? I still don't want to join."

"Come on, Patti," Mark said impatiently.

"Mark, you can join if you want. I won't be mad if you do. We can still be friends. Don't worry about me. I'll stop being a baby about it, okay?"

That's not the problem! He wanted to scream, but instead he struggled to think of another approach.

"If you're really my friend, you'll join," he said, knowing it was an unfair thing to say. But he was growing desperate.

Patti winced, as if he had struck her in the face. "What?"

"You heard me."

"I can't believe you could say that. What's wrong with you?"

"Nothing!" he snapped. "I just think you should join. That's all. If you're my friend, you will."

"That's not fair, Mark." Her tone was measured and adultlike. "That's as bad as saying I won't be your friend if you do join."

"Then join!" Mark said, his reasoning getting tangled up in his fear. If she didn't join, he didn't know what he would do. But he could bet his friendship with Patti would be over anyway.

Patti was firm. "I'm not joining, Mark. It's a matter of principle now."

Principles! What do principles have to do with anything? I can't win if she's going to drag principles into it, he thought.

Mark glared at her; then he strode toward the door.

"Where are you going?" she asked.

"I have to go," he snarled in a voice that didn't sound like his own. He stepped into the hall and lingered there for a moment.

Finally, he turned to her again and spoke in a more familiar tone. "Patti, I didn't mean for any of this to happen."

Mark ran down the stairs two at a time and shot out the front door.

He heard Patti call his name, but he didn't stop.

Chapter
Seven

MARK FUMED AS HE WALKED to Trickle Lake. He was mad at Patti. He was mad at himself. And he was mad at the Israelites. He was mad because his dad had never sent his bike from Washington, D.C., which was why Mark had to walk all the time. He was mad because he had to move to Odyssey in the first place. The list accumulated with every step toward the Great Tree.

He didn't know why Patti always had to be so stubborn. It would have been easy for her to join the gang. Why couldn't she join? Principles didn't have anything to do with it. She was being selfish. What kind of friend was she anyway? Not much of one to put Mark in this situation.

It's not her cave, he thought. *It's not like she owns a deed to it with her name on it. It doesn't belong to her. Anybody could have found the cave. Who is to say the Israelites didn't find it on their own? Patti doesn't have to know that I showed it to them. She'll just see that it's been taken over by someone else and probably go home and forget about it.*

"Hah! Patti forget about it? Not a chance," Mark muttered aloud to himself.

She would find out who had invaded her secret hiding place.

And she would blow a giant fuse when she discovered it was the Israelites.

"Oh, why doesn't she join?" he cried out.

Worse, why had he made the promise not to tell anyone about the cave? He would never make a promise like that to anyone ever again, he decided.

Mark reached the path to Trickle Lake. A hand-carved sign shaped like an arrow said "The Great Tree." The sign also mentioned in small letters that according to legend the person who could climb to the top of the tree could see as far as three counties.

Mark stopped on the path for a moment. *Maybe the Israelites won't show up,* he thought. *Maybe they've found another hideout in the meantime.*

Mark knew it was wishful thinking. They would be there. And he had better have something good to show them.

Maybe he should tell them the truth or part of the truth, he thought. He could explain that he had made a promise to Patti about this secret cave and . . . and . . . he had forgotten he had made the promise. And he could help them come up with another secret hideout. Not a chance. He could see Attai's smug look of satisfaction.

"See," Attai would say, "I told you Prescott didn't deserve to be a member."

Maybe Mark should turn around, go home, and not join the gang. Then he could keep his promise to Patti, so they could go on with the summer the way it had been.

But he would lose face with the Israelites for not showing. It was a no-win situation, all because of a stupid cave.

The path took Mark around a short bend that led to the Great Tree. Up ahead the Israelites were sitting by the tree waiting. When one of them pointed at Mark, they all stood.

The Israelites will get more use out of the cave than Patti, Mark assured himself. *All she wants to do is hide her dolls there. The Israelites will do important things, things that could help other people. The Israelites deserve to have that cave. Patti should understand. It's better to upset her than a whole gang.*

"You're late," Jonathan said as Mark approached. "We thought you might not show up."

Mark looked at him coolly. "I had to do a couple of things first."

Attai stepped forward and said, "Well, hotshot, where's this great hiding place of yours?"

This was the moment of truth, Mark realized. He looked at the faces of the Israelites. Were these the faces of his new friends?

"Well?" Attai prodded him.

"Follow me," Mark said.

Mark was silent as he led the gang up the trail. When they reached the spot, he spread aside the green curtain of ivy and stepped into the cave. Everything was exactly as Patti had left it the day before. Mark struck a match and lit the candle wedged in a soda bottle and set it on a crate in the middle of the cave. As the Israelites filed in, their faces registered the same excitement that Mark had felt when he first saw the cave. He knew their imaginations were jumping with the cave's possibilities as a hideout.

"This is an amazing place," said Jonathan.

Attai clapped Mark on the back and exclaimed, "You're all right, Prescott! You may be clumsy with tools, but you know a good hiding place when you see one."

Attai turned to the rest of the Israelites. "What do you think?"

The gang offered their approval through scattered praises: "Great!" "Wow!" "Fantastic!"

"I think we should vote him in," Attai announced.

This was better and faster than Mark could have imagined. What was he so worried about? He was going to become an Israelite.

Jonathan raised his hand. "Hold on, Attai, not so fast. The Israelites don't work that way. We don't vote people out because they make a mistake, and we don't vote people in because they happen to find a good hiding place. You remember the rules. Members are voted in based on their character. Members are seekers of truth. And, above all, they must have a desire to serve people in need."

"We know all that, Jonathan," Attai replied impatiently. "Look, didn't you say in the meeting this morning that Mark would be a good Israelite? Weren't you the one who stuck up for him when I was ready to vote him down?"

Surprised, Mark looked at Jonathan appreciatively.

"Yeah," Jonathan replied, "but I don't want Mark to get the wrong impression. If he is voted in as a member, it must be for the right reasons, not because he found a new meeting place for us. Is that understood? Mark was asked to join because of Mr. Whittaker's recommendation."

Again, Mark was surprised.

"Are you saying you don't want to vote?" Attai asked.

Jonathan shook his head. "We can vote. But I would like to ask Mark to leave for a couple of minutes while we do. Do you mind, Mark?"

"Nope," said Mark. They would vote him in, he felt sure. He was going to get what he wanted, the security of new friends, the prestige of a popular gang. Patti would have to understand. Somehow, he would make her understand. This was what he really wanted—Mark, the Israelite.

Suddenly the green curtain was pulled aside. "What's going on in here? What are you doing in my cave?"

Mark gasped and held his breath.

Patti looked around, bewildered, squinting as her eyes adjusted to the darkness. In her arms, she carried a small bag. Everyone remained still. Obviously no one knew how to react to her sudden appearance.

Patti scanned the gawking faces. Then she saw Mark, and her eyes widened.

"You told!" she cried out. The bag slipped from her hands. Dolls and keepsakes tumbled onto the ground. "You promised you wouldn't tell."

Her voice echoed through the cave and into the deepest part of Mark's heart. His mouth moved, but he couldn't force any words out. The eyes of the Israelites fell on him.

Patti started quickly picking up her dolls, stuffing them back in the bag as her tears began to fall.

"You told," she said again.

"What's going on?" Jonathan asked, assuming control.

Clutching her bag, Patti stood. "This is my cave. I found it. Mark, you promised." She choked on the words, turned, and ran from the cave.

Attai glared at Mark. "What did you promise her?"

Mark swallowed, his throat making a loud clicking noise. "I promised . . . I . . . I wouldn't tell anyone about this cave."

A collective gasp went through the Israelites.

"Why did you break your promise?" asked Jonathan.

"So you would let me join the Israelites," Mark replied softly.

Mark didn't want to believe this scene was real. He felt a terrible numbness working its way through him.

"I'm sorry you felt you had to do that," Jonathan said. He

paused, looking downcast. "As it is, we can't let you become a member, not like this."

Jonathan then turned to Obadiah. "Go tell Patti that her secret is safe with us. It's her cave. We'll find a hideout somewhere else."

The Israelites filed silently out of the cave. Jonathan was the last to leave. He placed his hand gently on Mark's shoulder. "I'm sorry, Mark. You shouldn't have done it. We probably would have voted you in without the cave."

Jonathan stepped through the green curtain; the flow of air caused the candlelight to flicker. Mark remained in the cave alone, thinking until the flame flickered, spat once or twice, and went out.

Chapter Eight

IT WAS THE LONGEST week of Mark's life.

After the showdown in the cave, he went home to self-imposed solitary confinement.

It's what I deserve, he thought.

He had lost Patti as a friend by betraying her. The Israelites surely wouldn't have anything to do with him since he was a dishonest promise-breaker. In either case, he couldn't face them. His shame was too great. He would stay home for the rest of the summer. Maybe he could make some new friends when school started. Maybe his mom and dad would get back together really soon, and they would move back to Washington, D.C.

His mother, sensing something was wrong, coaxed the story out of Mark right after it happened. At first she could only say, "Oh, Mark," over and over again.

That didn't make him feel any better.

Then she tried to explain that she understood how he must feel. "It's a lot like what happened to your father and me. We hurt each other. Now, we're paying for it in this time apart, in the slow, painful process of repairing our trust."

Again, Mark wasn't encouraged. He wanted to be able to go to Patti, apologize, and make everything the way it was before.

He knew better. It was a lesson he had already learned once. Things don't change back to the way they were before. Somehow, he had to deal with the way things were now. But how?

Mark wrote a letter to Patti, tore it up, started over, tore that one up. He started again and then gave up. He also tried to write a letter to the Israelites addressed to Jonathan, but he couldn't do that either.

He wanted to explain to them all. He wanted them to understand why he had done it. But the explanation didn't read right. Once he wrote, "I'm sorry," everything else seemed meaningless. And only the words "I'm sorry" on the page didn't seem like enough.

Mark had to pay some sort of penance. Punishment, that's what he needed, so he hid at home.

"This is a coward's way out," his mother said. "If you face up to what you did and apologize, I'm sure things will get better. You don't have to lock yourself in the house."

Mark simply nodded and returned to the book he was reading or the television show he was trying to watch or the letter he was trying to write to his father.

His mother couldn't even persuade him to go to town with her to run errands.

Whit's End was off-limits as far as he was concerned. He kept picturing himself entering the shop and facing a silent, staring crowd. "He's the one," they would say. "He double-crossed his best friend and tricked the Israelites." "Stay away from him." "He's trouble."

Then Whit would ask him to leave. "Sorry, Mark, we can't have kids like you in here."

More than once, Mark looked away from his book or the TV with tears in his eyes. Eventually his guilt gave way to a highly dramatic self-pity. He would be a loner from now on. A stranger to everyone. A boy without a name. Isolated and friendless, he would become nothing more than a shadow on the wall. Those feelings lasted for a day.

Later in the week, the isolation turned into boredom, and the boredom led to a quiet ache deep inside him. He didn't really care about the Israelites anymore. It would have been neat to be part of their gang. They were fun and exciting, but it didn't matter as much as it had before—not as much as Patti mattered. He missed her.

He lost count of the times he would be reading a book and wanted to tell Patti about the good parts. He remembered their walks in the woods when she introduced him to all the secret places of Odyssey. He thought about how they had met, how he had mistaken her for a bully and pulled her off Joe Devlin just as she was about to win the fight. Later, she had helped Mark solve the mystery of who had slashed the tire on Joe's new bike.

Mark couldn't remember when he decided to be friends with Patti. He probably never really decided at all. It happened the way friendships are meant to happen. They stopped trying to impress each other. They didn't need to pretend they were tough or cool or brave. They could tell each other things they wouldn't dare breathe to anyone else. They simply became friends.

Now the thought of losing Patti's friendship nagged at him. He didn't want to be an outcast or a loner or feel sorry for himself for the rest of his life. He wanted to make up with her. Somehow, he had to make her trust him again. It was a matter of principle. If only he could talk to her . . .

It was nearly dinnertime when Mark replaced the receiver on its cradle again; the phone was still busy. Someone at her house had been on the phone for a long time. His stomach tightened, wondering if Patti had taken the phone off the hook to keep from talking to him. It had been a week; would she do something like that after such a long time? He sat back on his mother's bed to consider the answer. It didn't matter, he decided. If she wouldn't talk on the phone, he would go to her house.

He had just stepped into the upstairs hallway when he heard someone knock at the front door.

He waited at the top of the stairs, listening to his mom walk to the door, open it, and then exclaim, "What a surprise! Come on in."

A deep, resonant voice responded with appreciation.

Whit! What's he doing here? Mark questioned.

He didn't move. His mind riffled through all the reasons Whit would come to his house.

"Is Mark home?" Whit asked.

"Yes, he's here. I'll go get him," replied his mother.

The banister rattled, and the steps creaked as his mother started up the stairs. She stopped halfway and called, "Mark? You have a visitor."

Mark's heart picked up its pace. *Is Whit going to talk to me about the Israelites? Will he lecture me for betraying Patti?*

Mark felt like he was walking in shoes filled with heavy stones as he went down the steps into the living room. Whit and his mom both turned with expressions of concern when Mark entered. His fear about what Whit might say increased.

"Hello, Mark," Whit said, extending his hand.

Mark took it, and they shook hands awkwardly.

"Hi, Mr. Whittaker."

"I haven't seen you around in a while. Whit's End isn't the same without you," Whit said with a smile.

"I . . . I've been busy."

Doesn't he know? Mark wondered. *Didn't anyone tell him what happened?*

"I stopped by to see if you've talked to Patti today."

"Patti? No, I haven't talked to her in . . . well . . . a week."

Whit raised an eyebrow curiously and then went on. "Oh, that's a shame. Then you haven't heard anything about her."

This line of questioning worried Mark. "No, why? Is something wrong?"

"We hope not," Whit replied. "Patti left early this morning. She was supposed to be home for lunch and a one o'clock dentist appointment, but she didn't show up. She's still missing."

"Patti's missing?" Mark asked with surprise.

Whit nodded gravely. "Her parents said it's not like her. They've been checking all the usual places, calling everyone they thought might know something. I think they tried here, but the line was busy."

"I haven't been on the phone," his mother said. "Mark?"

Mark thought of Patti's parents trying to call him while he was trying to call Patti.

"I was on the phone," he replied.

Whit continued, "The police are now looking for her. Some volunteers have joined the search, too."

The image of all those people searching for Patti made Mark realize how serious it was. What if something bad happened to her? Where could she be?

"Has anyone tried around Trickle Lake?" Mark asked.

"I'm sure they have," answered Whit. "Why? Do you know something we don't?"

For a moment Mark considered his promise to Patti. Just because he blabbed to the Israelites didn't mean he should blab to anyone else. But what if something had happened to Patti in the cave? It wouldn't be wrong to break his promise, would it?

Whit looked straight into Mark's eyes and said, "If you know something, Mark, it's important that you tell me. Anything could help."

Chapter
Nine

BOUNCING ALONG IN WHIT'S CAR to Trickle Lake, Mark told Whit about the cave and the painful story related to it.

Whit's face lit up with renewed understanding. "That explains a few things. You see, the Israelites didn't tell me why they voted you down for the group. And Patti hasn't been to Whit's End all week. I assumed she was with you."

Mark was surprised that everyone had kept quiet about what he had done to her.

"It must have been a miserable week for both of you," Whit observed.

"I'll bet she's glad to get rid of me," Mark replied dejectedly. "I don't know if she'll ever want to be friends again."

Whit glanced at Mark sympathetically. "I don't believe that for a minute. The ties that make up a good friendship are stronger than a single wrong."

"But I betrayed her," Mark cried helplessly.

"Yes, well, that will take some time to fix. But your friendship can be mended, Mark, if you're willing to work at it."

"I am! But I don't know if she'll want to."

Whit reached across the front seat and touched Mark's arm. "First let's go find her; then we'll see."

Mark gazed ahead as they approached the sparkling mountain lake and parked the car.

"There's a large flashlight under your seat. I think we'll need it," Whit said.

At the lake, the usual quiet was broken by a handful of volunteers who had spread into the surrounding hills and mountains to look for Patti.

"There are so many people," Mark observed.

"It's one of the advantages of living in a small town," Whit noted. "They don't waste any time when it comes to lost children."

Mark and Whit walked to a small dock on the north side of the lake, where a police officer was standing near his car.

The officer greeted Whit warmly and shook Mark's hand when they were introduced. Though he spoke directly to both of them, he kept glancing out at two powerboats moving in slow circles around the lake.

The officer's brow was furrowed into deep crevices. "I hate it when things like this come up. I have a daughter of my own, you know."

"Mark is going to lead me to a place where Patti liked to play," Whit explained.

"Holler if you find anything," the officer replied.

"Of course we will."

The officer looked back at the lake and sighed, "It's a sad business."

Mark watched the powerboats move through another cycle. Then he noticed people leaning over the sides of each boat, staring into the water. He trembled as he realized they were looking for Patti beneath the lake's gentle ripples.

Alarmed, Mark tugged at Whit's sleeve.

Whit nodded, said good-bye to the officer, and walked quickly to the path leading to the Great Tree.

"Do they really think Patti's drowned?" Mark asked with a quavering voice.

"They have to consider everything," Whit said matter-of-factly. "Patti's parents knew she often came up here."

"She's in the cave," Mark declared, willing it to be true.

They walked in silence, their breathing providing a natural rhythm to their steps. Mark motioned for Whit to follow him and took the lead as they navigated their way around the dense brush and trees.

"Here we are," Mark said when they were only a short way from the green curtain.

Whit glanced around. Spotting the camouflaged hillside, he remarked, "Ah, it's through there I'll wager."

"How did you know that?" Mark asked with astonishment.

Whit smiled as he moved toward the hill. "I used to be a Boy Scout."

They spread aside the green curtain and stepped into the cave. It was coal black. Turning on his flashlight, Whit went farther in, shifting the beam from object to object. Mark was jolted by the shining faces and sparkling eyes that peered back at them. *Patti's dolls*, he thought sadly.

She had obviously done some redecorating since Mark had been there a week ago. Not only were the crates still there, but she had also added small boxes that served as seats for the dolls. She had laid thick branches across evenly matched stones as shelves for knickknacks and trinkets.

"A home away from home," Whit said.

"Patti," Mark called. His voice sounded hollow and empty.

They stood still and waited.

"Patti, are you here?" Whit shouted.

No answer.

Mark's heart sank. He thought for sure she would be there. Where else could she be?

"I guess I was wrong," he said.

"This is such a well-formed cave. I wonder if . . ." Whit mused aloud, shining the light to the rear of the cave. "Hmm, an unfinished mine shaft?"

"It seems to go farther back, but Patti and I didn't go there," Mark said, failing to mention that they had been afraid.

Stooping to accommodate the incline of the ceiling, Whit followed the beam deeper into the darkness. Mark stayed close behind. They crept along for a short distance. The air was becoming noticeably thick with an earthy damp odor. They stopped before a wall of rock.

"It looks like a dead end," Whit observed. "Rock and shadow make it deeper than it is."

Again, Mark was disappointed. "We figured it went back for miles."

"A lot of the caves around here do, but not this one." Whit turned to Mark and said, "Let's get out of here."

Something about the movement of the flashlight beam on the cave wall caught Mark's eye. It bent into a particular shadow, he thought. Maybe it was a trick of the darkness. Whit didn't seem to notice.

"Watch your head," Whit advised as he started to leave.

Mark lingered a moment, and then said, "Whit?"

"Yeah, Mark?"

"I think there's something back there," he said timidly. If the shadow had been an optical illusion, he would feel embarrassed.

"What is it?" questioned Whit.

"I'm not sure." Mark pointed off to the side of the dead end. "Over there. It's a weird shadow."

Whit focused the beam on an area about ten feet away. "That's not a shadow!" Whit said, his breath quickening. "The cave bends around to the right!"

"No wonder we didn't see it," added Mark.

"An old miner's trick," Whit explained as they inched along. "Miners used to dig the entryway to the shafts at such an angle; then unwanted visitors would think there were no shafts at all."

Whit and Mark passed from the cave into a bigger area braced with large timber beams. The air thickened, and Mark found himself breathing harder.

"We have to be very careful," cautioned Whit. "Whoever dug this mine didn't do a very good job. To tell the truth, I'm not sure we're very smart to be in here."

Mark was about to protest when his foot struck something. It made a banging sound like he had hit metal. Mark jumped back, hitting his back against the wall.

"Ouch!" he cried out.

"What's this? A well-preserved lantern?" Whit asked as he bent to look at it. Then he answered his own question. "Nope, it's new. There's a price tag on it from McIntyre's Hardware in town."

"It's Patti's! She's got to be in here somewhere," Mark exclaimed, picking up the lantern. The glass surrounding the wick was shattered.

Mark stepped forward to continue his search.

"Mark!" Whit cried out, jerking the boy back.

"What's wrong?" Mark asked with alarm.

"Look!" Whit pointed the flashlight to the ground in front of

Mark. It continued ahead for three steps and then disappeared into a black hole.

"It's a deep shaft. Are you trying to break your neck?" asked Whit.

Mark gasped, fell to his knees beside the hole, and called out, "Patti!"

Whit knelt next to Mark and guided the light into the hole. A wooden ladder with broken rungs was hanging loosely until it almost touched the black gravel at the bottom.

"Twenty feet deep, I figure," Whit said.

Then Mark saw the sneaker on the bottom like a strange white spot in an ink well.

"There!" he shouted.

Whit adjusted the flashlight, so it would flood the area with a brighter beam of light. On the floor the small figure of a girl lay like a randomly tossed doll. It was Patti.

Chapter
Ten

MARK SAT IN THE HOSPITAL WAITING ROOM, battling the thick weariness that had threatened to take over his mind and body ever since he and Whit had found Patti. The numbness was winning. In a dream-like haze, Mark recalled everything that had happened.

Whit had sent him for help. Mark had run from the cave through the woods screaming as loudly as his aching lungs would let him. The police had come quickly. Then the paramedics. Under generator-powered lights, they had strapped Patti onto a stretcher and brought her out. Her parents, notified that she had been found, had stood nearby, watching anxiously. She was alive, everyone was assured, but no one knew how badly she had been hurt.

Mark's mother had appeared eventually; he didn't know when. Together, they drove to the hospital in nearby Connellsville, where Patti had been taken. Now Mark waited with his mother, Whit, and the Eldridges for word from the doctor.

Down the hall, someone laughed. *Nobody should laugh in a place like this, at a time like this,* Mark thought.

He didn't know much about hospitals, but he had seen movies and the laughter just didn't seem right.

What if Patti's so broken they can't fix her? he wondered. *What if she has to be in a wheelchair for the rest of her life? What if she isn't herself ever again? She could forget who she is. Would I, could I, still be her friend?*

"There could be brain damage after a fall like that," someone had whispered.

Mark squeezed his eyes shut, trying to block out the terrible thoughts. A tear slipped down his cheek.

What if she dies? What if the damage is worse than everyone thought it would be, and the doctor comes and says, "I'm sorry; we did all we could"?

Did people die from falls like that? Of course they did. Patti could die. Mark felt as if his mind were screaming with such awful possibilities.

Then he would never be able to apologize to Patti. This past miserable week would stretch into forever. And he would never have another friend like her.

Oh, God, Mark prayed silently, *don't let anything bad happen to Patti. Don't let her die. Please.*

He felt someone touch his hand and opened his eyes.

"Mark, are you all right?" his mother asked softly.

Mark's eyelashes were thick with tears. He had been crying and hadn't even realized it.

"Yeah," he sniffled.

Whit knelt in front of Mark and looked at him intently. "Mark, I hope you understand that no matter what happens with Patti, you're a good friend to her. We don't know how long she would have lasted if you hadn't known about the cave."

Mark couldn't accept a word of it. How could he? He had betrayed her.

"You broke a promise," Whit said, as if reading Mark's mind.

"But all of us hurt others at one time or another, especially those we care about the most. That's the risk of loving. We allow ourselves to get close enough to be hurt. Do you understand?"

Mark nodded, though he still wasn't sure he could be comforted.

Whit continued, "Friendship can seem fragile. But the love that creates friendship is made up of pretty tough stuff. That's the kind of love God gives us. And with that love, He gives the ability to forgive. I'm certain Patti cares for you and forgives you no matter how terrible you think you've been to her. Believe me."

Just as Whit stood, a doctor with a stethoscope draped around her neck walked into the waiting room and gestured to Patti's parents. They followed her to the opposite side of the hallway. The doctor spoke in a low whisper. She used her hands while she talked, as if referring to an invisible diagram. Shortly, Mrs. Eldridge began to cry and held her husband's arm tighter. Mark's mother, also watching the three of them, tensed and drew Mark closer.

This is how it happens in the movies, Mark thought. *This is how they break the terrible news.*

He prepared himself for the worst. He wondered if people would feel sorry for him, the best friend of the girl who had died so young.

Ex-best friend, he reminded himself. And it stung.

The doctor moved off down the hallway, and Patti's parents returned to the waiting room. Mark sat up and braced himself for the news.

Mr. Eldridge, struggling with the words, his voice catching, finally said, "She'll be all right. She suffered a slight concussion, bruised some ribs, and broke her right arm. But, all things considered, she'll be all right."

"We're so thankful," Mrs. Eldridge choked through her tears.

It was another day before Mark was allowed to see Patti at the hospital. It had been a long day to end a very long week. He rehearsed what he would say to her, imagining the scene over and over again in his mind. He checked and double-checked every word he would say. He had to say it perfectly with the right tone. Mark was desperate for Patti to know how sorry he was.

His mother waited in the hall while Mark went into the room first. Mrs. Eldridge opened the door and gestured for Mark to enter. Then she closed the door and joined Mark's mother in the hall.

Mark passed an empty hospital bed, the sheets starched stiff and white. He couldn't imagine anyone sleeping in such a hard bed. He peered around a curtain suspended from the ceiling by movable hooks. Patti was sitting on her bed, which was covered with get-well cards and gifts. Patti looked like Patti, Mark was relieved to see. Except, she had a small bandage on her forehead and a milk-white cast on her right arm that went up to her elbow.

"Hi, Patti," Mark said.

"Oh," she remarked, glancing at him with no special recognition, "hi."

He moved closer to the bed. "You have a cast," he observed.

She nodded. "It itches."

"Are you going to get everyone to sign it?"

She frowned. "No, my dad said he would draw a picture on it. Maybe ducks flying south for the winter."

"Ducks! On a cast? Nobody draws ducks on a cast. You want something cool," Mark contended.

"I'll have ducks if I want to. Don't tell me what to put on my cast."

"All right, all right. Have ducks."

This isn't how the scene is supposed to be played out, Mark thought.

Seconds passed as they both looked around the room awkwardly. Then Patti broke the silence. "Mom and Dad said you found me in that hole."

"Yeah."

"I guess I ought to thank you," she said without a hint of gratitude.

"Forget about it."

"Thanks, anyway." She let out a sigh and then said, "There. I wanted to be able to tell my parents I thanked you. You'll tell them, right? If they ask."

"Yeah, sure," he said. "How did you wind up in that shaft anyway?"

Patti shrugged. "I was unpacking some of my stuff, and a ball fell out of the bag. I thought it bounced to the back of the cave, so I went after it. Then I found that other cave. I got curious. I thought maybe I would find buried treasure. Pretty dumb."

"I would have done the same thing," Mark offered.

"Like I said, pretty dumb," she countered. "I dropped my lantern when I fell. I don't remember anything after that."

"Did you get your ball back?"

"No."

Mark brightened. "Maybe I can find it for you."

"You don't have to do that."

"I can if I want," he said. *Why is she being so difficult?* he wondered.

"Don't do me any favors," Patti replied. "I want to get my dolls and stuff out of the cave anyway."

"You do?"

"Yeah. What good is a secret cave when everybody knows about it? Tell your Israelite friends they can have it if they want it."

Okay, Mark thought, *she's still mad.*

"They're not my Israelite friends anymore."

"They aren't?" Patti asked with disbelief. "Why not?"

He shrugged. "Because I broke my promise to you. Didn't they tell you?"

"No," she said and then nodded. "It makes sense, though."

Mark just wanted to get out of there. He hesitated and looked out the window at nothing in particular. Now that he was finally in a position to apologize to her, he wasn't sure he could do it.

Yes, he had broken his promise, but did she really have the right to be mad after a whole week? After all, he was the one who had suffered sitting home alone, watching dumb TV programs. And what did she do? She decorated her cave like nothing had happened. It hadn't affected her one bit. He hadn't even gotten to be an Israelite either! The least she could do was be a little nicer when he was leading up to an apology.

He flinched. What was he thinking? Was he losing his mind? He took a deep breath.

"Patti," he began exactly as he had rehearsed at home.

"What?" Her tone was hard, as if she expected a fight.

He paused and glared at her. "I've been practicing all day, and this isn't working the way it's supposed to. You're making it really hard."

"What are you talking about?"

"This whole conversation," Mark complained. "I was supposed to tell you as soon as I came in."

"Tell me what?"

"Tell you that I'm sorry for breaking my promise to you. I . . . I betrayed you, and I've been miserable all week about it. I won't blame you if you don't want to be my friend anymore, but I'm . . . I'm still very, very sorry. Okay? I just wanted you to know that. I hope you can . . . you know . . . forgive me."

He considered making an escape right then, but he couldn't get his feet to move.

Patti shrugged indifferently. "I guess I can," she said.

"Huh?"

"Forgive you."

"You can?" Mark asked.

"Yeah, but . . ."

"What?"

"It still makes me mad when I think about it."

"That's okay."

"And it might make me mad for a little while after this," she added.

"That's okay, too," Mark said, glad to make any concession. "You can be mad and still be my friend at the same time, can't you?"

"Yeah, I guess I can. Mom and Dad do it all the time." She looked at Mark thoughtfully. "But it'll take a while. I mean, before we can be friends like we were. It'll be a long time before I can tell you any secrets again."

Mark relaxed. "Yeah, I figured. This kind of thing always takes time. I've been watching my parents."

Another lapse in conversation followed, but it was less awkward. Mark felt a peculiar sense of peace within. The room seemed brighter and warmer.

He considered what she had just said and asked, "What kind of secrets can't you tell me?"

Patti thought about it for a moment. "Any kind," she replied.

"You have some right now?"

"I might."

"Like what?" asked Mark.

"I can't tell you. That's why they're secrets."

"Come on," Mark said, coaxing her.

"No!"

"I won't tell anyone this time," he promised.

"Mark!" she glared angrily.

But Mark thought he saw a hint of a smile.

Chapter
Eleven

IT WAS A COUPLE MORE DAYS BEFORE Patti was allowed to go home. Mark had spent that time working feverishly. He wanted to prove he could be her friend again.

Exhausted, he stood on the Eldridges' front porch waiting for Patti's parents to bring her home that afternoon. When they pulled into the driveway, they lingered at the car, gathering her things from the backseat and trunk. As Patti mounted the steps to the porch, she still looked like the survivor of a battle. A smaller bandage now adorned her forehead; her cast was neatly cradled in a sling.

"Hi, Mark," Patti said. "What are you doing here?"

"I was in the neighborhood and thought I'd stop by," he replied.

"Oh, I guess you can come on in."

"If Mr. Prescott would be so kind," Mr. Eldridge said, as he dropped Patti's suitcase at Mark's feet.

"Patti, why don't you show Mark where you want this in your room?" suggested Mr. Eldridge.

"Lead on, Maid Marian," Mark said, gesturing grandly as he picked up the suitcase.

Patti shot him an uncomfortable glance. She wasn't ready to be Maid Marian yet, Mark concluded.

As she stepped into the house, she wrinkled her nose and sniffed the air. "Dad must be working on something in the garage again."

Mark didn't answer but followed her quietly down the hall and up the stairs. When they rounded the banister into the hallway, Patti's bedroom door was closed.

"Why did they close it?" she asked with a frown. Suddenly she turned on Mark. "All right, what's going on?"

"We all have our secrets, Patti," Mark answered with a smile.

"If this is some kind of trick, Mark Prescott," she threatened, "just remember, you're not on anybody's best-seller list this week."

"Hurry up, Patti, this suitcase is heavy. Will you just open the door, please?"

She growled, threw open the door, and gasped.

Her room was painted in a rich tone of forest green. The bedspread, canopy, and curtains were a complementary shade. At the foot of the bed, her dolls and keepsakes and everything she had taken to the cave were spread out in a carefully arranged display around three crates and the lantern with the broken glass. A copy of a book about Robin Hood and another one about pirates were propped up on two of the crates.

Patti exclaimed, "You? You did all this?"

Mark felt himself blushing. "Your parents helped."

"Mark!" she cried, tears forming in her eyes.

"Does that mean you like it?" he asked, hesitating. "I mean, it's not the cave."

Patti looked at him silently for several seconds, enough to make Mark squirm. He knew she liked it, but he wasn't sure what she was going to do. He tensed, thinking she might try to kiss him or something crazy like that. He didn't want her to get mushy. He just wanted her to be his friend again.

She smiled. Maybe she understood what he was feeling, because she didn't do anything to him or say another word. She simply walked into her room and looked it over proudly.

Book
Four

Behind the Locked Door

Chapter
One

MARK PRESCOTT STOPPED, pushed his dark hair back from his forehead, and looked up at the sky. The August sun ducked behind black and purple clouds. It had been playing hide-and-seek for a week now.

"It's going to rain," Mark said, resuming his stroll with Patti Eldridge.

Patti pulled her baseball cap down tighter on her head, as if bracing for an immediate downpour. Her blue eyes peered at Mark from the shadow of its brim. "Let's run back to my house," she said.

Mark nodded and shoved a flat, brown bag under his light jacket. "Okay. But let's take a shortcut," he said and bolted into a small cluster of trees.

"No, Mark! Don't!" Patti protested.

Mark dodged around the trees until he reached a wrought-iron fence with spikes along the top. He carefully climbed it and threw himself over. As he did, the brown bag fell out of his jacket onto the ground. Several brightly colored paperback books slipped out. They had titles like *Tales from the Tomb*, *Forbidden Mysteries*, and *Scream City*. Each had a menacing drawing to match its gruesome name.

Patti stopped on the other side of the fence while Mark picked up the books. "I don't know why you buy those things," she said.

Mark ignored her and slipped them back into the brown bag.

"Seriously, Mark! They're disgusting," she continued. "You'll warp your mind reading stuff like that."

Mark dismissed her comments with a wave of his hand. "Girls don't know anything about it," he said.

Patti glared at him.

He looked away. He knew it was an unfair thing to say to her. Since his arrival in Odyssey after his parents separated, Mark had found Patti to be a good friend. The fact that she was a girl bothered him at first. Boys didn't have girls as friends. At least, that's what he thought. But she remained friendly to him, even after he was impatient and rude to her.

In time, after several adventures together, he realized it didn't matter if she was a girl. He stopped thinking about it altogether—except when someone would tease him for being together so much or when Patti would do something he considered "girl-like." For example, she expected a compliment when she wore a new dress, and sometimes she would say that another boy was "cute."

"What do you mean, girls don't know anything about it?" Patti asked.

"Never mind," he said and turned to walk on. "Let's go."

"Oh, really?" she said, frowning at him.

Mark looked back at her with a blank expression. He thought she was going to nag him about the books some more, but then he realized she had something else on her mind.

"Well? How am I supposed to get over?" she finally asked.

Mark suddenly realized what the problem was. He had forgotten that Patti's right arm was in a plaster cast. She had broken it a few weeks before after falling into an abandoned mine shaft inside a cave. That was one adventure Mark was ashamed to think about. The cave was her secret hideout, and he had told people about it after promising not to. Although Patti never brought it up after he apologized to her, he still felt she blamed him. *Why wouldn't she?* Mark often thought. *I'd be mad if she betrayed me.*

"There's a gate over that way," Mark mumbled. They walked along together on opposite sides of the fence.

Patti sighed. "Look, all I'm saying is that you're gonna get in big trouble with your mom if she ever finds out you spent your whole allowance on those sick books!"

"But she *won't* find out unless someone blabs," Mark replied.

Patti frowned. "Nobody has to blab. The books are going to get you in trouble all by themselves."

"Quit nagging me!" Mark shouted.

They reached the gate in silence. A dark feeling hung over them just like one of the rain clouds above.

Patti walked through the gate. "You didn't have to shout at me," she said.

Mark lowered his tone. "Yeah, I know. Just drop it, okay?" It was the closest thing to an apology he could manage.

There wasn't anything else to say, so they walked on. Mark wondered how long it would take her to realize where they were. The thick grove of trees gave no clue, nor did the perfectly trimmed carpet of grass that cushioned their walk. But after a moment the trees gave way to a clearing, and the carpet of grass stretched before them dotted with gray, eroded tombstones covered with dark moss.

They were in the graveyard next to Saint Patrick's, Odyssey's oldest church.

Patti stopped in her tracks. "Oh no . . ."

"Oh, come on, Patti. It's just a graveyard," Mark said.

"I know it's a graveyard," Patti snapped. "Let's go around."

Mark shook his head. "Why go all the way around? It's a great shortcut! I found it the other day when I went to your house from Whit's End."

"I don't like it," said Patti.

Mark quickened his step. "We'll only be here a minute. Come on."

"I don't like it," Patti said again, wrinkling her freckled nose. But she followed Mark anyway.

They wove along the edge of the tombstones. Mark normally would have walked right through the center, but he didn't think Patti would dare. Her eyes, wide with fright, darted back and forth as if she expected a hand to suddenly reach out and grab her.

They were closer to the church now. It was a large building of sandy-colored stones fashioned like the old cathedrals Mark had seen in pictures. Washington, D.C., where Mark had lived before he moved to Odyssey, had a cathedral. It was bigger than this church, but it had the same kind of tower that jutted high into the sky. It even had working bells. Mark had never heard the bells ringing in this Odyssey church.

"Hurry up," Patti whispered.

But Mark was in no hurry. He wanted to see some of the names and dates etched in the tombstones beneath small crosses and statues of angels' wings. "Beloved son" . . . "Joshua David Penrose, 1877-1898" . . . "In the arms of Jesus" . . . "Victoria Simpson, 1860-1922." *They were all people who once lived like me,* Mark thought. *They went shopping and took shortcuts and jumped fences and . . .*

Patti suddenly gasped. "Look!"

Mark followed her gaze. Off in the distance, across the collection of weathered stones, Mark saw John Avery Whittaker leaning over a grave. Everyone in town knew John Whittaker— or Whit, as he was best known. He owned a remarkable ice cream parlor called Whit's End that housed room after room of activities and displays for kids. "A discovery emporium," Mark had heard some people call it. Kids could run the county's largest train set, perform on the stage in the Little Theatre, read through any of the hundreds of books in the library, or build an invention in the workroom.

Mark had experienced his share of adventures in and around Whit's End, including one with a time machine called the Imagination Station. He liked to think he and Whit were good friends. But he suspected Whit made all the kids feel that way.

"He's putting flowers on a grave!" Patti whispered.

"I wonder whose grave it is," Mark said, craning his neck to get a better look. The sight of Whit in a graveyard stirred a strong feeling of curiosity in Mark. It reminded him of a story in one of his books about a ghost dressed in black who waited next to a grave for a woman who would never arrive.

Drops of rain lightly splattered Mark and Patti. They only had time to look up before the sky gave way to a full-fledged downpour.

"I want to go home," Patti said. She moved to the shelter of a tree. Mark was a few steps behind her, but he kept his eyes on Whit.

"Did you hear me?" asked Patti.

Through the dull gray rain, Mark watched as Whit stepped back from the grave and slowly lowered his head. His white hair, normally wild and seemingly alive, lay matted against his forehead. Even his bushy, white eyebrows and mustache drooped under the weight of the falling water. After a moment, he turned and walked off in the opposite direction.

"It's as if he doesn't even know it's raining," Mark said.

"Well *I* do!" Patti complained.

"I want to know whose grave that is," Mark said as he took a step in that direction.

Patti grabbed his arm. "No, Mark. Let's get out of here. This place gives me the creeps!"

"There's nothing to be afraid of," said Mark.

"I don't care," Patti replied. "I'm not supposed to get my cast wet!"

Mark frowned and jerked his thumb at her cast. "You just don't want to mess up all those stupid autographs you got from everybody at Whit's End."

"So?"

"So—if you had left Whit's End when I wanted to, we wouldn't be caught in the rain right now," Mark asserted.

Patti's mouth fell open. "I can't believe you! You're not going to blame this on me. Getting people to sign my cast is the only thing that makes it bearable!"

"I just want to see the tombstone," he pleaded. "I'll only be a minute."

Patti was about to answer when suddenly a haggard old man appeared from behind a nearby tree. "Hey!" he shouted.

Mark and Patti cried out.

The rain had smeared dirt on the man's craggy face. His clothes were unkempt and torn. Mark thought of the cover of one of his horror books—a drawing of a corpse emerging from a fresh grave.

The old man stepped toward them and waved his fist. "This ain't no playground!" he shouted.

Mark and Patti ran for their lives.

Chapter Two

ONCE THEY WERE A SAFE distance away, Mark and Patti slowed down to catch their breath in the shelter of a covered bus stop. The rain falling against the roof sounded like a beating drum.

"I told you we shouldn't cut through there!" Patti shouted above the roar.

"It was just some old man," Mark said, then laughed. "You thought it was a monster."

Patti looked at him doubtfully. "Oh, yeah? If you thought it was just some old man, why did *you* run?"

"Because *you* ran," Mark replied.

"You were scared," said Patti.

"No more than you were," said Mark. They argued back and forth about who was more scared until it was obvious no one could win the argument.

"I'm going home now," Patti said. "My mom's gonna have a fit when she sees how wet I am."

Mark caught Patti's sleeve just as she was about to dash into the rain. "Whose grave do you think Whit was visiting?"

Patti turned to him impatiently. "I don't know, and I don't think it's any of our business, Mark. It's not right to spy on people in graveyards."

"Aren't you even a little bit curious?" Mark asked.

Patti didn't answer, but her expression told Mark she was. She held her cast close to her chest, lowered her head, and charged into the downpour. Before long, she disappeared into the watery haze.

Mark strolled out of the shelter as if it weren't raining at all. Getting wet didn't bother him. Not when his mind was on Whit. What was he doing in that cemetery? Whose grave was it? Patti had lived in Odyssey a long time. Why didn't she know? Why hadn't Mark heard that Whit knew someone buried there?

The questions swirled round and round in his brain like water down a drain. But there were no answers to be found. It only made him realize how little he knew about Whit. The pleasant and wise owner of Whit's End was now a man of mystery.

Mark threw open the front door to his house and stepped in. "Mom?" he called out. No reply. He took two steps and almost forgot to take off his shoes. His mom would have been angry if he had tracked mud on the carpet. He absent mindedly tugged off his shoes and dropped them next to the mat. He then pulled off his jacket, hung it up, and inspected his books. They were damp but not drenched.

"Mom!" Mark called again, wondering where she was. The loud ticking of the grandfather clock in the hall was the only response to his call. His socks made squishing sounds as he padded upstairs to his bedroom and threw the books into the top drawer of his dresser. Patti's words came back to him. One day, those books were going to get him in trouble.

He shrugged off the thought and ran back downstairs to the kitchen. As he reached for the refrigerator door to get a drink, he discovered a note stuck under a plastic magnet shaped like a cuddly kitten. The refrigerator was covered with those kinds of magnets. Mark thought they looked sissy.

"Don't go anywhere. Important news," the note said in his mother's handwriting. *Now what?* Mark wondered. He closed his eyes and took a deep breath. Ever since his mother and father had separated, Mark had prepared himself for all kinds of "news." First, it was his mother's news that they were leaving their home in Washington, D.C., to move to Odyssey. Then it was the news that his mother and father were getting a divorce. Then they had changed their minds and wanted to try to make their marriage work. Then it was the news that working out their problems would be a long and slow process. Maybe adults understood such things, but Mark sometimes felt as if he were on a roller coaster. All he could do was close his eyes and wait for the butterflies to stop flapping their wings in his stomach. Mostly he wished the ride would end and they could be a family again.

"News," Mark whispered to himself. He had no way of predicting whether the news would be good or bad. His parents had been talking on the phone a lot lately. Sometimes Mark's mom seemed excited; other times, she hung up the phone in tears. He never asked about it. He figured the answer would be more than he'd want to know.

The electric garage door opener suddenly groaned to life. In his mind's eye, Mark could see what his ears told him was happening. The car hummed and hissed its way into place. The brakes squeaked, and the motor cut off. With a loud click, the door opened. A soft dong-dong-dong announced that Julie Prescott needed to take the keys out of the ignition. Mark then heard some shuffling of paper bags—*probably groceries*, he thought—and went to the door leading into the garage. He opened it in time for his mother to step through with two large bags in her arms. They weren't groceries.

"Close the door, sweetheart," she said breathlessly. Mark obeyed and returned in seconds. His mom was still in her dripping raincoat as she carefully pulled a pink blouse from the bag. She held it up and smiled.

"Hi," he said.

"Hi," she replied. "What do you think?"

Mark shrugged. He couldn't decide if he wanted to press her for the news or wait until she chose to tell him.

Julie draped the blouse over the back of a kitchen chair. "Did you see my note?"

"Uh-huh," Mark said.

"I suppose you're wondering what the news is." She smiled.

Mark rolled his eyes. *I hope she isn't going to make me guess*, he thought.

She pushed him playfully. "Don't roll your eyes at me, young man. Otherwise I won't tell you."

"Mom!" Mark cried out, putting his hands on his hips.

"That's better," she said. She took off her raincoat and left it to drip on a coatrack next to the garage door.

"So?"

Running her fingers through her damp brown hair, she leaned forward to face Mark. Her hazel eyes danced. "I talked to your father today, and we decided I should go back to Washington for a few days. There's a counselor he wants us to see. I'll catch a flight tomorrow. This could be it, Mark."

"'It'?" Mark blinked.

His mom pushed a loose strand of hair away from her face. "If the counseling goes well, your father and I might . . . might . . . you know . . . *reconcile*."

The word didn't mean anything to Mark. Suddenly his mother realized it and said, "That means we'll get back together. We'll be a *family* again!"

Mark's heart jumped, but he told it to be still. He knew better than to get excited about this announcement. He'd heard such statements before. "But what about me?" he asked.

"Is that all you can say? Aren't you pleased?" Julie's mouth fell open with disbelief. It was her turn to put her hands on her hips.

Mark shrugged again. "I was just wondering where I'll stay while you're gone."

"I'll never figure you out. I thought you'd be happy." She went back to the bags and pulled out a charcoal skirt.

"I *am* happy," Mark said. "But you and Dad have been doing this *forever*. He comes here and you get counseling, or you go there and get counseling, and then you say you need more time and nothing happens."

Julie stopped digging in the bags and turned to Mark. "You're right," she said softly, reaching out to stroke his hair. "It's not fair to expect you to jump for joy every time something like this comes up. But it really is different now. You'll see."

Mark gazed down at his socks and wiggled his toes uncomfortably. The bottoms of his jeans were wet.

"I have some other news, too," she said.

Other news? Mark looked up at her. "What other news?"

"I arranged for you to stay with someone while I'm away."

At Patti's, I'll bet, Mark thought.

Julie's voice rose excitedly as she said, "You're going to stay at Mr. Whittaker's house!"

Chapter Three

WHILE JULIE PACKED FOR THE TRIP, Mark called Patti to tell her the news. She screamed into the phone so loudly that Mark had to hold the receiver away from his ear. "You're staying at Whit's *house*? You're staying at his *house*? You are going to stay at his own personal *house*?" she asked.

He wanted to sound casual, but he was pleased with her reaction. "Yeah, Mom's taking me first thing tomorrow," he said.

"Wow, I don't know *anyone* who's ever been inside Whit's *house*!"

Mark shrugged, even though she couldn't see it. He knew it was an honor to go to Whit's.

"I have some news, too," Patti said, lowering her voice. "I told my parents about seeing Whit at the graveyard."

"Why did you do that?" Mark asked sharply.

"Because I thought they might know something about it," Patti retorted.

Mark softened his tone. "What did they say?"

Patti hesitated, and for a moment Mark thought she might not tell him because he had spoken harshly. Then she said, "They think it might be Jenny Whittaker's grave. She died a couple of years ago."

Whit was married? Mark closed his eyes and tried to picture it. *Of course he was. Why wouldn't he be?* Yet, it was hard for Mark to imagine the Whit he knew having a wife and doing the kinds of things married people do. He just couldn't see it.

"Hello? Mark?"

"How did she die?" Mark finally asked.

"My folks weren't sure," Patti answered. She went on to explain she didn't want to press them with too many questions or they might lecture her about minding her own business.

Like you lectured me, Mark thought.

"Anyway, I have to go," Patti said. "See you tomorrow."

"Okay, thanks," Mark said as he hung up the phone. His stomach flip-flopped. Suddenly he was full of all the anticipation he often felt on Christmas Eve. He knew he wouldn't sleep well that night.

From the doorway to his room, Mark stifled a shriek. His mother was opening his dresser drawers. *The horror books!* he remembered. "Mom!" he called out just as Julie reached for the drawer containing them.

Startled, Julie looked up at him. "What's wrong?"

"I, uh, was . . ." Mark swallowed hard. "I was just talking to Patti. She's excited that I'm staying with Whit."

"Good. But you didn't have to shout like that," Julie said. She turned to Mark's bed, where his suitcase lay open like the mouth of a baby bird screeching for a worm. Julie fed it some of Mark's underwear, then looked around uncertainly. "I don't want to forget anything."

Mark was afraid she might reach for the drawer again. He stepped in front of it as if he merely wanted to lean against the dresser and folded his arms casually.

"What's wrong with you?" Julie asked.

"Huh?"

"You're acting very strange," she said, eyeing him warily.

"I'm just . . . you know," he replied.

Julie gently put her hands on his shoulders. "I know it's hard, Mark. All this going back and forth between your father and me . . . it seems crazy sometimes. I know it does. If I were you, I'd think we were the worst parents in the world."

"You are not!" Mark said defensively.

"Well, hang in there," she said with a smile. "Your father and I will meet with the counselor for two days of pretty tough talking. Then we'll decide if the time is right. Maybe this will be the happy ending we've all been praying for."

Mark didn't dare hope.

Julie kissed him on the cheek. "Take a look around to see if there's anything else you want to pack. I'll go downstairs and get us some lemonade."

She walked out of the room and down the stairs. Mark kept his position against the dresser until he was sure it was safe. Then he carefully opened the drawer and took out the horror books. The ghoulish face hadn't changed since that afternoon. Its peeling green skin, bloodshot eyes, and sharp fangs were as hideous as ever. Mark imagined the fright it would've given his mom if she had seen it. Then she would have grounded him for the rest of his life!

As he shoved the books into the bottom of his suitcase, he wondered if they were really worth all the fuss. Then he remembered he hadn't read the newest book in the *Tales from the Tomb* series.

❖ ❖ ❖

The next morning, Mark's mother gave him some last-minute instructions as they drove to Whit's house. He only heard fragments of what she said: "Be polite and respectful . . . don't talk back . . . come in when Whit says to . . . keep your room tidy." His mind was on the adventure that awaited him.

"Are you listening to me?" Julie asked.

Mark looked across the front seat at her. He was sure his blank expression said no. It didn't matter. He knew she knew he wasn't listening. Worse, he knew she knew he knew she knew he wasn't listening. Mothers were born with special radar to scope out daydreaming children.

"I didn't think so," she said with a smile. She put on the turn signal and cruised next to the curb. Mark glanced out the window and found himself staring at a large, Victorian-style house.

"Is this it?" Mark asked, hoping it was.

"Uh-huh. Nice, isn't it?"

Mark nodded. In some ways, the house resembled Whit's End; an odd collection of rounded and rectangular shapes all thrown together behind a spacious front porch and a large wooden door. Were there three stories? It was hard to tell, because the roof suddenly jutted upward at strange angles from other parts of the house. The small windows near the top looked like peepholes. He thought of slits he had seen in towers of old castles.

"It's so big," Mark said. "How many rooms do you think it has?"

Julie chuckled and answered, "I don't know. You'll find out before I will."

Mark threw open the car door, grabbed his small suitcase from the backseat, and walked quickly down the sidewalk to the house. Whit stepped out onto the porch just as Mark climbed the steps.

"Hello there," Whit said warmly. His eyes sparkled beneath bushy, white eyebrows, and he put out his hand.

Mark shook it. "Thanks for letting me stay with you," he said.

"I'm glad to have the company," Whit said, his lips stretching into a wide smile under his thick mustache.

Julie now joined them on the porch, took Whit's hand in hers, and thanked him for taking care of Mark. Whit said it was no trouble at all. He gestured for them to follow him into the house. "Come in. Would you like some tea or coffee?"

"No, thank you," Julie replied. "I'm going to be late for my flight." She turned to Mark and held his face in her hands. "Remember what I told you," she said.

Mark blushed.

"I love you," she said, and then she kissed him.

"Tell Dad I said hello."

She said she would, spun on her heel, and walked briskly back to the car. There was a light spring in her step. Mark couldn't help but think that sometimes she was more like a young girl than a mother.

Whit put his hand on Mark's shoulder, and they both waved. Julie touched the horn in reply. Mark felt a sudden catch in his heart—the kind of feeling he got when he knew he'd be separated from his mom for a while.

"Let's go inside," Whit said.

The house didn't look as big inside as it did from the outside. A small foyer by the front door instantly gave way to a hall, which led to the rest of the first floor. Next to it was a stairway. Whit grabbed Mark's suitcase and escorted him up the stairs to a landing, around a corner to another flight of stairs, and up to the second floor.

The stairwell was lined with frame after frame of photographs—one or two were of a younger-looking Whit, but most were of a woman and three children. Mark assumed Whit wasn't in those because he took the pictures. He wanted to ask who the others were but decided to wait. There was plenty of time for questions later.

Whit put Mark's suitcase in "Jason's room," as he called it. "This is where you'll sleep," he said.

The room was tidy and comfortable. A single bed was covered by a multi-colored quilt. Nearby, a nightstand held a lamp with a wood carving of an old sea captain. The captain wore a long coat, sailor's hat, chin beard, and a patch over his right eye. All these were intricately detailed by some woodcrafter's hand. Mark's gaze drifted above the bed to a painting of a ship. Its giant sails billowed in the wind as it cut through foamy waters. Similar paintings and pictures of ancient ships adorned the rest of the walls.

"He liked stories about the sea," Whit explained without being asked. "My son, Jason, I mean. *Moby Dick* was his favorite."

Again Mark had to rethink his image of Whit, not only as a man who was once a husband, but also a father. He tried to picture Whit sitting in this very room reading bedtime stories to his son.

Along the opposite wall from the bed sat a small desk surrounded by floor-to-ceiling bookshelves. Every inch of the shelves was stacked high with books.

"Wow!" Mark said. "It's just like the library at Whit's End! Jason must have read a lot."

Whit chuckled and answered, "My wife used to say Jason was the most like me."

"Your wife?" Mark asked.

"Jenny," Whit replied. "She was a wonderful woman. I'll have to tell you about her sometime."

Whit led the way out of Jason's room and pushed open other doors on that floor: a pink and lacy room that had once belonged to his daughter, Jana; a linen closet; the bathroom. Whit's bedroom was at the end of the hall. It was stark in its simplicity. It had a large bed, a dresser, and a tall wardrobe. All were made of the same rich, dark wood. As Mark expected, one wall was covered with shelves full of books.

"That completes our tour of the upstairs," said Whit. "How about downstairs?"

Mark nodded.

As they started down the hall toward the stairs, Mark noticed a door that hadn't been accounted for. *Whit must have forgotten about it*, he thought as he reached for the door handle. "What's this room?" he asked, turning the knob.

"Don't!" Whit snapped.

Mark jumped, backing away from the door.

Whit seemed to realize how harsh he sounded and spoke more gently. "That's just the attic. I don't want you to go up there."

"Oh," said Mark, his heart racing.

Whit looked at Mark and then at the door. "Just the attic," he repeated. He started down the stairs.

Just the attic? Mark wondered. *Then why did Whit snap at me?*

He sneaked a glance back toward the door.

Strange thing, Mark thought. *Especially since the door is locked.*

Chapter
Four

LATER THAT MORNING, Mark met Patti near the gate to the old cemetery. The cloudy sky made the sun look like a flashlight beam shining through a thin blanket.

"Why did you want to meet here?" asked Patti. "You know I don't like this place."

"I thought you wanted to know what was going on," challenged Mark.

"I do!" Patti said.

"Then come on," he said, walking into the graveyard. He wondered if the old man would suddenly appear to scare them as he did the day before. Mark couldn't see anyone. Except for the squish-squish of their feet on the thick, wet grass, all was silent.

After a moment, Mark said, "After I got to Whit's house this morning, he showed me around."

Patti shivered and said, "You can tell me on the way to town. Let's hurry up and get out of here."

Mark frowned at her but continued. "Whit told me about all his rooms—except one."

Patti looked at him expectantly. "Yeah? Which one?"

"The attic," Mark said. "I was going to open the door, and then he snapped at me."

"He did? Whit doesn't snap at people."

"He did this time. It made me jump."

"But why? I mean, if it's just an attic."

"Because he didn't want me to see what was behind that door."

"It probably had a lot of junk in it," she suggested.

"Oh yeah? Then why was the door *locked*?"

Patti wanted to know what Mark was getting at.

"I don't know," Mark answered quietly. "But it's like . . . he's hiding something."

"Mr. Whittaker? No way. You're making a big deal out of nothing."

Mark shook his head.

"It's those books you keep reading!" Patti said.

Mark swung around. "It is not! Why do you keep nagging me about them?"

"Because they're warped, that's why," Patti said sharply. "Ghosts, monsters, dead people . . . they're bad for you."

"What do *you* know?"

"I know your imagination will get out of hand if you read things like that," she replied. "They make you think weird things. I've heard Whit talk about it. We're supposed to fill our minds with good things, he said."

Mark had no defense against a quotation from Whit, and he knew it. "I don't want to talk about it anymore."

By this time, they had reached the grave Whit had visited the day before. It was Jenny Whittaker's grave, just as Patti's parents had said. "Here it is," Mark whispered.

"I still don't understand why you had to see her grave," Patti said.

"Because we didn't see it yesterday," Mark answered. The tombstone was a shiny gray with an ornamental design at the top—a slender angel with a long horn raised to its lips. *Guinevere*

Renee Whittaker, "Jenny," Loving Wife & Mother, the inscription read. A fresh planter of daffodils stood at the head of the grave. Mark noted that her birthday was February 20 and that she had died on August 17. The daffodils covered the years of her birth and death.

"That's probably why Whit was here," Patti said as she pointed at the second date.

Mark nodded. "It was the anniversary of her death."

"Great. Now let's get out of here," Patti insisted.

"Wait a minute," Mark said. "I just want to—"

"Back again are you?" growled a low voice behind them. A hand clutched Mark's arm; another grabbed Patti's. It was the old man.

Mark and Patti jumped back with a cry, but the old man held their arms tightly. "Let go!" Mark yelled.

The old man squinted and opened his mouth into a wide, brown-toothed grin that folded his face into creases. "Of course I will, of course I will," he said.

Patti screamed.

"Oh, be quiet," he hissed. "I'll do you no harm. No harm at all."

"Then let us go!" Mark said, straining against the old man's grip.

"It's not often we have kids your age looking around tombstones," the old man said. "Are you here to pay your respects, or are you playing games?"

"There's no law against looking!" Patti said. Her eyes mirrored both fear and defiance.

"Indeed there isn't, young lady. Indeed there isn't. But as caretaker, I have to know what you're up to. This isn't a relative of yours, is it? You're no relation to Whittaker."

"No. But Mr. Whittaker's a friend of ours," Mark said as he renewed his struggle. "We just wanted to see it!"

"A friend of Whit's, eh?" the old man mused. "Then you'll know all about Jenny Whittaker. All about her."

"We don't know *anything* about her," Patti growled.

"Interesting, it is," the old man said softly. "There are a few things folks don't know."

Once again, that strong feeling of curiosity rose within Mark. "Like what?" he asked.

"Mark!" Patti cried out with disbelief. "He's crazy!"

"The design at the top," the old man said, oblivious to Patti's words. "The angel, you see, with the long horn. Victorian, that is. A design called, 'Heralding the Hope.' It's about the hope of the resurrection in Christ."

Mark looked at the design and the angel with the horn lifted upward.

"And if you'll look just beyond the angel, you'll see a small cloud with a cross in it. Can you see it?" the old man whispered in Mark's ear. His breath smelled of licorice.

Mark squinted to see the small cloud, hardly aware that the old man's grip had slackened and his hand had fallen away.

Patti noticed instantly and started to run. She slipped on the wet grass with a loud splat, scrambled to her feet, and finally stopped at a safe distance. "Mark!" she called.

But Mark was fascinated by the tombstone. He took a step forward to get a closer look at the angel, the trumpet, and the delicate cloud.

"Mark!" Patti shouted again.

To his amazement, Mark could see a cross, nearly hidden by the billowy clouds so artistically carved.

"Nobody ever notices it," the old man said forlornly as he pulled a wooden pipe from his ragged coat pocket. "Something so pretty, and nobody stops to look. You kids certainly wouldn't take the time. Never do."

"Mark!" Patti shouted again, edging closer.

"Wow," Mark said. He reached out and touched the cold stone. It sent a startling chill through him, and he jerked back. Suddenly he realized he was standing on top of the grave. "Oh no!" he gasped, leaping to one side.

Patti waved frantically. "Come on, Mark! What's the matter with you?"

"I stepped on her grave!" he called out apologetically.

The old man clamped the pipe in his teeth and said, "You're not telling me you're superstitious, now are you? Walking on the dead—is that what you think you're doing?"

Mark's face went crimson. "I've heard that it's disrespectful, that's all," he said.

"Maybe it would be disrespectful if she was buried here," the old man said, producing a lit match like a magician who pulls a rabbit out of a hat. "But she's not."

Mark's mouth fell open. "What?"

The old man cleared his throat and placed the lit match against the pipe. "That's the other thing most folks don't know. Jenny Whittaker isn't buried here. This is a memorial."

Mark glanced anxiously at Patti, who now stood even closer.

"Then . . . where is she?" Mark gulped.

"Ah, but that's the question, isn't it?" the old man replied. "That's the question."

Mark looked at the tombstone again. The herald of hope. He stared at the name on the tombstone and found himself thinking of the locked door.

Chapter
Five

IF JENNY WHITTAKER ISN'T BURIED in her grave, then where is she? Mark wondered. Once Patti got over her scare at the cemetery and her anger at Mark for making her go there, she agreed to help him solve the mystery.

"How do we know the old man was telling the truth?" Patti challenged Mark as they watched a softball game at McAlister Park.

"Why would he lie to us?"

"Because he's a weird old man who likes to scare kids, that's why."

Mark shook his head. "I don't think so. Didn't you hear the way he talked about the herald of hope or whatever it was called? He's the caretaker of the cemetery—next to a *church*. He wouldn't lie to us."

"Yeah, but he wouldn't tell you anything else about it either," Patti countered.

Later, Mark and Patti went to a pond near Tom Riley's farm, where Mark swam and Patti lounged on the bank because of her cast. She dangled her toes in the water and asked why anyone would go to the trouble to have a grave but not put a body in it.

Mark floated on his back and considered the question. "The

old man said it was a memorial. People put up plaques and monuments without putting dead bodies underneath them, right?"

"I guess so," Patti said, then absentmindedly kicked water at Mark.

"So, where's her body?" Mark asked. "Why wouldn't Whit bury his wife in Odyssey?"

Patti leaned back and sighed. "Maybe she didn't like it here."

At Whit's End, their last stop of the afternoon, Mark and Patti watched Whit as he worked behind the ice cream counter. He laughed and joked with his young customers who had come from all over town to enjoy the food and fun of this discovery emporium.

Mark looked puzzled. "Where *did* he bury her, Patti?"

"I don't know, Mark. Why don't you ask him? He's right over there."

Mark grimaced.

"He's our friend, right?" she insisted. "He'll tell us. I feel like we're being sneaky, talking about him and making wild guesses about his wife. Let's ask him."

Mark rejected the idea. "Right. What would we say? 'Uh, excuse me, Whit, but could you tell us where your wife is buried?'"

"Well, it's better than all this creepy guessing. We're talking about a *body*. It gives me the chills," Patti said. "Besides, she could be buried anywhere."

"Or nowhere at all," Mark said thoughtfully.

"What?"

"Maybe she isn't buried," Mark said.

Patti's eyes widened and then narrowed as they always did when she got mad at him. She shook her finger at him, and Mark knew what she was going to say. *It's those horror books. They're warping your mind. Now you're thinking sick things about Mr. Whittaker's wife, and it's wrong.*

But Patti didn't say a word. She simply growled and turned away.

❧ ❧ ❧

That evening, Whit prepared some barbequed chicken, potatoes, and assorted vegetables for dinner. He and Mark sat down, and, after praying, they began to chat about the day as they ate their food. Whit explained that he was working on a new idea for the Imagination Station. He hoped to have it working well enough to bring it up from his workroom in the basement of Whit's End so all the kids could use it.

"What's wrong? Don't you like your chicken?" Whit suddenly asked.

Mark was surprised by the question until he realized he had just been picking at his food. "No, it's good," Mark said. He took a bite of the chicken just to prove it.

Whit cocked an eyebrow and said, "There's something on your mind."

"No, sir," Mark said after he swallowed his food.

"Are you sure?" Whit persisted.

It occurred to Mark that this might be the only chance he'd have to talk about Jenny, so he worked up his courage and did just that. "Patti and I took a shortcut through the cemetery yesterday, and . . . we saw you," he said softly.

"Oh?"

"You were putting flowers on your wife's grave."

"That's right," Whit said. "It was the anniversary of her death. Why didn't you say something sooner?"

Mark shrugged and said, "I don't know. I figured it was . . . you know."

"Hard for me to talk about?"

"Yeah," Mark said.

Whit reached over and touched Mark's arm. "Mark, I've always said that you should never be afraid to ask me about anything—and I mean it."

Mark looked at Whit sheepishly, suddenly embarrassed for making such a big deal out of nothing. "Will you tell me about her?"

Whit sat back in his chair, rubbed his mouth with his napkin, and then tossed it onto the table. "All right, I'll tell you."

Whit explained that he had met Jenny in Pasadena, California, when he was a student in college there. She worked in the library. At first, they didn't like each other much. They argued about books and philosophies and ideas, until one day they realized that something special was happening between them. They were becoming friends. In time, friendship led to a deeper relationship. Whit finally asked her out on a date, and a short time later they married.

"How did she die?" Mark asked abruptly, bypassing years of Whit and Jenny's life together.

Whit stroked his mustache and looked at Mark thoughtfully. "That's a more complicated story. Are you sure you want to hear about it?"

Mark assured Whit that he did.

"Well, Jenny's death and the creation of Whit's End are tied together. Did you know that?"

Mark shook his head no.

Whit began, "There was a building called the Fillmore

Recreation Center. It used to be a meeting place for all kinds of activities for the townspeople. But they built a new center in the middle of McAlister Park and left the old one to rot. It was falling apart, and some of the folks in Odyssey thought it should be torn down and replaced with a shopping center. My wife had other ideas. She was the leader of a movement to have the building restored and turned into a cultural landmark."

Mark asked what he meant by "cultural landmark."

"Have you heard how some cities have buildings that are real old, and people turn them into museums or give tours of them? That's what Jenny wanted the Fillmore Building to become."

"I get it," Mark said.

"Anyway, Jenny worked hard to save the building," Whit continued. "But not everyone in town agreed with her. In fact, *I* was one of them. I couldn't figure out why she was wearing herself down fighting for such a wreck of a building." Whit paused for a moment and chuckled at something he remembered. "Boy, we had some red-hot debates about it, you can be sure. I think she was just using me for practice before tackling the city council. She was very outspoken in those meetings. She was a determined woman."

"You mean she gave speeches and stuff like that?" Mark asked.

Whit nodded. "Uh-huh. All over town. She was desperate to win support. The town argued about it for months, but she never gave up. Then, at the town meeting when the city council was going to make its final decision, she collapsed suddenly."

"What happened?"

Whit was quiet for a moment, and Mark wasn't sure he'd answer. Finally he said, "At first I thought she was simply exhausted. She worked so hard, but . . . it was far more serious than that. She had a disease in her kidney that had poisoned her entire body. The doctors couldn't do anything for her and . . . she died that same day."

Again there was a long silence. Mark looked away, afraid that Whit might start to cry or something.

"I was crushed by losing her," Whit eventually said. "I felt bitter, too. I blamed Odyssey for her death. I locked myself away."

Mark glanced at Whit and was relieved to see he was dry-eyed. "What happened then?"

"A month or so went by, and I was visited by Tom Riley, my best friend. You know Tom."

Mark did. Tom Riley had once shot Mark in the rear end with a water pistol for picking apples from his tree.

Whit continued, "Tom was a member of the city council. He said that because of Jenny's death, the decision about the Fillmore Building hadn't been made, but that it would be the next day. He persuaded me that Jenny's fight for the Fillmore Building wasn't a waste of time, that she so often spoke of its potential as a place for kids to play and learn. He said the city council thought it would be a shame to lose the battle now.

"The building was doomed and the gavel was just about to fall when I burst into the room and said I'd buy the Fillmore myself." Whit chuckled as he added, "I've always had a weak spot for dramatic entrances."

"So the Fillmore Building became Whit's End?" Mark asked.

"Yep," Whit said with a smile. "A place of adventure and discovery where kids of all ages can just be kids. All because of Jenny."

A flash of heat lightning made Mark realize the sun was nearly gone. They had been talking for almost two hours.

Whit grabbed the dinner dishes and took them to the sink. "That's enough about me. How about a game of checkers?"

They laughed as they played checkers, particularly when they began to make up the rules as they went along. Then they played a game Whit had created to test the players' memories. The game turned the entire living room into a giant board game, with Whit and Mark as living, moving pieces. Finally, they found some man-sized cardboard boxes and turned them into "time-traveling" submarines. They decided to call it a night after Whit accidentally torpedoed an end table and broke a lamp.

When it was time for bed, Whit remembered that he wanted to give Mark a spare house key so he could get in and out during the day. "Come on. It's up in my room," Whit said as he turned off all the downstairs lights.

Mark watched as Whit fished through some keys he kept in a commemorative cup on top of his dresser. It struck Mark that the key to the attic might be in that cup, too.

"Here it is!" Whit announced, handing a key to Mark. Mark glanced at it, then shoved it into his pocket and said good night.

A few minutes later, while brushing his teeth in the bathroom, Mark realized he hadn't found out from Whit where Jenny was buried. Even though Whit had said he'd answer any of Mark's questions, Mark couldn't bring himself to ask. In the back of his mind, he knew Whit would think he was warped to even think of such a thing.

Mark went back to his room and gently closed the door. As he pulled pajamas out of his suitcase, his fingers brushed against his books. *Tales of Horror and Mystery* was on top. He tossed it onto the bed and pondered the cover as he slipped into his night clothes. "Shadows in the Night" shouted the subtitle. Under the subtitle, a stern-looking woman holding a candle climbed a dark stairway. Behind her, a menacing shadow with outstretched arms reached toward her.

Mark climbed into bed, opened to the first page, and stopped. It was the story of a man who returned from the dead to seek revenge on his wicked wife.

What would Whit think about this? Mark wondered as the moss-covered man—no longer a shadow—made his appearance during his wife's dinner party. *Would he approve or disapprove?*

Probably disapprove, Mark thought. He sighed and dropped the book next to the bed. He couldn't shake the image of Jenny Whittaker's empty grave and the locked door to the attic.

Another flash of heat lightning lit up the night. Mark shuddered. *Maybe Patti's right*, he ventured. His imagination *was* out of control. He grabbed the book and shoved it back into his suitcase.

He turned off the light on the sea-captain lamp and fell quickly into a deep sleep.

Thump.

The noise woke Mark up.

Someone just closed my door, he thought. He rolled over to look. For a moment, he thought it was his mom checking on him. Then he remembered it couldn't be his mom because she was in Washington, D.C. This wasn't his home or his own bed. He was at Whit's house. In Jason's room.

He sleepily rubbed his eyes and tried to focus them. The only light came from under the door. Somebody was in the hall. He saw the shadow of moving feet. *A shadow*, he thought, and his mind raced to the moss-covered man in the horror book.

He clutched the covers and looked around. Was something in the room with him?

The digital display on the clock across the room blazed at him with red eyes: *12:15*.

Thump.

The shadow beneath the door disappeared. Mark could hear gentle footsteps pad down the hall, then stop. There was a rattling sound, then a familiar click. *That's the sound of a key in a lock*, Mark thought. Then he heard the rasp of a latch and the turn of a doorknob as the door slid open on creaking hinges. The footsteps tapped up a flight of stairs until they faded into silence.

The attic, Mark thought. *Whit's gone up into the attic.*

He rolled on his back and swallowed hard with a spitless throat. It was like one of the stories he read in *Fright Frenzy* about a mad, wooden-legged pirate who haunted an inn looking for his dead shipmates. The tap, tap, tap of his wooden leg would echo through the hallways as guests tried to sleep. Years later, historians found skeletons trapped behind a brick wall in a secret room of the inn.

What in the world is up in that attic?

In the dark room, his mind turned to even darker thoughts.

Chapter
Six

"A MAD PIRATE . . . brick walls . . . shadows . . ." Patti mumbled and rubbed her cast as if she had an itch. Her eyes were fixed straight ahead, almost as if she were in shock. Mark chewed the inside of his lip. They were sitting on a bench in McAlister Park.

While he waited for Patti's response, Mark watched kids go in and out the front door to Whit's End. One boy waved to Mark before he disappeared inside. Mark halfheartedly waved back. The movement of his hand broke Patti's spell.

"You're crazy," she said, turning to face him without blinking. "You've lost all your marbles."

"I knew you'd say that," Mark said with a frown.

"What else am I supposed to say? You're trying to tell me that Mr. Whittaker is keeping *his wife* in the attic, and you think I'm going to agree with you?"

Mark spread his arms defensively. "Why not? Isn't that what happened in *Sleeping Beauty*?"

"That's a fairy tale!"

"And I read that the Russians keep the body of Lenin in a glass coffin. It's kind of a memorial. Isn't that what the old man said—Jenny was in a memorial?"

Patti looked disgusted. "Her *grave* is a memorial!"

"Yeah, but—"

"It's sick and *you're* sick, and I'm going to tell your mother about your scary books because they have *warped your brain!*"

Mark leaped to his feet and paced in front of her. "Will you quit badgering me about those books? I heard him sneak up the stairs to the attic in the middle of the night. Why would he do that? What else could he have up there?"

"Old books, model airplanes—how should I know? But it never occurred to me that he might—" She stopped as if choking on the words. "I don't even want to say it. You're sick."

"I am not," Mark said. "And you better not say anything to my mom about those books."

Patti sneered at him, "I won't have to say anything. You're acting so weird that she'll figure it out for herself."

"Look, Patti—"

"Look *nothing*, Mark! You're getting really weird about this, and I don't want anything to do with it. Understand?" She folded her arms as if they would somehow lock out any further discussion.

"Then what am I supposed to do?" Mark pleaded. "How am I going to find out the truth?"

"Why don't you ask the old man in the cemetery since you're such good pals with him now," she mocked.

Mark kicked a stone angrily and looked in the direction of the church. Its tower rose high above the trees of McAlister Park.

Mark was certain the old man would see him and suddenly appear from behind a tree or a tombstone. But he didn't. So Mark stood in front of the church and debated with himself about whether to go inside. He decided to circle around first, just in case the old man was outside working. He felt safer talking in the light of day anyway. A dark church seemed too spooky to Mark, considering his present frame of mind.

"Hello?" Mark called out. "Mr. Caretaker?"

A large blackbird squawked at him. Mark jumped, then continued on. Eventually, he heard the scraping sound of a spade in dirt. *He's digging a grave*, Mark thought with a tremble. He stopped where he was and had another debate with himself. Did he really want to know about Whit's wife *this badly*?

Yes, he thought. *It's just an old man shoveling dirt, that's all. Nothing to worry about, nothing to fear.* He forced himself to go on.

Near the rear of the church, Mark could see the top of the old man's head. Then he heard grunting and more digging and saw an occasional shower of dirt as the shovel was hoisted above the hole.

Mark approached cautiously and peered down. The old man was wearing the same ragged clothes he had worn the day before. The wooden pipe jutted out of thin, compressed lips that were hardly distinguishable from the other lines on his face.

The old man looked at Mark and said, "What do you want now?"

"I just, uh, wanted to, uh—" Mark stammered, then composed himself. "Are you digging a *grave*?"

"Maybe my own if I don't find that leaky water pipe soon," he snorted. "The basement's flooded."

"Oh," Mark said, a little disappointed. Digging a grave was far more exciting than digging for broken water pipes.

The old man wiped his brow with a dirty handkerchief. "I know why you're here," he said.

246 ＶBEHIND THE LOCKED DOOR

"You do?"

"I do, I do," he cackled, then coughed harshly. "Your mind's been working hard since you were here yesterday, hasn't it?"

Mark blushed. "Well . . ."

"Got a whiff of a mystery, didn't you?" The old man poked the shovel into the ground, rested his elbow on it, and fished in his pocket for a moment. He found some matches and relit his pipe. "A real mystery."

Mark felt annoyed as he suddenly realized the old man was playing some sort of game with him. "Are you teasing me?"

"What do you think?" The old man laughed and coughed.

"You said Jenny Whittaker wasn't buried here," Mark complained.

"Well, she isn't," he said. "You think I lied to you? A liar, am I?"

"No, sir," Mark answered more quietly.

"You kids think you know it all, don't you? Well, you don't," he grumbled.

"Yes, sir."

The old man chuckled again. "Couldn't work up the nerve to ask Whit, could you?"

Mark wondered how the old man knew so much. Was this a game he played with other kids who happened through the graveyard? "No," Mark replied.

"Nope. Knew you wouldn't," the old man said proudly. "Even Whit can't get the kids to talk to him about *everything*."

Mark resented that the old man spoke with such pride—as if he had accomplished some small victory for himself. "Where is Whit's wife?" Mark asked directly.

The old man shook his head. "Not here, that's for sure. Nope. She's not buried in Odyssey at all."

"Then where is she? Please tell me."

"I should make you guess, but I've got work to do." The old man mopped his brow again. "She's in Callee-forn-eye-a."

"What?"

"California!" the old man snapped.

Mark stared at him as if he didn't understand.

"Pasadena, California. Whit had her put in her family's mausoleum in Pasadena, California," he said as he picked up the shovel.

"A mausoleum?" Mark wondered aloud.

The old man looked at Mark impatiently. "Are you deaf? I said a *mausoleum*. A crypt. A vault in the middle of a cemetery. Rich folks use them to bury their dead, you know—stone houses for their mortal remains."

"She's buried in California?" Mark asked numbly.

"Where'd you think she was—Whit's basement?" the old man growled. Then he returned to his digging.

Not exactly, Mark wanted to say. Instead he asked, "Why didn't you tell me yesterday?"

"That woulda been too easy. Too easy by a mile. I thought I'd give you something to chew on. I know how you kids are. Get bored in the summertime and you get in trouble. Take to wandering around my cemetery. Bet you like ghost stories, don't you?"

Mark turned and walked away. He felt as if a cruel trick had been played on him.

"You wanna hear about ol' George McAlister's grave?" the old man said with a laugh and a cough. "There's a story that'll keep you awake nights!"

❦ ❦ ❦

Mark found an empty corner booth in Whit's End where he thought he could brood in peace. Across the room, Patti stood at the center of a small group of kids. One was signing her cast.

Mark looked away. At the moment, he didn't care much for Patti. She had lectured him for ten minutes after he told her what the old man said. She called him twisted and mean and a disloyal friend to Whit. He thought she was being extremely cold-hearted, considering how ashamed and embarrassed he already felt for thinking such morbid things about Whit's wife.

They stood in stony silence in front of Whit's End for a few minutes, each waiting for the other to apologize. Neither one would. Then, when she said she wanted to go into Whit's End to get people to sign her cast, he angrily said she was just using it to get attention. She called him a creep, he called her conceited, and they stormed into Whit's End and went their separate ways.

Mark knew he should apologize. The argument was his fault. But he had suffered enough humiliation for one day and couldn't bring himself to do it. So he was wrong about Jenny Whittaker. That still didn't explain why Whit was being so mysterious about the attic—why he locked the door. And, for the first time, it struck him that he had only a few more days to sort it out.

He lowered his head, tore a napkin into little pieces, and tried to come up with a plan.

"Making a nest?" Whit asked as he slid behind the opposite side of the table.

Mark jerked his head up. Shame and embarrassment washed over him anew.

Whit pointed to the scraps of napkin now collected on the table. "A nest," he repeated with a smile.

Mark shook his head and glanced away. Patti had found someone else to sign her cast. But her eyes were on Mark. She watched with interest now that Whit was with him.

"Is something wrong?" asked Whit.

Mark considered coming right out and asking Whit about the attic. It would be the smart thing to do, he figured. Whit was his friend. He would be honest about it. And if it wasn't any of Mark's business, Whit would say that, too. Wasn't that how friendship was supposed to work? Maybe so. But maybe the old man was right. There were some things he couldn't say, even to Whit.

"I had a fight with Patti," Mark finally offered.

"I guessed," Whit responded. "What was it about?"

Mark thought carefully, scrambling for an answer other than the truth. "She . . . she blames me because her arm's in a cast."

"Does she?"

"Yeah. And I know she's over there right now telling everybody how it happened and how it's my fault."

"I don't think she'd do that," Whit said. "Besides, it wasn't really your fault, was it?"

"Sort of," he replied. "Even when she doesn't say it, I know that's what she's thinking."

"You're a mind reader now?" Whit said with a chuckle.

Mark shrugged.

Whit burrowed into the napkin remains with his finger and said tenderly, "I wouldn't pretend to know how Patti feels about you or the things that led to her breaking her arm. You'll have to talk to her about that. But you knew it would take a while for her to trust you again."

"Yeah, I know," Mark said softly. This wasn't what he wanted to talk about, yet he felt glad that they were.

"It's possible that the cast makes you feel guilty about what happened—even if she doesn't say so out loud," Whit observed.

"People often have a hard time letting old wounds heal. Sometimes it's even harder when you have something that serves as a reminder. Like a cast."

Mark's expression betrayed his confusion.

"I didn't realize my pearls of wisdom were so hard to understand. I'll have to work on that," Whit said with a laugh. "All I'm saying is, let it go. Don't let her cast bother you. And don't assume she's thinking something that she's not."

Mark looked across the room again. Patti was still watching them. Though he wasn't a mind reader, at that moment Mark was sure he knew what she was thinking. She was thinking he should ask Whit about the attic. *I should*, he thought. The old man didn't have to be right.

He opened his mouth to do it. He even silently formed the words. But he couldn't ask. He would look for another chance to ask—or another way to find out. Not now. Later. There was still time.

Whit slid out from the table and stood up. "There's something else I need to tell you," he said.

Mark looked up at Whit's round and friendly face.

"Your mother called this afternoon. She wanted to talk to you. I guess she thought you'd be here."

Mark searched Whit's face expectantly. *More news*, he thought. *They decided to get back together.* His stomach tightened.

"We've arranged a flight for you," Whit said.

"A flight?"

"Your parents want you to join them in Washington for a few days," he said with a big grin.

Mark's heart began to pound. "They want me to fly to Washington? Why?"

Whit shrugged and replied, "I suppose they want you to be with them. She didn't say. I'm sorry."

That didn't dampen Mark's excitement. "When do I go?" he asked.

"Tomorrow."

Chapter Seven

MARK LEFT WHIT AND PATTI at Whit's End. His excuse was that he needed to go back to Whit's house to pack for the flight. The real reason was that he felt mixed up about leaving and was afraid he might blurt out everything about the attic, Jenny's grave, and his suspicions.

How could he feel happy and sad at the same time? He was happy because he would fly to Washington to be with his parents. He was sad because now he would never find out what was in Whit's attic.

He should've asked Whit directly, he knew. But he realized how stupid it would sound. Real stupid.

Patti's probably right, he said to himself. *There's probably nothing in that attic but old books or model planes or a stamp collection. Why make a big deal about it? I should curb my curiosity. If the old man wanted to give me something to think about to keep me out of trouble, he gave me the wrong thing. In fact, my whole brain is filled with the wrong things.*

As he reached the handle to Whit's front door, Mark made a vow to himself. He promised to throw away all the horror books. "And," he continued out loud, "it doesn't matter what's in the attic!" He pushed open the door, never suspecting the temptation that awaited him.

The sky rumbled ominously. It began to rain again.

✤ ✤ ✤

Large raindrops lashed at the window in Jason's room where Mark packed his suitcase. The fading light bled through the pane and swirled like haunted shadows on the bedspread.

Mark shoved another shirt into his suitcase and felt the books at the bottom. He considered throwing them away right then, but he didn't want Whit to find them later. He'd wait until he could find a large outdoor trash can.

The phone rang. Mark stepped into the hallway, unsure of where the phone was. He followed the sound into Whit's bedroom and found it on the nightstand next to the bed. He picked up the receiver and said sheepishly, "Hello, John Whittaker's residence."

"Hello, Mark," Whit said above the din of Whit's End. "I'm glad I found you."

"Was I lost?" Mark asked innocently.

Whit laughed heartily. "I meant—oh, never mind. I'm really sorry about this, but I got a call from Tom Riley, and there's a zoning meeting I have to attend at City Hall tonight. Do you mind?"

"It's okay," Mark answered as he turned and casually scanned the room.

"There's a plate of food in the refrigerator for you. Just warm it up in the microwave. Three minutes should do the trick. All right? I won't be very late."

Mark's gaze fell on Whit's dresser and the cup full of keys. "Okay, thanks," he said.

"Bye-bye."

"Bye," Mark said and hung up the phone. *Keys*, he thought. *Whit won't be home for a while. The attic.* He walked around the bed to the dresser and, for a moment, argued with himself. *Don't touch the keys*, his conscience said. But that strong feeling of curiosity rose up once more to remind him this was his only chance to find out what was in the attic.

By the time he reached the cup, he knew he couldn't turn back. It was too perfect. He would find the key, go up to the attic, satisfy his curiosity, and come back down. No one would ever know.

Still, his heart hammered against his chest as he picked up the cup and began to search for a key to the attic door. He had no idea what it should look like. There were copper, gold, and silver keys; round, rectangular, and square keys. Mark figured it would take half an hour just to try them all in the lock.

His eye caught a long, slender key with a hollow circle on one end and a simple cut of teeth on the other. A "skeleton key" he remembered his grandmother calling this kind. They had one or two stuck in closet doors back at his house. He decided to try it first.

His hands trembled as he approached the attic door and aimed the key at the lock. Maybe Whit would suddenly appear behind him. Or an alarm would go off. Or someone would scream at him maniacally from the other side of the door.

He hesitated, took a deep breath, and then slid the key into the lock.

Ring!

Mark nearly leaped out of his skin, sure that he had been caught.

Ring! the sound came again.

He leaned weakly against the wall as he realized with great relief that it was the phone. *The phone!*

He raced to answer it, his mind ablaze with apologies and excuses in case it was Whit and he somehow knew what Mark was up to.

It was Patti.

"Hi, Mark," she said.

"Hi, Patti," he said curtly.

"I heard you were leaving tomorrow and, well, I thought it might be a couple of weeks before I see you again because I might be at camp by the time you get back, and you know, I was thinking about . . ."

Mark held the phone away and tapped his foot impatiently. Didn't she realize he was busy? He pressed the phone against his ear again. Too late, he realized she was apologizing.

". . . it was all really silly and, well, I hope we can still be friends and forget about the whole thing, because I'd hate it if you left and we were still mad at each other."

"Yeah, okay," Mark said quickly. *Whit could come home any minute!* he thought, chewing the inside of his lip.

"Yeah, okay," Patti said. She seemed surprised that making up could happen so quickly. "So . . . I guess you're sorry, too."

"Uh-huh," Mark said. "I'll see you when I get back."

"What?"

"I said I'll see you when I get back."

Patti's tone went hard. "You want to get off the phone, don't you?"

"Well, uh—"

"Mark Prescott, you are one of the rudest boys I've ever known in my life!" Patti hung up with a loud click.

Mark listened to the buzz of the receiver. For a second, he

thought he should call her back and apologize. But only for a second. He dashed back to the attic door, where the key still waited for his attention. He held his breath, turned the key, and heard the lock click! As he clasped the doorknob, it was cold to his touch. Every muscle in his body tightened involuntarily. He looked down at his hand on the knob and felt as if it belonged to someone else—in a picture, maybe.

Do you realize what you're about to do? his conscience asked. *You're about to go into a forbidden room.*

That's right, Mark replied. *But I'll only be in there a minute. Just long enough to see what's there. Then I'll come out and never think about it again. I promise.*

Mark didn't give his conscience another chance to argue. He opened the door and walked into the dark passageway.

Chapter
Eight

AT THE BASE OF THE STAIRS, Mark fumbled for a light switch, found it, and flipped it on. A dim light shone at the top of the stairs. Mark pondered the yellow glow and the ten wooden stairs he had to climb to see what waited for him. With lead feet, he took the first step. A musty smell drifted down and got sucked past him by the fresh air in the hallway. He took another step. Then another.

It hadn't occurred to him that he might be putting himself in serious danger. Not until now.

But it's Whit's house, he reasoned as he slowed his pace.

Yeah, sure, his conscience suddenly spoke again. *Just like you reasoned that Jenny Whittaker might be up here.*

Mark shivered as his skin went goose-pimply. Although Mrs. Whittaker was safely buried in Pasadena, California, Mark couldn't easily shake off the notion that she might be in the attic.

Nah. It's just a cold attic, he assured himself as he rubbed his arms. But he knew it was a lie. The attic air was thick and warm from the summer heat.

Frightening images from his collection of paperback books paraded before him. Closets of skeletons, basements of madmen, attics of . . . *of what?*

He stopped to consider his options. What if something hideous suddenly lunged at him? What if he saw something so terrible that he would never have a decent night's sleep again? What if Whit's secret was so disgusting that he could never go back to Whit's End or look Whit in the eye?

He listened carefully. Secretly, he hoped the slightest sound would give him an excuse to run away. But he heard nothing except the thumping of his heart and the occasional creak of the steps beneath his feet.

This bolstered his courage enough to climb a couple more stairs. He was now eye level with the attic floor. He pushed up on his feet and peered cautiously over the wooden planks. To his surprise, it looked like most attics. Wooden beams stretched up to the peak of the A-frame. The mustiness was stronger and carried with it years of pink insulation, scattered junk, cardboard boxes, unused clothes, outdated appliances, and yellow paper—spread throughout in various clusters and with no apparent order.

Just an attic, Mark thought, disappointed.

He climbed the rest of the stairs and stood confidently in this room that had consumed him for the past few days.

Just an attic, he thought again.

Then he saw it. A section in a far corner was set up as a room. It was furnished with an immaculately made bed, shelves full of books, high school pennants tacked to the wall, a small student's desk and study lamp—all carefully placed on a large, antique rug. It was a well-ordered island in a sea of clutter.

Wide-eyed, Mark walked to the room and browsed like a patron in a museum. This, in fact, is what it reminded Mark of: a museum. Except this one had a small layer of dust all over it.

The pennants on the wall, the "high adventure" books on the shelves, and the sports trophies lining a small dresser were dead giveaways. It was a boy's room. But it was a boy's room from another time. Mark had seen rooms like it on television shows from the late 1950s and 1960s.

He spied three framed photographs on a shelf. One was a black and white of a freckled, light-haired boy playing happily in a sandbox. The second, also black and white, was of the same boy—older now—with a dark-haired, mustache-free Whit proudly holding up a large fish.

Who is this kid? Mark wondered.

He looked at the third photo. It was in color but faded, and it showed the boy—a teen now—wearing a Santa Claus hat and hugging a dark-haired, mustachioed Whit in front of a brilliantly decorated Christmas tree.

Mark felt that catch in his heart again—the same one he felt when his mother left.

His eye caught a yellowing newspaper clipping on the small student's desk. "Jerry Whittaker Killed in Action," the headline shouted. The article had a photograph of a more-adult version of the light-haired boy. He was wearing a uniform. Behind him was the American flag.

Jerry Whittaker.

He looked closer. The article explained that Jerry Whittaker, son of John and Jenny Whittaker, was killed in a skirmish in Vietnam. *Killed in a skirmish.*

Mark's head spun with the news, and he suddenly remembered the photos on the wall of the second-floor stairwell. They pictured Whit, Jenny, and *three* kids. But Whit only spoke of Jason and Jana. *Why?* he wondered.

Mark picked up a paperweight fashioned from red clay to look like an Indian head. It was obviously handmade and crudely done. His fingers felt ridges on the bottom, so he turned it over.

There, in youthful script, it said: "To Dad, with all my love, Jerry." Mark closed his eyes and pictured it. Whit came up to this room and sat at this desk to read the article, hold the handmade gift, and drift into memories. Mark understood. He sometimes did the same thing in his own room after his mother and father split up. He would hold the baseball glove his dad bought him and let his mind sail to better times.

Mark wondered if Whit cried the way he sometimes did. He looked again at the article. Near the bottom, the ink sprayed out in several circles. Fallen tears.

Bang! A door slammed like a gunshot.

Mark gasped and dropped the paperweight. It broke into three pieces with a dull crack.

"Mark?" came Whit's muffled voice from far below.

Oh no oh no oh no oh no oh no, Mark's soul cried.

Panicked, he grabbed up the three pieces and, glancing around quickly to see where to hide them, decided to shove them into the back of a desk drawer. He dashed on tiptoes across the attic to the stairs, then down to the hallway, bracing himself for Whit's appearance.

"Mark!" Whit called again.

He's in the kitchen was Mark's frenzied guess as he closed the attic door as quietly as possible. He wasted precious moments searching in his pockets for the key, only to realize it was still in the lock.

"Anybody here?" Whit called again, this time from the front hall. He was making his way to the stairs.

Mark couldn't get the latch to turn. *Oh no oh no oh no oh no oh no.* His silent moan was fast becoming a shrill scream in his head. Whit was in the foyer now, and Mark pushed on the attic door. The latch clicked.

"Mark," Whit called from the bottom of the stairs. Just around the corner. So much closer now.

Mark searched the hall for an escape. Instantly he knew that if he tried to get to his room, Whit would see him from the landing and suspect something. Instead, Mark turned in the opposite direction and ran into the bathroom. He quietly closed the door, waited a few seconds, then flushed the toilet. *Whit will think I've been in here the whole time and couldn't hear him*, Mark hoped.

Turning the faucet on, he shoved his hands under the cold water. *This will make it look authentic*, he thought. He dried his hands and turned to the door. Bracing himself for whatever might happen next, he opened the bathroom door and stepped back into the hall. Whit stood at the top of the stairs.

"There you are," Whit said with a smile.

Chapter Nine

"ARE YOU SICK?" Whit asked.

"No," Mark answered, surprised by the question.

"You look pale," Whit said.

Mark rubbed his face self-consciously. "What happened to your meeting?" he said. "I thought you'd be home later."

"Cancelled," said Whit. "Are you sure you're all right? You look like something's wrong."

"I do?" Mark touched his face and wished he had checked himself in the bathroom mirror.

Whit reached over and pressed his hand against Mark's forehead. "You don't feel like you have a temperature. What were you doing?"

"I was just getting ready to leave tomorrow," stammered Mark.

"Ah, yes," said Whit. "You're leaving in the morning. Are you all packed?"

"Uh-huh."

Whit stroked his mustache thoughtfully. "Well, I may as well say it now. I'll be sad to see you go."

"Really?"

"Of course! You've always been good company, Mark."

Mark didn't know what to say.

Whit winked at him, then rubbed his hands together. "I think you should have a bath so you'll be clean for the flight in the morning. Then we'll see what kind of trouble we can get into."

"Trouble?" Mark squeaked.

Whit chuckled. "Fun, Mark. Are you absolutely sure you're all right?"

"Yeah," Mark said.

Whit stepped past him into the bathroom and ran the water. It roared in the hollow of the tub—an old-fashioned, snow-white type that was long and sloped and sat on stubby feet. "There you go," Whit said as he walked out of the bathroom. "Just shout if you need anything."

Mark closed the door and began to undress. His heart was still beating fast. *What am I gonna do? Whit'll find that Indian head sooner or later, and he'll know I broke it!*

He dropped his clothes on the floor as an agonizing thought struck him. *What an idiot I am! I should've left the Indian head on the floor! Whit would assume it fell off on its own or something. Now it's tucked in that drawer; he'll know someone put it there on purpose.*

Mark stepped into the hot tub. It was a little too hot, so he adjusted the faucet handles accordingly. The continual roar of the water was soothing. It was as if the sound protected him, hid him. He leaned back, stretched out, and let the water cover him.

How am I gonna tell Whit? Mark asked himself over and over. He knew he would have to. There was no returning to the attic to disguise what he'd done, no chance to fix it before Whit discovered it.

He tried to picture himself breaking the news to Whit. *I'm sorry, Mr. Whittaker, but I stole your key, snuck up into the attic after you told me not to, and, while I was there, broke your prized Indian head that your dead son made for you when he was little.*

Oh brother.

He let himself soak for a long time before applying any soap. *Maybe I can leave for Washington, and he won't go up there for a long time. When he finally does, he'll forget I was here and think he broke it himself and . . .*

No way.

After giving himself a thorough wash, Mark climbed out of the tub, pulled the plug by the beaded chain, and dried off. *Maybe Mom and Dad really will get back together again, and we'll stay at our home in Washington, and I'll never have to face Whit or explain what happened.* Mark shook the thought away.

As he stopped to pick up his clothes, he noticed an old-fashioned key in the bathroom door lock. *It looks just like the attic door key*, he thought.

Then he put his hand over his mouth in horror as he realized, *The attic door key! I didn't put it back in the cup!*

Mark tossed his towel aside and snatched up his clothes. He checked the pockets and folds and shook them in hopes that he would find the key. Not once, not twice, but three times, just to be sure. Then he searched around the bathroom—the tub, the sink, the bathmat, and every inch of the tiled floor. Nothing.

Oh no oh no oh no oh no oh no, his soul cried again. He had left the key in the lock to the attic door! He knew it as surely as he knew his own name. He grabbed the towel, wrapped it around himself, and carefully inched the bathroom door open. Maybe, just maybe, he could retrieve the key before Whit noticed that it wasn't where it should be.

Mark stuck his head into the hallway and looked to his left, in the direction of Whit's room. The door was open, but the room seemed to be empty. He turned to the right and instantly felt something hot shoot from his stomach and through every nerve ending in his body. The attic door was open.

Mark's jaw dropped, and he wasn't sure whether to scream or cry. He heard footsteps on the stairs. Whit emerged from the stairwell with a stricken look on his face. In his hands were the broken pieces of the Indian head paperweight.

"Do you know anything about this?" Whit asked, his face turning red.

Mark stammered, "It . . . it was an accident!"

"An accident!" Whit countered angrily. "You *sneaked* up there and . . ." His voice trailed off into a low growl.

Mark looked at the carpet, the burning in his stomach getting even hotter.

"Do you know what this was?" Whit asked, his voice now a hoarse whisper.

Mark shook his head, even though he *did* know. Then he changed his mind. "Yes," he said softly.

"It was the only thing he ever made for me," Whit said. The edge of anger gave way to a sorrowful tone.

Mark stared at the carpet. Its pattern twisted and turned like snakes as his eyes filled with tears. His knees felt weak, but they were locked in place. He couldn't move even if he wanted to.

"Just go to bed." Whit strode past Mark, went into his room, and slammed the door.

Mark wasn't sure how long he stood there, but it felt like a very long time.

Chapter
Ten

MARK SLEPT FITFULLY. He seemed to be stuck in a netherworld between dreams and reality. Once, he thought Jerry Whittaker was leaning over his bed. Another time, he suddenly sat upright in his bed without knowing why, only to find that his cheeks were wet with tears. Still later, he thought he found the broken Indian head paperweight under his pillow and panicked because he wasn't sure where to hide the pieces. Then a cadaverous woman pushed open the closet door, shook a bony finger at him, and said, "You shouldn't have gone up to the attic."

I'm going to throw away those horror books at the airport, Mark vowed.

The sun finally rose on yet another cloudy day. Mark was already awake and dressed by the time he heard Whit come out of his room. He listened as Whit passed by—*did he stop outside the door for a moment?*—on his way to the stairs.

When he was sure it was clear, Mark crept out of Jason's room and into Whit's. He placed a note on the pillow. It said "I'm sorry" with Mark's signature underneath. He crept back out again, picked up his suitcase, and walked downstairs. He considered walking out the door and back to his own house, but he realized he wouldn't have a way to the airport, nor did he know how to get his airplane tickets. So he put the suitcase down and walked into the kitchen.

Whit silently laid out breakfast for Mark. Worse than his silence was that Whit wouldn't look at him. Mark wanted to cry all over again. But he didn't. Instead, he simply picked at the ham and eggs.

Mark looked at the clock. 7:45. His flight left at 9:30. The airport was only 15 minutes away, so Mark wondered how they would spend the time. Sitting in this stony silence? *Please, Mr. Whittaker . . . yell at me or something*, Mark thought. *Just don't ignore me like this.*

As if by magic, Whit spoke. "Let's go," he said.

It was a relief for Mark. Maybe Whit would just drop him off at the airport and end their misery.

It rained as they drove, and the hum and swish of the windshield wipers were the only sounds. Mark cleared his throat a couple of times, wanting to say something, but he didn't dare. He began to see signs for the Odyssey Municipal Airport, and his worry increased. *I can't leave Whit like this*, he said to himself. It would be torture. It would ruin his life. A note wasn't enough. He had to apologize out loud. *Now.*

Whit drove into the airport parking lot, pulled a ticket from the machine, and glided into a parking place. An airplane roared overhead.

"Here we are," said Whit.

His voice broke the dam of Mark's emotion. "I'm sorry, Mr. Whittaker," he said. "You don't know how sorry I am! I never should've gone up in the attic. I know that now. I should've listened to you. And I didn't mean to break Jerry's paperweight. It was a stupid accident because I was stupid for being there in the first place, and I'll do anything you want me to do to make it up somehow if I can, but I know I can't, but I'll try if—" Mark's voice was strangled by tears, and he pushed them out with heaving sobs.

Whit raised his hand. "Whoa, hold on," he said.

Mark lowered his head, and Whit gently placed his hand on his shoulder. Mark got control of himself and lifted his eyes. For the first time that morning, he looked Whit full in the face. Whit's eyes were red and puffy as if he'd been crying, too.

"I'm really, really sorry," Mark said again.

Whit managed a smile, but it didn't have its usual brightness. "I know you're sorry, Mark. I know. And I accept that. Okay?"

Mark nodded.

Whit sighed. "I loved Jerry very much. And when he died in Vietnam, I was devastated. It was more than I could take. My whole family was thrown into a very dark time.

"We were living in the Chicago area when it happened. We decided to leave. I suppose we thought we could escape the memories. In a way, we did. We found Odyssey and thought we could start over again."

Whit stared out at the passing cars for a moment. He seemed preoccupied by a man and woman saying good-bye at the curb in front of the terminal. "Odyssey was good for us," he finally continued. "We didn't even buy a house with enough room for Jerry's furniture. It got stored away in the attic. It was our way of saying good-bye to him, I think."

Again Whit paused as the couple at the curb kissed and the woman rushed into the terminal. The man watched her for a moment, then climbed into his car and left.

"After Jenny died, I was heartbroken all over again. But this time Jana and Jason were grown up, so I had to grieve alone. Maybe because she died near me, instead of in a faraway country, I found I could handle it better. But the pain of Jerry's death came back again. One day, I was up in the attic and saw all the furniture from his room. I set it up the way you saw it—a re-creation of the way his room looked when he went off to war. It became my secret place. I was wrong to do it."

"There's nothing wrong with having a hideout," Mark offered.

"This secret place was different, though," Whit replied. "Maybe it was a way to cope with the loss of two loved ones, but I found myself spending a lot of time up there. Just sitting. Remembering. Losing myself in the past. That can be a dangerous thing to do. I wanted things to be the way they used to be."

Mark closed his eyes. Those were familiar words to him; an echo of the feelings he had when he first moved to Odyssey. It took Whit and the Imagination Station to make him realize you can never make things the way they were before.

"Nobody knew about my secret place—until you came along. And I was very angry with you for finding it. It hurt. I resented the intrusion."

"I know, Mr. Whittaker, and I'm sorry. I'll never tell anyone about—"

Again Whit held up his hand for silence. "Last night, after you went to bed, I thought about it and prayed and . . . realized *I* was wrong to get so emotionally tied up in my memories—in Jerry's old life. A life that's gone. It brought back sweet memories, but it brought back pain, too. And loss.

"With that room, I was keeping open the old wounds, not giving them a chance to heal."

"Just like I've been doing with Patti's cast," Mark said, suddenly remembering their conversation the day before.

"Yes, just like that," Whit agreed. "So, I decided that I'm going to dismantle the room."

The announcement took Mark by surprise.

Whit nodded and continued, "It's time to let go of the past and let old wounds heal. And I want to thank you for helping me realize that."

Being thanked for what he did was another surprise for Mark. *I'll never understand adults as long as I live*, he thought. But he was relieved, too. Now they could be friends again.

They picked up Mark's ticket at the airline counter. There was still time to kill, so they went to the airport cafeteria and had some disgusting, watered-down orange juice. Afterward, Mark suddenly remembered one other important detail. While Whit watched him curiously, Mark dug into his suitcase and pulled out the horror books.

"You're kidding," Whit said. "You *read* that trash?"

"Not anymore," Mark said as he dropped them into a nearby trash can.

Whit walked Mark to the gate and—the third big surprise— hugged Mark good-bye just before he boarded the plane.

"Have a good trip, Mark," he whispered.

"Thank you, Mr. Whittaker," Mark replied.

Whit reached into his pocket, produced a small package, and slipped it into Mark's jacket pocket. "Don't look at it until you get to your parents' house," he said.

Chapter
Eleven

SOMETHING WAS WRONG. Mark knew it instinctively when his mother and father picked him up at National Airport in Washington, D.C. Yeah, they were all smiles and gave him long hugs and asked how the flight was, but it didn't ring true. They seemed tense and ill at ease.

Mark felt deflated. He didn't realize until the plane landed that he had expected his parents to scoop him up in their arms at the gate, announce that all was well, and promise they'd all live happily ever after.

He sank further into disappointment when his mom and dad began to argue during the ride from the airport. Their comments were too adult and veiled for Mark to guess what their problem was, but it was all too familiar. Just like old times. He sank into the thick cushion of the backseat and fingered the mysterious gift Whit had given him.

Mark entered his old home like a stranger. It was the same as he remembered, but it didn't feel as if it belonged to him anymore. It could have been a next-door neighbor's house for all he cared. *Odyssey is my home*, he realized.

Julie kissed him again and said how glad she was that he was with them. Richard, his father, agreed and added, "Why don't you take your suitcase up to your old room?"

Mark did, hoping his old room might spark something within him. It did—but not the feeling he expected. Through the vent, he could hear his parents' voices from down in the kitchen. They were fighting. Mark felt a rush of nausea as he was transported back in time to those mornings and nights in the spring when he played up in his room, hoping to drown out their bitter words. It was happening all over again. Nothing had changed between them. All the counseling and promises and wishful thinking hadn't amounted to anything.

Mark tossed his suitcase on the bed and walked to the window. It perspired as the outside humidity clashed with the air conditioning inside. The familiar scene overlooking his backyard was blurred. Maybe it was the window. Maybe it was the tears that filled his eyes.

He wanted to leave. He wanted to be back in Odyssey with Whit and Patti. But he wanted both his mother and father to be with him. Together. Was it too much to ask?

For comfort, he reached into his pocket and touched Whit's gift.

From downstairs, Mark could hear his parents shout about something that happened when they first got married. *That long ago?* Mark wondered. *Why would they fight about that now?*

He decided not to cry anymore. Nor would he leave. Nor would he join their fight. He simply walked down to the kitchen and poured himself a glass of milk. By that time, Julie and Richard had moved their fight to the living room. Once, Julie suggested that they continue their conversation later—"for Mark's sake." That triggered another argument about whether

Mark was old enough to understand how adults argue with each other.

"It's nothing to worry about," Richard called in to the kitchen to assure Mark.

Mark shrugged and sipped his milk, then casually took off his jacket and threw it over one of the chairs. The small present from Whit fell out of the pocket. He picked it up and decided that now was a good time to open it. The wrapping paper was off in a flash. Underneath was an oblong box. He took off the cover and looked inside. A smile stretched across his face.

It was the key to Whit's attic door.

Mark clutched it tightly in his hand and held it to his chest. *I'll find a special place for it*, he thought—somewhere so it would always remind him of what had happened and what he had learned.

Richard and Julie were nose to nose in a renewed shouting match when Mark walked into the living room. Their fight had something to do with something Richard had said one night after Mark's third birthday party, which Richard didn't think was any worse than something Julie had said to him during Mark's second-grade Christmas pageant.

Mark stood in the center of the room and watched them quietly. Julie noticed him first and looked at him with a curious expression on her face. Richard, catching on that Julie wasn't listening to him anymore, did the same.

"You know what?" Mark said quietly. "Maybe it's time to let old wounds heal."

Richard and Julie looked at him, then at each other.

Mark slipped the key into his jeans pocket and took another drink of milk.

About the Author

PAUL MCCUSKER FOR MANY YEARS WAS PRODUCER, writer, and director for the *Adventures in Odyssey* audio series. His work includes over 40 published novels, full-length plays, skit collections, screenplays and lyrics.

Works by the Author

Novels
Strange Journey Back (Focus on the Family)
Danger Lies Ahead (Focus on the Family)
Point of No Return (Focus on the Family)
The Passages series (Focus on the Family)
A Season of Shadows (Zondervan)
The Mill House (Zondervan)
The Faded Flower (Zondervan)
Epiphany (Zondervan)

Instructional
*Youth Ministry Comedy & Drama: Better
Than Bathrobes but Not Quite Broadway*
(co-author Chuck Bolte; Group Books)

Plays
Pap's Place
(Lillenas Publishing Co.)
A Work in Progress
(Lillenas Publishing Co.)
Snapshots & Portraits
(Lillenas Publishing Co.)
Camp W
(Contemporary Drama Service)
Family Outings
(Lillenas Publishing Co.)
The Revised Standard Version of Jack Hill
(Baker's Play Publishing Co.)

Catacombs
(Lillenas Publishing Co.)
The Case of the Frozen Saints
(Baker's Play Publishing Co.)
The Waiting Room
(Baker's Play Publishing Co.)
A Family Christmas
(Contemporary Drama Service)
The First Church of Pete's Garage
(Baker's Play Publishing Co.)
Home for Christmas
(Baker's Play Publishing Co.)

Sketch Collections
Sixty-Second Skits
(with Chuck Bolte; Group Books)
Void Where Prohibited
(Baker's Play Publishing Co.)
Some Assembly Required
(Contemporary Drama Service)
Quick Skits & Discussion Starters
(co-author Chuck Bolte; Group Books)
Vantage Points
(Lillenas Publishing Co.)
Batteries Not Included
(Baker's Play Publishing Co.)
Souvenirs
(Baker's Play Publishing Co.)
Sketches of Harvest
(Baker's Play Publishing Co.)

Musicals
The Meaning of Life & Other Vanities
(with Tim Albritton; Baker's Play Publishing Co.)
Season Tickets
(Lillenas Publishing Co.)
A Time for Christmas
(with David Clydesdale, Steve Amerson,
and Lowell Alexander; Word Music)

Don't Miss the Next
"Adventures in Odyssey" Collection!

On the following pages, you'll find
chapter one of *Lights Out at Camp What-A-Nut*,
the first story in the next "Adventures in Odyssey"
collection, *Danger Lies Ahead*. We hope you
enjoy the preview of this book and will then
want to read the rest of the story.
Don't miss it!

Chapter
One

THE BANNER "Welcome to Odyssey Municipal Airport!" stretched across the airline gate, ready to greet the passengers on the approaching plane. Mark Prescott leaned across his mother's seat to get a clear look out the window. Although the pane was dotted with raindrops from yet another late August storm, he could see the banner and felt his heart leap at the name "Odyssey."

"Are you glad to be back?" Julie, his mother, asked.

Mark nodded.

Julie rubbed Mark's back. "I was just thinking how nice it is to be home again. Funny, huh?—thinking about Odyssey as home."

Mark understood what she meant. When his parents separated the previous June, Mark was sure nothing worse could ever happen to him. That is, until Julie moved Mark to his grandmother's house in Odyssey, halfway across the country from his father, Richard, and their home in Washington, D.C. Then Mark *knew* it was the end of the world.

But that was last June.

In the almost three months since then, he had made new friends, enjoyed Odyssey's gentle charm, and taken part in some exciting adventures (including taking a trip in a time machine and solving a mystery). Slowly, Mark felt less like a stranger and more like a welcome friend. By August, it was as if he'd always been there—and always would be.

Mark and Julie followed the crowd of passengers from the plane to the baggage claim area. A horn sounded a warning blast, and the conveyor belt loudly whirred to life. Mark stood nearby, grabbing their luggage when it came past. They tossed the suitcases onto a cart and pushed it to the long-term parking area where Julie had parked the car only a few days before.

Only a few days? It seems longer than that, Mark thought, then said so aloud.

"Did it seem long because you didn't enjoy yourself?" Julie asked as she closed the trunk.

"I guess so," Mark said with a shrug. "It wasn't as much fun as I thought it would be. It's like . . . our house wasn't ours anymore."

Julie nodded her head, a lock of her long, brown hair falling across her face. "I understand. Everything looked the same as it did before we left, but it seemed different somehow. Once or twice, I felt like I was a visitor in a museum." She started the car and backed out of the parking space.

"All my old friends were either away on vacation or they didn't want to see me," Mark added. That bothered him a lot. Somehow it didn't seem fair that they went on with their lives without him being there to give his approval.

Julie paid the parking attendant, wound up her window, and pulled away. "That's the hardest part. When you go away, you think everyone should suddenly stop in their tracks and never do anything important without you. You think you're the only one who can change or make new friends or have new experiences. And when you come back, it's a shock to find out that their lives kept going—just like yours did."

"Yeah, but Mike Adams is hanging around Tom Nelson! They couldn't stand each other before!"

Julie laughed and said, "Just like you never thought you could have a girl as a friend."

His mom was referring to Patti Eldridge, a girl who had become Mark's closest friend in Odyssey during the summer.

"That's different," Mark replied. He stared out the passenger window thoughtfully. "And I thought you and Dad . . ." He glanced down at his lap uncomfortably.

"You thought your dad and I would get back together again. I know."

She was right. The reason they had gone to Washington, D.C., in the first place was so that Mark's mom and dad could iron out their differences. But by the time Richard dropped Mark and Julie off at the airport for their return trip to Odyssey, it was clear that wasn't going to happen.

"I'm sorry, Mark," Julie said. "I really thought your dad and I would work it all out. I thought this trip would be the end of our separation. I know you're disappointed."

"Wars have ended quicker than you two getting back together," Mark said as they drove away from the airport.

Julie smiled wearily in return. "You have to be patient. You may not see the improvements, but they're there."

"Then why aren't you together again?"

"Because we're not ready," she answered. "I won't get back with your father until I'm sure we're ready."

"But that's what you and Dad keep saying!"

"I know. But some things came up in our counseling session that we have to figure out." Julie sighed. "You wouldn't understand."

"What wouldn't I understand?" Mark snapped. "Why do you always think I don't understand?"

Julie glanced at Mark, a pained expression on her face.

"I'm sorry," Mark said. "I didn't mean to be so sharp."

Julie acknowledged the apology with a nod, then reached across the seat to touch Mark's hand. "It's all leading somewhere, Mark. You have to trust us. We've needed this time to mend our wounds."

Mark shot her an ornery look, then said, "Maybe you should buy some Band-Aids."

She pinched him playfully and drove on.

FOCUS ON THE FAMILY®

At Focus on the Family, we work to help you really get to know Jesus and equip you to change your world for Him.

We realize the struggles you face are different from your parents' or your little brother's, so we've developed a lot of resources specifically to help you live boldly for Christ, no matter what's happening in your life.

Besides exciting novels, we have Web sites, magazines, booklets, and devotionals . . . all dealing with the stuff you care about.

Focus on the Family Magazines

We know you want to stay up-to-date on the latest in your world — but it's hard to find information on entertainment, trends, and relevant issues that doesn't drag you down. It's even harder to find magazines that deliver what you want and need from a Christ-honoring perspective.

That's why we created *Breakaway* (for teen guys), *Brio* (for teen girls), and *Clubhouse* (for tweens, ages 8 to 12). So, don't be left out — sign up today!

Breakaway
Teen guys
breakawaymag.com

Brio
Teen girls
briomag.com

Clubhouse
Tweens ages 8 to 12
clubhousemagazine.com

Weekly Radio Show
whitsend.org

 Phone toll free: (800) A-FAMILY (232-6459)

BP06XTN

THE LAST CHANCE DETECTIVES ®

Their town is Ambrosia . . . their headquarters is a vintage B-17 bomber . . . and they are The Last Chance Detectives . . . four ordinary kids who team up to solve mysteries no one else can be bothered with. Now, for the first time, the three best-selling episodes in the series are available in one DVD gift set.

Request this collector's edition set by calling the number below. And see if you can crack the cases of *Mystery Lights of Navajo Mesa*, *Legend of the Desert Bigfoot*, and *Escape from Fire Lake*.

And for the latest audio exploits of The Last Chance Detectives, call that same number. Request your copy of *The Day Ambrosia Stood Still*, *Mystery of the Lost Voices*, and *Last Flight of the Dragon Lady*.

Phone toll free: (800) A-FAMILY (232-6459)

PASSAGES™

What if history repeated itself — with you in it? "Passages" takes familiar stories and retells them from a kid's perspective. Loosely based on the popular "Adventures in Odyssey" series, "Passages" books begin in Odyssey and take you to a fantasyland, where true belief becomes the adventure of a lifetime! Look for all the exciting "Passages" adventures, including *Darien's Rise*, *Arin's Judgment*, *Annison's Risk*, *Glennall's Betrayal*, *Draven's Defiance*, and *Fendar's Legacy*.

Request the entire set or each book individually at *www.whitsend.org/passages*.

Phone toll free: (800) A-FAMILY (232-6459)